To Ni

The trilogy

SILENT MONEY

Is complete!

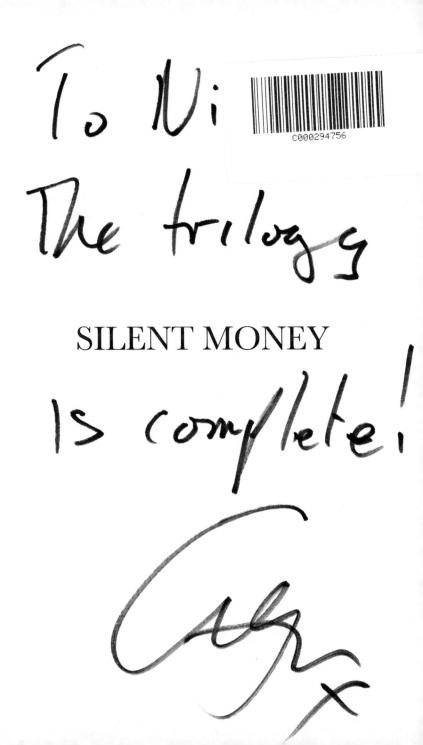

GD Harper is a past winner of a Wishing Shelf Red Ribbon for adult fiction, and has been shortlisted for the Lightship Prize for first-time authors and longlisted for the UK Novel Writing Award.

Also by GD Harper:
Love's Long Road
A Friend in Deed

SILENT
MONEY

GD HARPER

Matador
9 Priory Business Park,
Wistow Road, Kibworth Beauchamp,
Leicestershire. LE8 0RX
Tel: 0116 279 2299
Email: books@troubador.co.uk
Web: www.troubador.co.uk/matador
Twitter: @matadorbooks

ISBN 978 1838590 291

British Library Cataloguing in Publication Data.
A catalogue record for this book is available from the British Library.

Printed and bound in the UK by TJ International, Padstow, Cornwall
Typeset in 11pt Aldine401 BT by Troubador Publishing Ltd, Leicester, UK.

Matador is an imprint of Troubador Publishing Ltd.

November 1972
Glasgow

chapter one

Things had been going well, almost too well. Until the letter arrived.

As Michael read it, his teeth clenched. If anyone had seen him at that moment, they would not have recognised the suave assistant manager of the Byres Road branch of the Royal Clydeside Bank. Michael Mitchell, the friendly face of banking. But he was alone, the door of his office closed.

He picked up a pencil, grasped both ends, pushed his thumbs against it until it snapped. It gave him a moment of respite as he clawed back control of his emotions. The searing anger began to subside, replaced by something more enduring – a deep and brooding resentment. That he held on to, nurtured, let it fill his soul.

Anyone else would have thought it an overreaction. The letter said he had been passed over for promotion, that was all. He had only been with the bank four years, assistant manager a few months. It was not unreasonable that the new manager would be from another branch. It was even to be expected that a Kelvinside Academy old boy would be chosen over someone with his background. But Hector Duffy? A buffoon. A talentless plodder. Another wave of fury stoked his bitterness.

Michael looked at the two halves of the pencil lying on the desk. He slid them into his jacket pocket and glanced over at the office door, checking it was closed. No one had seen.

He picked up the phone, at the same time looking up Duffy's number in the company directory. He would make the first contact with his new boss, to allay any suspicions of resentment. It would be easy. Duffy was too brainless to spot any deceit.

'Duffy,' he heard the voice say. He could picture Duffy's sweaty, red-cheeked countenance, still smug from the news. He pushed away the image and leant back in his chair. It was important the conversation sounded relaxed.

'Hector. It's Michael. Congratulations are in order, I believe. When are you moving?'

'Oh, you've heard?' Duffy gave a throaty chuckle. 'I wished they'd told me the cat was out of the bag. Yes, big surprise. Condolences, old chap, can't think why they chose me. Buggins' turn, I suppose.'

'Plenty of time for me to move up. There's a lot I can learn from a wise old head.'

'It sounds to me like you've been doing a splendid job holding the fort these last few weeks,' Duffy replied. 'I've been looking at the numbers. That's a lot of new customers you've brought on board. Well done. Numbers, Michael, they're what count. Keep up these results and you'll be next. Mark my words.'

'Very kind of you, Hector. I'll do my best.'

Michael had been acting manager at the branch ever since the previous manager had done the unthinkable and accepted a job with a competitor. Shown the door straight away. It had been September, a critical time for the branch, with new students arriving at the university and looking to open accounts – Byres Road was right next to the university buildings. He had been told he would be acting manager until candidates for the job could be interviewed. A few nods and winks suggested that things could land very nicely for him.

These few weeks had been a firestorm of activity. Michael was in the bank at six every morning, getting the paperwork and analyses completed before the rest of the staff turned up. He made a point of inviting every student asking for an application form into his office for a chat, gently nudging them to sign up. By the end of October, the bank had as many new customers as in the last three years combined.

None of that mattered, he had discovered. It was who you knew that counted, who you could rely on. Who the powers that be thought was the kind of chap who wouldn't let the side down, wouldn't rock the boat. A dullard like Hector Duffy.

'When can I bring you up to speed with what's been happening here?' Michael said. 'There's a couple of initiatives I'm putting in place while the new undergraduates are still opening accounts. I'd love to hear what you think.'

'Initiatives, eh? Maybe we should talk about them now. I won't be able to move right away, need to make sure there's an orderly plan here at Maryhill. You'll find I'm a stickler for doing things by the book. So, what have you planned? Nothing too controversial, I hope?'

'We're well below our bad debt provision for the year. Since I've been assistant manager, I've personally checked and followed up on any red-flagged accounts every week and that's meant we've spotted any potential problem before it's become a liability.'

Michael heard a murmur of approval down the phone. He took a deep breath. 'So, I thought I'd have an informal arrangement where we turn a blind eye to any new student customers who run up a small unauthorised overdraft after they open an account.'

No confirmatory murmur this time. Only silence. He ploughed on. 'Waive the charges. Give them a chat about managing their money better, a breathing space to get themselves sorted out. We lose a small amount in fees and take on a small debt risk, but I reckon it will be repaid in loyalty to the bank for years to come. And give us a better reputation on campus than any of the other banks, too.'

'Oh dear, Michael. Informal arrangements? A blind eye? Not sure about this at all. There are procedures, you know.'

Michael spoke in a carefully controlled tone. 'Of course. I had thought branch managers could use their discretion, bend the rules a bit if they saw fit. But if that's not your style, no problem.'

'Good, good. We're seeing a lot of council-house students turning up at university nowadays. The place is going to the dogs. We can't let these sorts of people think we're a soft touch; they don't have the upbringing to understand the meaning of responsibility and discipline. Not that I'm a snob you understand. It's just that if we do help someone out, we need to know they come from a family we can rely on to do the right thing.' Duffy chuckled. 'Don't quote me on that. We do have to cater for the riff-raff and the great unwashed these days.'

Riff-raff. Rabble, scum, trash, the lowest of the low, the dregs of society, good-for-nothings. The badges Michael had worn himself after leaving school at fifteen. The second he could support himself, he did. Twelve years washing dishes in hotels around Scotland, living in the staff quarters with just about enough money to have some sort of life, if he put in the hours.

That's who he had been, and the bank would never let him forget it. Going to night school to get the O levels and Highers he'd missed out on had secured him a job as a teller. A finance diploma, also from night school, was enough to convince the bank he was management material, or so he had thought. But he had been kidding himself. It was people like Duffy the bank wanted.

Michael forced himself to play along. He laughed and said, 'Don't worry, Hector; discretion is my middle name. The other thing I'm working on is what I call our helping hand project. I attend student events in the evenings, mainly charity things, and use them as an opportunity to network for new customers and show the bank supports worthy causes. Make a small donation at the end of the evening – making sure that everyone sees me do it. All approved by head office. Not a penny of the branch's client hospitality budget has actually gone on hospitality for six months. I've been using it for this instead.'

'Charities, eh? Very noble. Excellent idea, Michael. No problem at all with that. As long as your interactions with the students are strictly professional, no problem at all.' There was a pause, and Michael sensed Duffy was weighing up what to say next. 'Might have to put a stop to the donations, though. I'm of the school that says good relationships with the top customers are all-important, and that's what I see most of my time being taken up with. Got to keep those relationships well oiled, if you get my drift.'

'If that's everything,' he said quickly, giving Michael no time to respond, 'when do you want me to tell the rest of the branch staff? Should I come over tomorrow?'

'I can handle that, if you like,' Michael replied. 'The word is bound to get out, so I thought I'd tell everyone after we close for business today. Save you the trip.'

Duffy agreed, and Michael savoured a small victory. He would be able to communicate the news on his terms, control the reaction and the impact on his reputation. At three thirty he called everyone together.

'I thought you'd want to know the news about the new branch manager,' he said. Grins broke out, and Michael allowed himself a split second of satisfaction. They thought it was him. 'Hector Duffy. Some of you might know him if you've spent any time at Maryhill. Once he hands over at Maryhill he'll be starting here. In a few weeks.'

A leaden silence filled the room.

'It should have been you, Michael,' someone said eventually.

Michael affected a studied nonchalance. 'Not at all,' he said. 'I've been delighted to get the chance to help out over the last few weeks. But that's it. I want you all to give Mr Duffy your full support when he moves here.'

He went back to the barren office, pleased that he'd never really moved in. It would make the prospect of the office pool less painful. He forced himself to adopt a more positive frame of mind. His results as acting manager spoke for themselves. It wouldn't be too long before another opportunity came up. They wouldn't pass him over a second time, and Duffy was a time-server who was probably ten years behind the pace with his career progression. A momentary setback, that's all. Branch manager at Byres Road wasn't an option for the foreseeable future – Duffy was never going to get two promotions in the same decade – but there were lots of other branches. It was just a question of working harder and biding his time.

When Duffy arrived, Michael found that, although he had only run the branch himself for a few weeks, Duffy's failings were abundantly clear. He didn't understand the fundamentals, was too lazy to be bothered to master the details, too pompous to make any effort to understand the people around him – Duffy was the embodiment of someone who ascended to high places without any discernible ability. His plan as branch manager turned out to be to introduce his pet bureaucratic procedures, wine and dine his favourite business customers, and have Michael do as much of the actual work as possible.

Michael slowly built up an army of defences to hide his contempt and frustration. He weighed up every word, measured every gesture; developed a carapace of detachment with his peers, a veneer of faux subservience to those above him. He slipped into this new persona like an actor donning his costume. Who he really was would never be seen again.

Duffy was delighted to have such a talented and respectful subordinate. Whenever someone from head office was to pay a visit, Michael was always pulled into his office a few minutes before they showed up.

'Remind me why this fellow's got a bee in his bonnet, would you, old chap?'

Michael became practised at giving him a one-sentence summary of what the meeting was to be about, as well as a gentle reminder of what to say and not to say. Anything beyond the most basic of issues and Michael would find himself sitting in on the meeting, clarifying Duffy's utterances, subtly making it clear which one of them knew what was going on.

'Got me out of that sticky wicket, again,' Duffy said after one meeting. 'Don't know what I'd do without you, Michael. My number-one man.'

'Very kind of you to say so,' Michael replied. 'If people know the branch is doing well, that's good for all of us. If there's any way I can help, I'm always glad to do so.'

He congratulated himself on his deception. With every gullible beam of gratitude from Hector, with every growth in his stature in the eyes of those who met him, Michael was channelling his contempt into a positive force, to show yet again what he was capable of.

★ ★ ★

He was completing the quarterly reconciliations when Duffy's secretary came over and hovered at his desk.

'Michael, Mr Duffy would like a word with you in his office when you have a minute.' She giggled. 'I'd get in there straight away. He's been on the phone to the personnel director for the last twenty minutes. I think you might be getting some news.'

Michael gave a conspiratorial nod of thanks and walked over to Duffy's office. This was it. The manager of the Edinburgh student branch had just been promoted, and he was the obvious candidate for the vacancy. The last few months had been hell, but it was about to pay out.

He walked in. Something was wrong. Duffy looked shifty, defensive.

'Ah, Michael, good of you to pop by so quickly. Some news.'

Ian Mason was to be the new Edinburgh branch manager. It was going to be announced next week. Not even the pretence of a selection process. Twenty-six, seven years younger than Michael. He would be the bank's youngest-ever branch manager.

Duffy floundered as he followed up on the bare facts. 'Don't take it personally,' he said. 'Mason's father and grandfather both made the board, it's obvious he's being groomed for high places. It's no reflection on you or your ability. I've had personnel on the phone, and I've told them just that. You're doing awfully well for yourself for a chap who left school at fifteen. It's only a matter of time.'

Michael assured Duffy he was fine with the news, that he completely understood and appreciated his support and words of encouragement. He didn't let his mask slip for a second.

Work hard, do better, and you'll be rewarded. What he'd wanted to believe was true was now proven beyond all doubt to be a cynical lie.

Society didn't play by these rules. So he wouldn't either.

chapter two

Michael knew what to do. Get Duffy to trust him implicitly, become totally reliant on him to do his job. Then destroy him.

It would be child's play. Duffy's day revolved around lengthy chats and even lengthier lunches with the few big business customers the branch had. What was going on with the rest of the branch's clientele passed him by. He had jumped at Michael's offer to deal with all the other customer issues and hassles. Michael always completed the weekly letter to head office; went over the branch management reports and dealt with all the queries. Everything Duffy should have been doing. Duffy believed he had found a hard-working and conscientious subordinate who appreciated his view that a branch manager's job was all about projecting the right image and schmoozing the fat-cat customers.

'Just so long as you keep me in the loop, Michael,' Duffy had told him. 'And make sure the correspondence to head office always goes out in my name.'

'No problem at all. The minutiae of the job are what I enjoy. All the little details that show what a good job the branch is doing. I have a lot to learn from you, Hector. I appreciate you letting me get so close to the numbers so I can see how a well-run branch operates. Leaves you more time to concentrate on the big-picture stuff. Drafting your reports is the least I can do.'

Then the whispering started. Michael started making asides to the other branch employees, especially those he knew were well connected to the company gossipmongers and feeders of the rumour mill. Anecdotes about Duffy's aloofness, his lack of any grasp of what was going on. He would check Duffy's mail every morning, intercepting memos, selecting the ones that would remain unanswered. The ones important enough to cause irritation that they hadn't been dealt with, but not so crucial that it would draw attention to the fact that a growing amount of mail was going astray. And Duffy was forever missing some key point or vital piece of paperwork when he went off to regional meetings, so that he fell flat on his face in front of his peers.

But try as he might, nothing happened. Duffy cheerfully blustered his way through the office day, seemingly without a care in the world. No matter to what depths of incompetence he plummeted, he seemed untouchable. Michael's only solace was a new type of memo that started arriving for Duffy, sealed in the brown intracompany envelopes with red edges that signified confidential information, marked *Addressee Only*. Michael ached to know what they contained; if they were merely some sensitive financial or personnel information, or whether they were the beginnings of the recriminations and warnings that would give him hope that his strategy was working.

But the consequences of opening them were too great, the risks too high. Every time Michael saw one, its presence would gnaw away at him. Duffy never mentioned them. Whenever one arrived, whatever was inside the envelope was never on display when he stopped by Duffy's office later in the day. Spirited away into some filing cabinet somewhere, Michael concluded, but no sign of where. Duffy locked the door each evening, and there were too many comings and goings to look for the memos during the day, even if the room was empty. Finding and reading them would be tricky.

Tricky, but not impossible. There was one opportunity. Duffy never locked his door when he went for a business lunch, as his secretary was always popping in and out to drop off whatever she had finished for him. Michael realised he could go into his office on the pretext of leaving a note on his desk about some matter or other. There would be a precious thirty seconds, a minute at a push, when he could open a filing cabinet and check the contents. It would take ten, maybe fifteen visits, but eventually he would have the briefest of glimpses of what was in every drawer.

After the third sweep, he found what he was looking for. Every folder in the filing cabinet immediately behind Duffy's desk had a neatly typed label, and they were arranged alphabetically by Duffy's diligent secretary. But one was labelled *Correspondence* in Duffy's own handwriting. Michael glanced inside. Sure enough, an *Addressee Only* stamp on each memo.

He steeled himself. To complete the next stage of his plan, he would need time to read what was in there. That meant swiping the folder from the office when Duffy went for lunch, finding a place where he could read it without fear of detection, and getting it back before Duffy returned. The next business lunch seemed like a long time coming, but then one Friday, around midday, Michael glanced up from his desk and saw Duffy struggling into his Gannex raincoat. This was it.

He stood outside Duffy's office door, gave a quick look to left and right. Everyone had their heads down, focused on their work. He slipped in, went straight to the filing cabinet, dropped the correspondence folder into a manila envelope, placed a note with some anodyne update on Duffy's desk and was back outside the door, all in a few seconds. A quick catch of his breath and he headed for the gents. He locked himself in a cubicle and gave a long exhale as he opened the envelope.

Memo after memo, more and more frequent – initially, gently pointing out to Duffy that he needed to get a grip on things, then becoming increasingly terse. Michael smiled as he read the one about the debacle at the last managers' meeting. He had intercepted a memo telling Duffy about an imminent interest rate rise in response to a Bank of England base rate hike, only for his ignorance to be exposed at the meeting. The admonition was all the more telling for being curt and direct, lacking any of the pleasantries of the earlier correspondence, which had tiptoed around raising the ungentlemanly notion that Duffy wasn't up to the job. Michael felt an unalloyed satisfaction that his strategy was working. It looked as if one more push would be all it would take to send Duffy on his way.

But first, he needed to return the folder. Duffy's secretary was peering at a handwritten memo, obviously having difficulty in deciphering some handwriting. Michael slipped into the office, glancing back at her to check his presence had gone unnoticed. Then he turned and saw Hector Duffy sitting at his desk.

'Hector. Gosh. Sorry, should have knocked. I thought you'd gone for lunch.'

'Turned up at the restaurant and found the bugger had cancelled. Bloody bad manners if you ask me.' Duffy gave a grump of annoyance. 'Anyway, you look in a hurry. What can I do for you?'

'Never stops,' Michael said, giving himself some time with a chuckle of exasperation. 'I left a note on your desk to ask if you wanted any help getting ready for the regional meeting this week. I was going to add that the revenue forecast is also due, in case you need any input.' He leant over to point to the note he had left earlier, tucking the envelope under his other arm.

'Ah yes. I was going to talk to you about that. Maybe I should be doing more of this stuff myself,' Duffy said, his face reddening. 'I need to spend more time at the coal face. Can't have you doing all the work.'

'I don't mind,' Michael replied. 'You shouldn't be getting tied up in the day-to-day stuff. I'm happy to handle it.'

'And I'm happy to let you.' Duffy sighed. 'But it seems I need to be a walking encyclopaedia about the habits of every single one of our customers these days. I'll be expected to know what they've had for breakfast next.'

'Very unfair, these information requests that keep coming in. When do they think you'll find time to run a bank if you have to deal with all that nonsense?'

'Quite. And that forecast you mentioned. "Where will the business be every month for the next year?" How the bloody hell am I supposed to know?' Duffy shook his head. 'I mean, who do they think I am, Nostradamus? I tell you, Michael, this banking lark is changing out of all recognition. Used to be about people. Now it's results, results, results. Very wearing.'

'I tell you what, let me do the forecast. Don't worry; I'll keep it between ourselves. It will be good for me, great learning experience.'

Duffy didn't need convincing. 'Would you? Not my cup of tea doing that sort of thing. But mum's the word if you don't mind. I've got to make it look like my work.'

'No problem. Only too glad to help. Do you want me to be a bit bullish, or err on the side of caution?'

'Good God, dear boy! Caution. I know you're an ambitious fellow, but I don't want to create a rod for my own back. This job is tough enough already.'

Michael headed back to his desk, clutching the stolen file so tightly his knuckles were white. He slipped it into the top drawer of his desk and waited for Duffy to vacate his office. And waited. The knowledge that at any moment Duffy could open the filing cabinet made it impossible for him to concentrate on anything else. If Duffy found the folder gone, even he would be suspicious – he might even have the wit to start speculating on who had taken it, and why. Michael cursed the man's pomposity. He never ventured from his office. Everyone came to see him.

But he was still human. When Michael saw him heading for the toilet, he slipped in to replace the file. No time to wait until he was sure no one would come in behind him. He closed the door to give himself a few precious undisturbed seconds to replace it, already prepared with his embarrassed chuckle that he'd closed it absent-mindedly, should Hector return too soon. But the operation went smoothly. Michael collapsed into the chair back at his desk, a few seconds before Duffy emerged from his ablutions.

He worked on the forecast that evening, finishing it in the early hours. It showed a massive drop in business to anyone who was familiar with the recent state of the branch's revenue. Which, of course, was not Duffy. He grinned as he finished it. The finest suicide note any bank manager would ever produce.

Michael slipped it surreptitiously to Duffy the next morning. Duffy disappeared into his office to rewrite it, so that it would be in his handwriting when he handed it to his secretary to type up.

'Sounded very professional,' he confided to Michael. 'And I'll have it in before the deadline. Keep the buggers off my back for a while at least.' He patted Michael on the back. 'Thanks again, old chap. Wish you could share in the glory, but needs must, eh? Rest assured, my man, I'll remember your help when the time comes.'

★ ★ ★

It was a red-faced Duffy that called Michael into his office when he came back to the branch after the meeting.

'I think there was a communication breakdown between us, old boy. When I said "conservative", I didn't mean that conservative. Caruthers had it in for me. Made me swear blind I'd done the calculations myself, that I totally believed in the numbers, and then he showed me the branch would effectively be closing down if what I'd forecast became a reality. Asked me to explain myself, and I must admit I floundered. For God's sake, Michael, what were you playing at?'

'I gave you the worst-case scenario, so you could top it up to a level you felt comfortable with.' Michael fished out a carbon copy of the covering memo from his briefcase. 'Just there.'

Duffy groaned. Michael's eyes widened.

'Surely you didn't present the base case numbers? Hector, it's my fault. You did say you wanted to be left alone with the report, finish it off yourself to make sure it looked like it came from you. That's why I left you that last bit to complete. I'm so sorry. I should have made everything clear.'

'Yes, you should. But no use crying over spilt milk. Maybe I should have checked the numbers before sending them on, but it was a busy time. Anyway, I know when to do the decent thing. They want me to quit the branch, do some office job in Edinburgh. Said yes, I'd be delighted, even though I couldn't for the life of me understand what the job was. World's getting too complicated. Don't understand a bloody word of most of what I read from head office these days.'

'You and I both know you've done a fine job at the bank. And I'll tell anyone who asks just that.' Michael gave his assiduously cultivated smile of support. 'And your efforts won't be wasted, Hector. I've run the branch at short notice before. Happy to do it again. Make sure the ball doesn't get dropped.'

Duffy sighed. 'If only things were that simple, Michael. I'm afraid all my flannelling about trying to explain the numbers has led them to believe the branch is all over the place. They're catapulting that bloody whizz-kid in from Edinburgh. Ian Mason, you probably know him. Crisis management, they call it. Bloody cheek. I told them you would have my full confidence to run the branch; that I'd taught you all I know and I'd stake my reputation on you doing a splendid job. But they were having none of it. Sorry, old bean.'

Michael's smile turned into a bitter grimace. Just when things couldn't get any worse, they just had.

chapter three

Michael was alone in his flat. Shostakovich's Symphony No 10 filled the air, the music whirling with a mad frenzy, the brooding strings reflecting his despair, the fury of the brass and percussion fuelling his anger. He had torn off his tie and was slumped down in a chair. The light was fading; he sat motionless as the room descended into darkness.

The record finished playing and the stylus stayed nestled in the playout groove, replacing the soaring music with a repetitive, insistent click, like a clock ticking away the seconds of his life. He let the turntable turn twenty, maybe thirty times before he stirred himself into action and switched it off.

'I will not let them beat me,' he said aloud, each word filled with the fire of conviction. 'I will not let them beat me.'

That evening there was to be a Second Chance charity event. Duffy had stopped Michael using the bank's money to make showy donations, so now he would do so from his own pocket. It was an expensive ritual he couldn't really afford. Away from other people he tended to live an ascetic existence, but in the public gaze he was cultivating a new image; someone successful, generous, with taste and culture. These trappings did not come cheap, and he had to scrimp and save to afford the silver cufflinks, the monogrammed cigarette case and the tailored suits. Charity events gave him a stage to play out his new persona, to be fêted as a dignitary, a favourite of the fresh-faced impressionable young students who formed the bulk of the volunteers. Second Chance had made Michael a trustee, a big responsibility for someone in their early thirties, and at every fundraising event he was treated with deference and admiration, a champion of the disadvantaged and underprivileged. For a few hours at least, he could step into a world where he enjoyed everyone's respect and esteem.

And he was, if he could ever admit it to himself, even a little supportive of what the charity was about. He saw a lot of his own background in the failed lives of the people they were trying to help. He remembered his confusion as a child, when his mother tried to cover up her alcoholic stumbling when he came home from school, and when the domestic chaos of her addiction brought out his father's violent temper. Michael would hide in his room until the shouting and screaming subsided. He had never touched alcohol as a result.

He took a long shower to wash away the negativity of the day, then slipped on a blazer with a pocket square over his crisp white shirt and skinny tie; plaid trousers and loafers completing the look. He still had the hard, muscular body he had developed from his years doing the physical work of a kitchen porter; the clothes hung well on him. It was maybe a touch too formal for the occasion, but he liked it. It gave him gravitas.

The event was at Drumchapel, a thirty-minute drive, and when Michael turned off the A82 and onto the litter-strewn streets of a vast pebble-dashed housing estate, it occurred to him that whatever the desolation of his own upbringing, this was an even more brutal existence. Broken-down cars on every street, random pieces of industrial machinery rusting away on patches of front gardens choked with overgrown weeds. Smashed windows patched up with sodden chipboard, litter blowing over the broken, sagging fences. He parked his Ford Cortina under a street lamp and headed into the community hall.

The evening was based around a talk by Kenny McGowan, a regular speaker at rallies to do with crime, rehabilitation and social injustice. He had been a career villain who had gone straight after serving a lengthy spell in Barlinnie, 'Bar-L' as it was known to the criminal community. McGowan had been notorious in the 1950s and 60s, a razor-wielding thug who had terrorised the mean streets of Glasgow's East End with his gangland antics. Now he was a reformed character and gave talks about that time, as well as campaigning for prison reform and offender rehabilitation.

The place was packed. A hundred and fifty people were crammed into the hall twenty minutes before it started. A small group of students from the university branch of Second Chance huddled together in a corner, the girls' maxi skirts and the boys' loon pants and tie-dyed shirts marking them out as a different tribe to the rest of the audience, who were clad in a drab monotony of brown and beige. A group of men in crumpled, ill-fitting suits and wide kipper ties looked to Michael like criminals; acolytes there to pay homage. He stared for a few seconds at a small man with the pocket-atom frame of a retired featherweight boxer, who was chatting somewhat incongruously to a burly colossus in a long overcoat. He smiled and turned back towards the students, recognised one of the charity volunteers and went over to join them.

Someone walked up to the microphone and tapped it a couple of times.

'Good evening.'

Everyone ignored him.

He tried again. 'Good evening.'

A few heads turned but the conversations continued.

Kenny McGowan walked up to the microphone, strutting like Jimmy Cagney. 'You're no' listening,' he said to the crowd, a flat tone to his voice. 'He said "Good evening".'

The crowd fell silent. McGowan smiled and handed the microphone back to the embarrassed charity worker.

'Um, thanks, Kenny,' the man said, fiddling with his tie. He cleared his throat. 'It's a very special night for Second Chance this evening, because we have two important guests. Michael Mitchell, one of our trustees …'

He indicated Michael with an outstretched arm and there was a polite round of stuttering applause. Michael raised his hand in acknowledgement, nodding a half-smile around the hall. He caught McGowan's eye and saw a look of penetrating appraisal. McGowan's lips loosened into a furtive smile. He knew exactly what game Michael was playing, and Michael looked away first, unsettled.

'… And the person who doesn't need any introduction at all, Drumchapel's own Kenny McGowan. Over to you, Kenny.'

The hall erupted with cheers.

McGowan addressed the crowd with practised ease. He talked about his life of crime, starting at the age of eight, stealing sweets from the local corner shop, and graduating to smashing open cigarette machines by thirteen. Then crying for his ma when he was sent to a notorious List D school. But it was the story behind his life sentence that impressed Michael. McGowan was jailed for the murder of a fellow villain after refusing to name the friend of his who did the deed.

'I'm from the Don't grass on your mates school of thought,' he said. 'Meant I had to eat porridge for fifteen years. I'm no' saying that's right and I'm no' saying that's wrong. It's just who I am.'

The men in ties led the applause.

'Aye, it's good to see you agree with that.' McGowan caught the eye of the pocket atom and they exchanged a meaningful look. 'Because it's all about respect. I had a fierce temper on me, especially when I'd had a dram or two, and I knew how to use my fists and even a chib if I had to. But that sort of respect disnae last. Any hard man can put the fear of God into the punters and get respect for that, until the next hard man comes along to take him out. But real respect, respect that lasts, that disnae come from your fists, that comes from in here.' McGowan pointed to his head. The crowd applauded again.

He was in full flow. 'I had rules, even when I was at my worst. A philosophy, you could call it if you wanted to get poncey. I'd never burgle or steal from my own people. My motto was, "If you want it, take it", but only from the rich buggers – the shops, the banks – where taking a wee something for myself wouldnae cause any hardship.'

That got hoots and hollers. McGowan held up a hand to quieten the crowd. Instant silence.

'Heard o' Fredrick Nietzsche?' he asked.

No response.

'Thought so.' He gestured over to the students. 'That lot would know about him, but they're too feart to say a dickey bird in a crowd like this.'

A murmur of laughter spread around the room. Michael took a step away from the students, staring at his shoes.

'Nietzsche. The man. Asked himself what was right and what was wrong, tried to go beyond words like "good" or "evil". See, if you're a caveman, and your wife and bairns are starving and you go and kill another caveman to get his food, then it's the right thing to do. If the consequences of doing something are right, then that makes the action right. If you then shag all the other cavemen's birds so the strongest genes get passed on, all that shagging would be all right as well. It's no' the morality of the action that matters; it's how beneficial it is. The morality of consequences, the end justifying the means. Nowadays, none of what that caveman did would be acceptable. But it was back then, that's how society worked. If the world was treating you badly, doing what it took to make that right was just fine and dandy. Nobody would have expected you to do otherwise.'

Michael wasn't staring at his shoes now. Every word that McGowan uttered seemed to throb with significance. This was a credo he could live his life by.

The charity guy introduced Michael to McGowan after the talk, describing him as a big supporter from the business world, a bank manager from the Royal Clydeside. Michael didn't correct the job description.

'Bank manager, eh?' said McGowan. He asked Michael to wait behind for a few minutes so he could have a word. Curious, Michael agreed.

Michael returned to the student group. They were talking loudly to each other, congratulating themselves for daring to venture into this part of Glasgow, but at the same time completely isolating themselves from the community they purported to understand and help. The youngest-looking amongst them, a pretty brunette, was standing slightly apart from the group, vigorously nodding to all that was being said.

Michael asked them a few questions about McGowan's speech. Two young men were doing most of the talking so he asked one about the thoughts of the other and stepped away, letting them debate without him. He turned to the young woman, asked her name and took another step away from the group. When she answered, he cupped his hand to his ear, pretending not to hear over the hubbub. She stepped closer.

'Mary,' she said, swaying on her feet – a combination, it seemed, of nervousness and enthusiasm.

'Your first time in Drumchapel?'

'Yes,' she replied. 'I'm looking to make a difference while I'm at uni. Second Chance seems to offer the sort of practical support young people in this part of Glasgow need.'

It was a reply straight out of the charity's flyer. The base of her neck started to redden.

Michael went into his well-practised routine about being a major figure in the banking world, tasked by his bank to spearhead their efforts to put something back into the communities they served.

'It takes a lot of my time,' he said, 'but it's worth it.'

He encouraged her to start talking about herself. She was nineteen, she told him, studying sociology and still living with her parents, like a lot of the other students at the university.

'But that's only until the end of term,' she told Michael. 'I've got a summer job at Butlins, down in Ayr. Next year I want to get a flat. I think I'm missing out, living at home. I'm counting the days until I move out.' Then she spluttered and quickly added, 'But that doesn't mean I don't love my parents, or don't appreciate everything they've done for me. You mustn't think that.'

Michael found her awkwardness endearing. 'Don't worry, I didn't think anything,' he said. 'You want to be independent, nothing wrong with that. And you're doing something about it, not waiting for it to happen. That's the right thing to do.'

Mary beamed.

Someone came over to tell Michael that McGowan was ready to talk. Mary looked impressed and started to stumble out a goodbye, but Michael interrupted.

'I'm enjoying our chat, Mary,' he said, and noticed a flush of pride that he had remembered her name. 'Look, I've got my car parked outside. If it's still there, that is. Why don't I have a quick word with Kenny and then I'll give you a lift over to an Underground station? We can talk some more as we drive. Save you having to wait ages for a bus.'

She looked uncertain, but only for a moment. 'Are you sure? Thank you.'

Michael walked over to McGowan and the cast of *The Lavender Hill Mob*. McGowan beckoned him towards the corner of the room. They dragged two chairs over and sat down to talk. Michael glanced over at Mary, and whatever she was saying to the group was causing some surprised glances to be cast in his direction.

'Thanks, pal, for hanging back for a wee natter,' said McGowan, his eyes betraying a keen intelligence.

'No problem. But if you're looking for an insider to help with your next bank heist I'm not available, sorry.'

'Nice one, pal. Good to see a suit with a sense of humour. But that's no' what I wanted to talk to you about. It's about opening an account.'

'No problem.' Michael was slightly disappointed. 'Come into the branch on Monday and we can fill in all the forms, get you sorted.'

'No' for me, you eejit. I'm a celebrity now; I've no problem. I'm talking about all the guys that get let out of Bar-L. You banks look at them like they've crawled out from under a stone when they try to get on the straight and narrow. I want you to do something about all the prejudice that exists about ex-cons. Tell your toffee-nosed tellers not to send them packing when they come in to bank their giros.'

'Getting them a line of credit might be a problem in the short term, but there's no reason why we should refuse anyone who wants to open a simple bank account. Here's my card. If any of your … colleagues want to open an account, tell them to make an appointment to see me. I'll do all I can.'

'Way to go, pal, that's brilliant. Wish there were more like you. Owe you one for this. If you've ever got something that needs sorting out, just let me know and I'll do all I can. Here's my number, call anytime. But legal, like. I'm a reformed character these days.'

They shook hands and their eyes met, a spark of recognition between kindred souls. Half-formed dreams began to take wing in Michael's imagination. What McGowan had described was a world with codes of honour, self-imposed no-go areas about where the boundaries were on the crimes committed, conventions and rules about solving disputes and exacting revenge. It was like a parallel society alongside the one he knew, where the moral code was not handed down from on high but came from the people themselves. He found it unnervingly exciting.

Mary was waiting for him as he returned, her friends long departed.

'This is very kind of you, Mr Mitchell,' she said. 'You really don't have to go to all this trouble.'

'Michael, please. It's no trouble. Like I said, I've enjoyed chatting to you.'

'And me too … Likewise … Chatting.' She shook her head and laughed. 'If I can get a sentence out.'

Mary lived in Paisley and Michael suggested she take the Underground from Kelvinbridge to St Enoch to get the train home. Neither of them mentioned it was a rather circuitous route. He turned the car off the Great Western Road about a mile before the station.

'Plenty of time until the last train,' he said. 'Let's stop off at my place to continue our chat. If you've got time.'

Mary turned to look at him, her eye contact steady now.

'The last train is at eleven-ten,' she said. 'Plenty of time.'

At the flat, Michael took a Barry White album from his album rack, carefully removed the vinyl from its cover and placed it on the turntable. He switched the record player on and watched the needle drop down onto the first track. The deep growling voice filled the room. Michael turned to Mary, who was perched on the edge of the sofa. He sat down next to her.

'You look uncomfortable, sitting there,' he said to her. 'Come closer.'

They started kissing, gentle and tender. It had been just over a month since Michael had finished his last relationship, a clandestine affair with one of the bank tellers which had ended when she had started getting too close, wanting him to open up. He had always craved physical intimacy, hungered for the love and affection denied him as a child, but he baulked at giving too much of himself to any lover. Every relationship floundered on the cusp of becoming more serious.

As the kissing became more frenetic, Michael slipped his hand under Mary's camisole, cupping her breast and brushing the hard pearl of her nipple with his slim, pianist-like fingers. He felt her body spasm and slacken, then she closed her eyes and pulled him towards her. As he started to trace the length of her spine with his nails, she released her grasp and, with one fluid movement, pulled her camisole over her head. She gazed at him with dark brown, virginally-wide eyes, a look of innocence that could not have been in starker contrast to the boldness of her actions. This was not the time to start another relationship, Michael knew. He needed to be on his own, keep a clear head, avoid distractions. That thought lasted no more than a split second. He unzipped her jeans, put his hands behind her knees and manoeuvred her to the edge of the sofa. Gliding his fingers down the sides of her waist, he gently slipped her jeans down to her ankles and, as they fell to the ground, slowly finished undressing her. He drew her knees apart and breathed in the sweet bouquet of what the French would call her *cassolette*, the scent of a woman, the aroma of arousal. Michael buried his head deeper between her legs. The taste was even sweeter.

She got dressed afterwards, looking at Michael in a daze of dreamy satisfaction that only partly covered the apparent pangs of worry that she'd done something she'd later regret. He was careful to reassure her, to make sure she knew that this wasn't the one-night stand she feared. He wanted to meet again. The next evening, and the one after that. She looked happy, relieved. He knew it was foolhardy, but he was already looking forward to the next time.

Michael insisted on driving her to Paisley, parking around the corner from her parents' house as they said their goodbyes. As he returned to his flat, reality began to intrude. Still assistant manager despite all his plotting. Now with a new boss, humiliatingly younger than himself and not as easy to deceive. He was too old to start another career, lacked the university degree that all the other banks insisted on for a management position. He was trapped – in a world he was growing to despise.

The bubble of prestige and importance he'd been in all evening burst and the intolerable reality returned. He deserved better, no matter what it took to achieve it.

The morality of consequences.

chapter four

Ian Mason wasted no time transferring to the branch. He came over from Edinburgh in the afternoon, introduced himself to the staff and disappeared into Duffy's office for the handover. It lasted thirty minutes. They came out, Duffy headed off somewhere, and Michael was called in for a chat.

'Looks like I was talking to the wrong person trying to get a handle on what's going on here,' said Mason. 'I think old Hector has been out of his depth. It's valiant of you to carry him for so long. Must have been an impossible workload.'

Michael's shrug gave little away.

'I hope I can make things easier for you from now on,' Mason said. 'You'll find I'm very hands-on, a bit of a stickler for detail. If you help me with the management reporting first time around, you won't have to worry about half the things you've had to put up with once I get up to speed. I've scheduled a few hours this afternoon for you to brief me. Let me take a lot off your plate, give you more time to do your job.'

'Very kind of you, Ian,' Michael replied. 'But it was no problem. Happy to keep doing it, if you like.'

'No, that's okay. One place where I do want you to keep up the good work is signing up these new accounts. This branch's enquiries-to-acquisition ratio is outstanding.' Mason smiled, and Michael tried to smile back. 'You seem to have a real knack for charming students into signing on the dotted line. That can be your baby. It's very important for the bank to win as many student customers as possible, and I want Byres Road to be the best university branch in Scotland – and I don't just mean within the Royal Clydeside. I'm an ambitious man, Michael, and I know you're ambitious too. Let's make this happen together.'

A lot of new accounts were opened in the next few weeks and Michael was pleased that Mason didn't scrutinise them too closely. Michael was true to his word with Kenny McGowan, and a steady stream of slightly dubious characters came into the bank, mainly on a Wednesday afternoon when Mason headed off for the weekly management meeting. Michael opened current accounts for all of them, apart from one guy who was a notorious con artist, but even with him, Michael had agreed to a deposit account, flagged for close monitoring. New student accounts, all that Michael had left of the job he was doing before, also continued to multiply. Mary moved her account to Royal Clydeside and persuaded a few of her friends to do likewise. Sleeping with prospective customers was not a technique he'd come across in the bank's marketing manual, but it was effective nonetheless.

However, Mason's first pep talk to the branch staff had confirmed Michael's worst fears. According to the new manager, the key to efficiency was clarity. Everyone should know who did what; there was to be no duplication of responsibility. Every management decision was to be made by him, and him alone. For the first few weeks, when other staff members would go to Michael out of habit to get the okay for a customer issue if Mason was not around, Mason would make a point of contradicting Michael when he heard of it. It had the desired effect; Michael was back to being a glorified bank teller. He wasn't sure what angered him most, the insincere attempts by Mason to praise him when no one was around, to try to con him into thinking he was valued, or the constant humiliating reminders to the rest of the staff that he had no authority around the branch anymore.

'I've got the company magazine chap coming in tomorrow,' Mason told Michael a few weeks into the job. 'Bringing a photographer. He wants to do an interview with a new branch manager.' He gave a nonchalant shrug. 'Bit of a pain, if you ask me. But if I have to do it, I may as well do it right.'

He waited for Michael's response but was met with silence.

'Anyway, that's what's happening,' said Mason, flustered. 'They want photos of me in action and I thought I'd take over one of your new student customer interviews tomorrow to give them something photogenic. If that's all right with you.'

Without waiting for a reply, Mason picked up Michael's appointment diary. 'Ah, good. An appointment at two o'clock.' He peered at the entry. 'Medical student. Excellent. And a woman, very modern. Can you get me her application form? I'll tell everyone to get the office smartened up in case they want another few photos around the place. Don't worry, it'll all be over in a couple of hours and then we can get back to normal.'

Mason puffed and preened around the office the next day. Michael found it laughable that he complained about the disruption but was loving his moment in the limelight. He harboured a delicious fantasy that the medical student's application interview would turn out to be a disaster and even toyed with thinking up ways to sabotage it, but in the end decided it was too risky. Mason wasn't as much of a fool as Duffy. If he suspected any disloyalty, Michael was sure it would backfire on him. He gritted his teeth and kept his head down. Let Mason get his ego trip over with as quickly as possible.

Two months later the article appeared in the company magazine. Mason on the front cover, hailed as the bank's rising star, a photo of him inside shaking hands with the new student customer. The article was full of his boasts of the branch being the top performer in winning new customers. Not a single mention of Michael Mitchell. As he read it, Michael felt he'd been kicked in the stomach. The only thing at the bank that he could still call his own, and Mason was taking all the credit.

He decided. He could take no more, even if it required giving up on his dreams. No matter what platitudes came his way, where he had come from meant he wasn't for the top. He had to get out. Anything was better than this.

★ ★ ★

It was a chance look through some paperwork that led Michael to the discovery that Royal Clydeside Bank had a criminal as a customer. A real criminal, operating right under their noses, and not one of McGowan's referrals.

When Mason had told Michael after the magazine article that it was best he saw the new account applications going forward and have one of the senior tellers handle the paperwork, he lamely tried to sell Michael on the new responsibility he would have in its place: the annual check of business customers' bank records to spot any warning signs. Michael could see why Mason had given the job to him. Boring, repetitive and invisible. Nothing that could take the shine off Mason's own career prospects.

At first glance, Ron's Taxis looked okay. Quarterly revenues up forty per cent on the previous quarter, total annual income a more than respectable £60,752. But almost no outgoings. Money paid in as large lump sums, rather than daily takings. It was not the way a taxi firm did business.

He went to get the City Taxis file for comparison. As he suspected, money paid in daily; direct debits to the garage that supplied the diesel; payroll payments to the drivers, and a loan account to purchase new vehicles. Ron's Taxis had no employees; the taxis drove on air, and there was only one actual vehicle on the books. He checked the file history. Every previous year showed the same picture. Every one initialled and signed off by his predecessors.

He permitted himself a small smile of self-congratulation. This would be the chance to show he was able to do more than just charm impressionable students to open their bank accounts with Royal Clydeside. And criminal activity reports went straight to head office, so there was no way Mason could steal his glory. Michael reached for the phone before realising that he should probably mention it to Mason in any case. No point in causing unnecessary friction when he found out Michael had filed a report. He slipped on his jacket, an act of false deference, knocked on Mason's door and entered when called.

'Oh, it's you,' said Mason, barely looking up. 'Come back later, will you? I'm in the middle of something right now.'

Michael recoiled at the abrupt dismissal, and a feeling of rebellion stirred within him. Ron's Taxis, he decided, was safe. He walked back to his desk and slipped the file into his briefcase.

Mary came around for a meal that evening. She had looked surprised when he told her he enjoyed cooking, that it relaxed him. To an extent it was true, but projecting an image way beyond his means meant balancing occasional fancy restaurants with more frequent entertaining at home. A cheap curry would be a giveaway. Cooking at the flat was both romantic and economical.

She was turning out to be the perfect girlfriend. Fun and lively, she was a welcome escape from his troubles, besotted by his charm, as enthusiastic in bed as she was with life in general, and always eager to learn more. Michael, in turn, was enamoured by the transformation that happened every night as her demure demeanour gave way to passionate lovemaking. And, most of all, he was pleased that she respected his need to be left alone and didn't try to pry into his inner thoughts.

The only thing she tried to influence was Michael's steadfast refusal to have anything to do with the counter-culture music and fashion that she was part of.

'Come on, Michael,' she would implore him. 'Let's go to a gig together. Gentle Giant are playing Green's Playhouse. You'll like them.'

The compromise they reached was that she would bring some of her favourite LPs and Michael would dutifully give them a listen. Wishbone Ash and Van der Graaf Generator only got one playing, but Michael grudgingly admitted that the rhythmic abstraction of Soft Machine and Can could be tolerated if played quietly in the background. Michael liked that she was trying to influence him, to get him to loosen up a bit. He promised himself he'd do so, once he was in the right frame of mind.

Usually, Mary stayed until eleven, when Michael would drive her back to her parents' house in Paisley, but this night he wanted her to leave early. The meal had been perfunctory, the sex by usual standards rushed, and he took Mary to the train station two hours earlier than usual, with an apology. Michael had some thinking to do.

When he returned to the flat, he sat down to read through the file again. He could just about recollect who this Ron character was. Pale and tall, like a henchman in a Hitchcock movie. He jotted down the last few months' transactions and added them up. No wonder he was putting money in the bank. Wherever he was getting it from, it was too much to stuff under the mattress. That was the risk of being a criminal. Danger getting the money, danger holding on to it, and danger spending it. You could just as easily be brought to justice by an eagle-eyed bank employee as you could by a clever detective.

Michael pulled out a pad of paper and wrote *Ron's Taxis* at the top. It already felt like a piece of incriminating evidence. He added a question mark. A police siren suddenly pierced the silence in the room. He walked over to the window in time to see a blue light turn the corner and disappear.

'Haven't got me yet,' he said aloud. The joke made him smile.

He turned to the record player, found his Bach Sonatas, slid the album out of the sleeve and sat it on the turntable. After a second of pristine silence, the contemplative profundity of the music filled the room.

Michael sat down at his desk. The abstract architecture of Bach's music helped frame his thoughts. He would be logical, dispassionate. Nothing would be left to chance.

He tried to imagine himself committing a criminal act, and the photograph of a disgraced bank manager from the *Glasgow Herald* weeks before leapt back into his mind. The ashen-faced police mugshot of a previously respectable banker, sentenced to five years for stealing customers' money. He could imagine every ounce of anguish that pitiful wretch must have felt.

Folly. Michael shook his head and tore off the page. He ripped it in half. Just to be sure, he threw it in the fire and watched as the paper leapt into flames. He lit a cigarette, but that didn't seem to help. This was a waste of time, he told himself. If he was paranoid about the implications of two innocuous words written on a sheet of paper, he would be driven crazy by taking any real risk.

An involuntary shake of his head spurred him on to think again. Cowardice. If things were going to change he couldn't be weak. Doing nothing was always an easy option. When the magazine article came out, Mason had pretended it didn't exist. The right thing would have been to apologise, to show he realised he had got credit for something undeserved and promise to put things right. But Mason was a coward. He had taken the easy way out, hoping if he did nothing, nothing would be said. Michael despised him for that. If Michael wanted things to happen, he needed to be bold, he needed to be daring.

The phone rang. That would be Mary, letting him know she'd got home safely. It rang for a minute or so before going silent. Michael picked up the pad of paper again. Wrote *Idea* at the top of the page.

Idea. If he was to be a criminal, he had to be anonymous. No one should ever be able to penetrate the disguise of the successful businessman, always under control. He inhaled on his cigarette and blew out some smoke in the direction of a poster on the wall, a print of a Magritte painting he'd bought in Woolworths, a bowler-hatted man with a green apple covering his face, Blu-Tacked to the wall where it covered a damp patch. The inscrutability of the image always resonated with him, the businessman's real self invisible, the outside world seeing only the apple.

Idea. His mind played with possibilities, as fitfully and discursively as a musician runs his fingers over a keyboard. Ron has trouble concealing his ill-gotten gains from view. That must be a common problem. Maybe there's a way to hide and launder criminal cash. With an accomplice, perhaps, to deal with other criminals who want a similar service? He would never come into contact with the clients. Michael smiled at the word 'clients'. It sounded very respectable. Yes, an accomplice. A partner. They would be the visible side of the operation; he would be in the shadows.

He wrote, *Handle cash. Run operation back office.* on the pad and put a tick beside it.

Michael picked up the bank file again. An accomplice would be high risk. Ron, the taxi man – could it be him? Could he confront him with what he'd found out, deal with whatever unpredictable response he received, determine if he was the right partner and if it all felt wrong, pretend that it never happened?

Michael's mouth was parched; he went into the kitchen for some water. He drank it in one gulp, feverishly, like he'd been in the desert for days. He remembered his mother drinking gin like that when she was stressed, like she was trying to put out the fires of some unquenchable hell. He shuddered. One day, he promised himself. One day he would be free of his past.

He sat down again. *Ask McGowan*, Michael wrote on the pad. He could do that. Another risk, but a manageable one. McGowan knew everyone. He kept secrets. If he warned me off making contact, Michael reasoned, the exposure would be minimal. Michael recalled McGowan's speech in Drumchapel, the irony of a hardened criminal spouting a moral code he could believe in. The morality of consequences. This plan fitted that philosophy exactly. Yes, ask McGowan.

Meeting 1: Introduction and confrontation. Get Ron into the bank, tell him what he knew, say there was a proposition that might interest him. Suss him out. And if he decided to walk away, so what? Ron's word against his, and why would Ron want to say anything? The worst that could happen would be the loss of a customer.

Meeting 2: Proposition. Starting to get in deep. *Could still walk away.*

Michael wrote on the pad one final time. *Meeting 3: Decision*. He stared at the words. Would that day ever come? He tore the page out of the notepad. Glanced over to the fireplace. He hesitated for a second, then slipped the page into a desk drawer and placed the pad on top.

Michael thought back to that evening he'd seen McGowan. Fifteen years in jail because his code of honour prevented him from grassing on one of his friends. He could be trusted not to reveal one incriminating, but theoretical, conversation. It was a gamble, but any business proposition came with risk.

McGowan had said that he owed Michael for helping the ex-cons. It was time to take him up on his offer.

★ ★ ★

Michael arrived ten minutes early for their meeting in an East End pub, the conversations of the customers a mix of gregarious banter and whispered confidences. When he asked for a club soda, the barman stared in disbelief, his reaction picked up in an instant at more than one table. The buzz of chatter perceptibly hushed, everyone on full alert. Michael felt the hostility crackle in the air.

He went to an empty table and could feel the eyes boring into him. The miasmic fug of cigarette smoke was suffocating. A one-armed bandit in the corner suddenly paid out, its celebratory bells and jangling of coins cutting an incongruous note through the tension.

McGowan walked in. Someone proffered a handshake. The buzz of conversation returned as he glad-handed his way to the bar, like a politician working a crowd. A pint of Belhaven was already poured as he got to the counter. Michael saw McGowan go through the motions of offering to pay for it, the barman laughingly declining.

He spotted Michael and came over. A disbelieving mutter went around the bar. The two men sitting nearest them stood up, and with a deferential nod to McGowan, moved to another table out of earshot.

'You're treated like a king here,' Michael said.

'Aye, respect.' McGowan looked around. 'As you heard me say, that's always been a big thing with me. Respect is the only thing that keeps folk loyal to you.'

'Was that how you kept out of prison for so long?'

McGowan stiffened at the directness of the question, then relaxed.

'Definitely,' he replied. 'Just about every gang member gets nicked eventually. No' because they get caught, but because they get betrayed. My folks would do anything for me, because they love me.' He leant forward until his face was a few inches from Michael. 'And because they fear me.'

McGowan sat back in his chair having made his point. 'But you still need to know what you're doing to make a killing at this game. Get inside information, think ahead, always have a plan B. And never get greedy.'

'How do you know who to trust?' Michael was inching towards deciding whether to take McGowan into his confidence. For all he knew, this could all be an act. McGowan could be someone who shouted his mouth off when he felt in the mood. He could even be a police informer these days.

'I don't trust anybody,' McGowan said, with a shake of his head. 'Everybody's got some wee scam going on in their life that they don't want to be found out. And I definitely don't fucking trust you, young Michael. I can see you're up to something, so why don't you stop fannying about and tell me what it is? You didnae come all the way out to Shettleston to enjoy the delights of a club soda.'

Michael flinched, but didn't hesitate. 'You're right. It's time I told you why I asked to see you. Have you ever heard of a man called Ron Smith?'

There was a long pause.

'Ron Smith? Common enough name. Why would I know a Ron Smith?'

'He's a customer at the bank. Runs a taxi firm. At least that's what his file says. But I think there's more to him than that. I'm thinking of approaching him with a business proposition, but I wanted to find out about him first.'

'Now why would I happen to know a taxi driver and even if I did, why would I tell you anything about him?'

'Because he's in trouble and he doesn't know it. His banking record has a funny smell about it. I want to help him fix it.'

McGowan frowned. 'Planning a shakedown, Michael? I must say you disappoint me. And all these bank accounts you've been opening? Are these poor wee sods next on your list?'

'No, you've got me wrong. Not a shakedown.' Michael hesitated for a second, testing himself to see if there was any doubt in his mind about what he was about to say next. But he'd never felt more sure.

'A partnership. I'm not talking about looking the other way with Ron. I'm talking about showing him how to stash his money better. And if it works for him, finding the contacts that let me help others in the same boat.'

McGowan's grim face was like a carved mask, simultaneously inscrutable and menacing.

'*Do I know Ron Smith*? You don't come here and ask me questions like that, pal. I'm no' a pimp you can use to chat up whatever villain takes your fancy. Who the fuck do you think you are, asking Kenny McGowan to finger a criminal, be your lackey to introduce you to some punter so he can kiss your feet because you want to do him a favour? You have no fucking idea what you're getting into. And if you expect me to help you, you're off your trolley.'

Michael didn't back off. 'I'm sorry if I offended, Kenny. I've got nothing but the deepest admiration for you. I agreed with every word of what you said in Drumchapel. I want to live by that code. That's why I'm here, out of respect. I don't expect you to help me, but I'd be honoured if you did. I'm about to make the biggest decision of my life, and what you say matters to me. And yes, I need your advice. Will you help me?'

McGowan smiled. Michael had the uncomfortable feeling that he had just passed a test.

'Let's say I do know Ron Smith. If you want me to tell you if he's a crook, you can fuck off. Just as I'd say the same to anyone who asked me if you were planning to become a bent bank manager. But if you want to know what he's like as a bloke, aye, I could do that.'

'And? What's he like?'

'Old school. Rare to find these days. Plans well. Smart, discreet. Got a good brain; no' a nutter like so many of the yobs doing jobs these days. Has a lot of respect on the street. But he's small beer. He keeps out of trouble from the big boys, never looks like someone who wants to run an empire. I'm talking about his taxi business, of course. Just so we're clear.'

There was a glint in his eyes. McGowan obviously liked playing matchmaker.

'He might be street smart,' said Michael, 'but he's going to draw attention to himself if he doesn't watch out. There's a new manager at my bank who's itching to make a name for himself. He's pretty astute. Only a matter of time before he notices what Ron's up to.'

'New manager? I thought you were the manager there?' McGowan chuckled to himself. 'Now it's becoming a bit clearer what's going on. Had a knockback, have you, wee Michael? Found out the world can be a cruel place sometimes?'

'Since you ask, yes. Been passed over twice now for a job I can do standing on my head. I'm taking my destiny in my own hands. So, Ron Smith. Should I talk to him?'

'As I've told you, I'm retired now, straight as an arrow. But you could do worse than Ron if you want to go down that road. Aye, give him a proposition. He'll no' like it at first, but he's smart enough to see if it makes sense.'

'Can I mention your name?'

'No, sorry, pal. That's me getting involved, and I don't do that.' He leant over and squeezed Michael's arm. 'I … don't … do … that,' he repeated. 'You'll no' forget, will you?' The squeeze was getting painful. McGowan let go and took a sip of his beer. 'Let's say this was an … off-the-record chat. A character reference, if you like. Just between you and me.'

Michael waited until the next day before taking any action. The conversation with McGowan was as good a green light as he was ever going to get. There was no reason not to progress to stage two. But it was a big moment. It was all he had thought about since meeting with McGowan, but no new perspectives or alternatives had come out of his endless internal debate. He toyed with calling Ron directly, but that wasn't office protocol. And he didn't want to start the conversation over the phone; he wanted to be face to face to read the signals he was getting before he said too much. He told the office secretary to call Ron, asking him to make an appointment to review his account, any time in the next few days.

'Certainly, Mr Mitchell,' she replied. 'Should I give a reason for the meeting?'

'Say I want to discuss bank procedures. If he asks why, say I'm not around at the moment but that I did say we should discuss it in person. Wednesday would be good for me, if that gives him enough notice.' Mason's Edinburgh day.

She made the appointment for two o'clock on Wednesday. For the rest of the day, anxiety and excitement tore through his body as he thought about what he had set in motion. As time went on, the tension faded and an eerie calmness took over. He felt a sense of freedom, of liberation, that he had never experienced before.

He had spent all his adult life trying to succeed in a world where his talents were not valued. Now, for the first time, he was going to do something about it.

chapter five

Michael woke early. Other than that, his morning routine was as exactly choreographed as usual. He gave his shoes a quick polish, selected one of the five identical white shirts from his wardrobe and put on a silk tie and matching cufflinks. With time to kill, he arrived in Byres Road and headed off to University Café for breakfast. He glanced at the front-page headline in the *Glasgow Herald*. The government was warning of petrol rationing. His scrambled eggs on toast remained untouched.

The seconds crawled by. It was still not too late, Michael told himself. When this Ron character turned up, if he had any doubts, he could say the meeting was only about the account irregularities. Ask Ron to explain himself and watch him disappear into the distance, never to be seen again.

Or he could even abandon the whole harebrained scheme before it got started. The possibility flooded Michael's body with relief. He cut the corner off a piece of toast, his appetite returning. Then he looked outside again, at the early morning commuters scurrying by the window, their heads down and their collars turned up to protect them from a biting, cold rain. Rushing to start another day of their miserable existence, all because they didn't have the courage or imagination to do anything about it. He pushed his plate away, drained his coffee and stood up. He was going to see this thing through.

Ron Smith arrived at ten sharp. Michael got a glimpse of him as he was shown into the meeting room. Late thirties, with a bad haircut that did nothing to improve his ferret face. He looked wary and focused, his body rigid with tension. A good sign. Whatever bluster he might try on, this was a small-time crook who was apprehensive that he was about to find out he'd been rumbled. He had to be approached carefully, like a cornered wild animal.

Michael let him stew in the meeting room for a few minutes and then got up and walked in to meet him.

'Mr Smith, a pleasure to meet you,' he said. 'Thanks very much for being so prompt. Got a busy day so it's much appreciated.'

'I'm busy too.' Ron gave him a fixed stare. 'Can you tell me what the problem is?'

Michael produced a ledger pad and opened it at the front page. He'd got a new pad to do this analysis; one which he would dispose of afterwards. There would be no record of today's meeting.

'We have three taxi firms who use this bank. I want to show you a comparison between the three of you. I've called the other two firms A and B, and of course I can't tell you who they are for client confidentiality reasons. But I think what I'll show you will be quite clear.'

Ron remained silent.

'You see, when I look at their statements over the last three months, their outgoings on average are sixty per cent of their income. It varies between forty-five and seventy per cent. With your business, it's less than ten. Can you explain that?'

Ron stood up. 'No, I can't. If all you've got me here for is to ask bloody stupid questions, then I'm leaving. If you've got a problem with my business, I'll go elsewhere.'

Michael's question had been exactly what any diligent bank employee would have asked when investigating a suspicious transaction. Even what he was going to say next could easily be explained as a misunderstanding. Michael felt his skin prickling. He uttered the words he had rehearsed the night before.

'Please, Mr Smith. Sit down. I want to help you. Even a cursory glance at your accounts raises more questions than it answers. That might be a problem for you one day. Not with me, you understand. I'm all for people doing well in their line of work. But I'm not the only person who looks at these numbers. I want to help you to make them appear as above board as of course they are, so that they don't attract … unwanted attention. That's all.'

The last sentence hung in the air, filling the room with an atmosphere of conspiracy.

'That's very good of you,' was Ron's icy reply. 'And just why would you want to do that?'

Michael laughed. 'You've obviously never seen what an audit looks like. Extremely tiresome, I can assure you. I thought if I invested some effort to help you while the numbers in your account look a little … unbalanced, shall we say, it would save us both a lot of paperwork later on.'

His relaxed demeanour did nothing to betray that his senses were on full alert, picking up every tiny clue in Ron's reaction. The whitening of Ron's knuckles as his hands made a fist. The tensing of his body. Eyes narrowing as he tried to work out whether he was dealing with a bumbling incompetent, a corrupt official. Or both.

'Shoot,' Ron said. 'What's the deal?' He spat out the words. 'Go on. I'm all ears.'

Michael's first concern, that Ron would walk out without hearing another word, seemed to have passed. McGowan had been right: Ron liked to listen, rather than act impulsively.

'Frankly, Mr Smith ... Ron, may I call you Ron?' Michael didn't wait for a reply. 'Frankly, Ron, there's something not quite right about your bank account. It's a time bomb. If anyone from our audit office looked at it, they would see it as a classic cover for criminal activities. Now you don't look like that sort of person to me, so I want to help you avoid unnecessary suspicion.'

Ron glared. 'Look, pal, what's your point? If you're looking for a wee sweetener to look the other way, you're way out of your league. You don't want to mess with things that don't concern you. Understand?'

'I hate when people get something for nothing.' Michael gave a dismissive shake of the head. 'I'm not trying to do that. I want to offer you a proposition.'

Ron lowered his eyes; his brow wrinkled in suspicion.

'You have a very successful, if slightly unconventional, taxi firm,' Michael said. 'You seem to be good at what you do; you're doing well. But what you're not good at is being discreet about your success. That's where I come in. Working at the bank has taught me a lot about discretion. I want to share that knowledge with a customer who would value it. You.'

Ron said nothing, the slightest nod of the head telling Michael he was interested.

'I'd like us to meet again, away from the bank, where I can offer you … let's call it a consultancy service. Something that could help your business and others like it. That's what this is about. No threats. No blackmail. I do it for free, as a way to get to know each other. To explore whether working together, the two of us, we can make your business look above suspicion to anybody who takes a look, for whatever reason. And if it works for you, to consider whether it might be a service that other individuals might be interested in. People who might pay handsomely to demonstrate that their money is squeaky clean. And to see if I can trust you. And, of course, if you can trust me. Interested?'

Ron paused and looked around. 'You're one cool customer, pal. You're either a nutter, or this is a set-up. Look at you, mister bank manager, in your pinstripe suit. What makes you think I would trust you an inch? How do I know that that this is not your bank's way of stitching me up? Why should I tell a poncey git like you how I run my business? *Consultancy service*? Yeah, right.'

'Why should you trust me?' Michael nodded to himself as if to acknowledge the reasonableness of the question. When he spoke again, his voice became more intense. 'Because this is not the way banks work. Do you think it would be acceptable for my superiors to ask me to take the sort of personal risk a conversation like this might entail? Your account sticks out like a sore thumb. If it had been spotted before now, it would be the Fraud Squad you'd be talking to. Not, as you say, a poncey git like me.

I'm the one taking the risks. It's me that should be asking for the reassurances. Think about it and get back to me.'

Michael stood up to signal the meeting was at an end.

'I think that covers everything, Ron. Please call me Michael, if we meet again. And if you do want to meet, give me a call and we'll arrange something.'

He opened the door and Ron walked out, shaking his head. Michael went back into the meeting room, closed the door and leant against it, taking a deep breath. Everything would be okay. Ron wouldn't want to draw attention to himself by reacting to what he had told him. Even if there had been a legitimate explanation for his finances and he reported Michael to the authorities, Michael could deny the conversation took place.

All he had to do now, was wait.

★ ★ ★

In the meantime, there was Mary to distract him. He was in the uncharted waters of a five-month-old relationship. He had always resisted letting anyone stay around long enough to get to know him, but with everything that was going on, he told himself he didn't want to waste any energy moving on. There was more to it than that, though. Every night with Mary was as intense as the last. She'd arrive at his flat as fresh as the fragrance of a crushed herb, and leave with the earthy muskiness of a fulfilled Aphrodite, the glazed look in her eyes betraying the night's pleasures. Tonight promised to be no different.

As usual, their passion started the moment he opened the door, their lovemaking beginning on the hallway floor, as they slowly, inexorably and pleasurably made their way to the bedroom. After their bout of frenzied lovemaking had ended, Mary jumped off the bed, following the trail of discarded clothes back to the hallway, where she scooped up her bag and scampered back to the bed, giddy with excitement.

'I have a present for you, my darling,' she said, her eyes sparkling with pride. 'Open it.'

It was a Peruvian angora sweater she must have spent weeks doggedly knitting. Michael slipped it over his naked body and sat up on the bed, looming over her. 'What do you think?'

She reached up and pulled him towards her. 'I knew I'd guessed your size. I've been knitting it since that very first week we met. Do you like it?'

'Love it,' Michael replied. 'No wonder it took so long.' He tugged at a sleeve to stop his arm from itching.

'Mum and Dad were full of questions about who I was knitting it for. I'd like them to meet you, Michael. Would you do that for me?'

His gaze wandered around the room. This was the problem with letting relationships go on for too long.

'I'd love to,' he said, a flat tone to his words. 'But I'm not sure it would be a good idea, not yet. I'm twelve years older than you, don't forget. That's a lot when you're nineteen. I think it might be awkward. For them, not me.'

'I think you're being silly,' Mary replied. 'And Mum and Dad are different. They don't like who I usually hang out with. Dad says they're all hippies and communists and a spell in the army would do them the world of good. I told them you were older, a bank manager. They didn't mind at all.'

'I'm not sure, Mary. Let's think about it, okay?'

'Okay, but they can't object. My dad's ten years older than Mum and he was a police superintendent when they met. She wasn't long out of school.'

Michael tried not to look surprised. 'Your dad's in the police force?'

'Fraud Squad. Something important there, but I'm not sure what. Doesn't talk about it much.'

Michael was still taking in this news as he spoke. 'If you think it's a good idea, then maybe it wouldn't be too bad to meet them. As you say, how can they object?'

The pros and cons of meeting her father occupied his mind as he took off the sweater and let it drop to the floor. What was it McGowan had said, about how important it was to get inside information to stay one step ahead of the game? Yes, very useful. He had worried that he had no idea how to get an early warning signal he was doing anything that could be detected. Mary's father was going to find that Michael was an avid listener.

Decision made, he gave Mary his full attention.

★ ★ ★

It was a week before Michael saw Ron again. When he came into the branch he looked around furtively, waiting until he could catch Michael's eye. Michael spotted him and gave the briefest nod of acknowledgement. He went over to one of the empty teller windows and motioned Ron to come over.

'Necropolis, 6 p.m. Underneath John Knox's statue,' Michael whispered, handing Ron a leaflet on business loans as a cover. Their eyes locked. Ron turned and left.

Glasgow's necropolis sat high on Fir Hill, a testament to the city's Victorian business fathers' yearning for immortality. Moody gothic tombs and mausoleums were scattered everywhere, a myriad of paths weaving their way past the statues and the final resting places of the great and the good, everything maintained in immaculate order. 1970s Glasgow didn't care much for the living, but it really looked after its dead. Dismal rain hung in the air, keeping the visitors down to a few dog walkers.

Michael stood beside the low wall next to the Knox statue, sheltering under an umbrella. He had wanted to meet somewhere where they could walk and talk at the same time, with less chance that someone nearby could overhear. He looked up at the religious firebrand, who stared down at him in frozen admonition. Michael just smiled.

Ron arrived, gave Michael a nod, and they wandered over to one of the mausoleums to shelter from the rain. Ron was curt. 'Let's hear what you're offering.'

'There are three things they tell me to look out for with suspicious business accounts,' Michael said. 'Unrealistic growth; cash businesses with little or no outgoings; and large lump-sum lodgements on an irregular basis. Ring any bells?'

'What's your point?'

'I need you to do three things to make your business look less conspicuous. You need to set up a parallel banking operation to give you some outgoings. Open an account at another bank for a company that sounds like a diesel and garaging business. That company needs to start invoicing you for the running costs of your taxi fleet, about half of your turnover would be about right. And when that business gets above ten grand a year, you open a new bank account for a different business. Then you can cascade down fictitious expenses until they are too small to be noticed.'

'Sounds like you've done this before, pal.'

'Maybe. Then we have a second plan to take care of any additional funds that this first scheme won't cover. You take that extra cash and divide it by the percentages on this sheet.' Michael handed Ron a typed-up table of numbers. 'You go to the bookies and find a row that matches the odds in a race the next day, so the odds aren't changing very much, and spread your bet based on the percentage number underneath each of the odds number. A separate slip for each bet, in two, ideally three, different betting shops. When the race is over, you collect the winnings and keep the betting slip, simple as that.'

Ron looked incredulous. 'This is a joke, right? Put my hard-earned dosh on the gee-gees? What if they lose?'

'That's the point. The money is allocated across all the horses, using different bookies, in proportion to the odds of each horse winning. No matter the result of the race, you've picked a winner. A gambler doing this for real would lose four per cent of his money every time, that four per cent is how bookies make their money. But it's also what it takes to make the rest of the money legitimate. For every winning bet, you get a receipt from the bookies that matches what you pay into your saving account. The losing bets you tear up. You're just a smart horses man, someone who can study the form and is sharp at picking a winner. You get the bookies to pay out your winnings by cheque to show where the money is coming from. Everyone loves someone who can get one over on the bookies.'

'Yeah, but I don't like losing money. Four per cent goes to the bookies? I'm doing just fine without them. And without you, for that matter.' Ron turned up the collar of his coat. 'I've wasted enough time listening to your harebrained schemes. Just keep well away from me, do you hear? And if I pick up that anybody's been snooping around my affairs, I know where you work. Keep well away.' He turned and left.

Michael stood alone, staring out over the city of the dead, a hollow sensation building in his chest. For a second, he contemplated running after Ron but realised that would be futile. He started shuffling down the hill, head bowed as the sudden squall built in intensity.

He was surprised to see Ron waiting for him at the Merchants' House gates by the entrance.

'You've got some balls, I'll give you that,' he told Michael. 'How exactly does this bookies scam work?'

'Follow the instructions on the form I gave you. It should be clear.'

'I'll try it out. If it works, I might be back in touch. Might be, I say. Don't hold your breath.'

Ron disappeared into the now driving rain. Michael watched, oblivious to the icy rivulets tricking down the back of his collar. He could do no more. With a shrug, he headed back to his flat.

★ ★ ★

Michael's next meeting with Ron was in the slightly more comfortable surroundings of Shettleston's Golden Egg, the sort of fast-food restaurant people ate in who couldn't afford the gastronomic delights of a Wimpy Bar. Michael was studying the numerous glossy photos of egg-based dishes on the menu, none of which bore any resemblance to the fare being served up around him, when Ron slid into the seat opposite him.

There was no small talk.

'Seemed to work,' Ron said, passing the crumpled grid sheet over to Michael. 'Total bets £5,000, £5,020 back, betting slips and all. Came out ahead because I didn't put a bet on a no-hoper, even though your grid told me I should.'

'You've got to cover every eventuality, no matter how unlikely you think it is,' Michael replied. 'But anyway, it's showed you it works. Do you want to try the next step?'

'Which is?'

'Set up the parallel companies. You've got betting slips that explain how you came by five grand, but there's still the rest of your money to deal with.'

Michael spent the next twenty minutes explaining how things would work. Customer service wasn't a high priority at the Golden Egg and they were left undisturbed by the waitress as he went through the details. When they had finished, Michael could tell Ron was impressed. He decided it was time to tell Ron more.

'The betting grid is a process in place to launder big one-off incomes from your activities that wouldn't be explainable for a taxi firm. But the taxi business is the best way to handle income from other customers, especially if it's coming in all the time. Hopefully, there will be a lot of it, so first we need to put in place a story that will explain why the business is going to skyrocket. I'll need you to come into the bank and meet my boss, Ian Mason. Tell him about your big expansion plans, spin him a tale about a major programme of buying other taxi firms and merging them with yours. Ron's Taxis is going to become part of a newly formed holding company, let's call it Alba Transport, that's going to be buying up similar operations all over Scotland to create a new group. That will explain the rapid growth when we open our operation up to new customers.'

Michael saw a flicker of concern on Ron's face.

'Don't worry, Ron. The meeting's at least three months away and you'll be giving Mason the chance to brag about having a big new customer. He's not going to ask too many questions. And it'll give you a chance to see how you feel about having to tell a few tall tales – because that's the business we're going into. You'll be fine. I presume you've never met him before?'

'No. I kept a low profile until you came along.'

'And you will in future. But just for this one meeting, I need you to front up the operation to the bank. After that, I'll be able to handle everything on that side once it's safe for me to quit my job at the bank and move Alba Transport to another bank. But at the moment, I need it to stay at Royal Clydeside, so I can keep an eye open for any suspicions about what we're up to. Once we've proven to each other that we can make this scheme work, then we talk more about how we can make money from it. Real money. Happy with that?'

'Okay.' Ron shrugged. 'You tell me what to say and I'll say it. Just keep it simple.'

'Excellent. Let's see how this works out and we'll take things from there. That's why this new business has got to look legitimate from the start, nothing about it should raise suspicion. Once we get going, it's our passport to bigger things.'

'Well, you've got me interested. I got a phone call after our first meeting, let's say from a mutual friend. He told me it might be a smart move to listen to what you had to say. That's the only reason I'm here today. You don't look like a chancer, pal, but I need to make sure. Let's keep the bookies scam going, and if looks good, well yeah, I've got a couple of pals who might be interested in finding a smart way of stashing some cash their old grannies might have left them.'

McGowan couldn't help but get involved. Michael felt strangely flattered by the news. The bosses at the bank didn't think he had what it took to succeed, but a career criminal did.

Michael shook Ron's hand. His new life was about to begin.

1974

chapter six

Michael checked the accounts every couple of days. Ron was faultless. Money was moving between the accounts precisely in line with the ratios that Michael had laid out. Then it was transferred to a transit account in another bank, from where it could be sent to any bank account he wanted it to end up in. There were also some big bookmaker cheques getting paid into his personal deposit account. Ron's income was impressive, and he was only a small-time crook. Michael was beginning to realise the scheme he was setting up could be massive, even if only a small part of Glasgow's underworld took part in it.

With the new system up and running, there was only the flawed history of Ron's bank account to deal with. Michael needed to erase the past, so no matter how far back in time somebody looked, there would be nothing that seemed questionable. He smuggled out blank monthly statement forms and spent his evenings typing up a new set of records he could use to replace the old ones in the files. They wouldn't tally with the bank's central records, but he could deal with that later.

It was a painstaking process. Everything that needed to be typed was always done by one of the secretaries at the bank, never a manager. Sitting in his flat, bashing away on two fingers into the early hours, it was several weeks before he completed the new statements to his satisfaction. Then over the next few days, as frequently as he could without attracting suspicion, Michael set about swapping over the statements in the branch's archives. He created what looked like a completely legitimate taxi firm, its accounts a textbook example of a well-managed business. Now he could begin.

Michael met up with Ron in a bar deep in Glasgow's South Side, well away from either of their usual haunts, sitting at the end of the horseshoe to distance themselves from the noisy chatter of the pub's regulars. He produced a set of carbon copies of the newly fabricated bank statements for Ron to keep with his business files, along with a document showing the transaction summaries of half a dozen of the bank's business customers, with some calculations in the margins showing liquidity ratios, net present value calculations and gross operating margins. Ron's Taxis was nestled securely and anonymously in the middle of the pack.

'I haven't got a clue what any of this stuff means, but all that business jargon sounds spot on to me,' said Ron. 'Looks like you've put a nice respectable window dressing on what some nosey parker might think looks dodgy. I feel quite the businessman.'

'Good, because now you've got to act the part. We've sorted out your accounts, so your business doesn't look suspicious. Now we can start to use it to launder other people's money. It's time to have that meeting I told you about. Make an appointment to see the manager, tell him you've got big plans to expand the business. So that when the money comes flooding in, the bank will have been expecting it. Think you can handle that?'

'Don't forget, it might look like I run a big taxi firm, but I know bugger all about the business. But yeah, I think I can handle it.' Michael picked up an unwelcome bravado in Ron's reply.

'You'll be fine. But get in and out of that meeting as quickly as possible, and say only what I tell you beforehand. No embellishments.'

Ron set up the meeting for the following Wednesday, 10 a.m. Michael had chosen the time carefully. Mason had to leave at eleven and Ron was instructed to turn up twenty minutes late, making profuse apologies, to keep the time when they would be talking as short as possible. After the introductions and pleasantries were out of the way, Ron would have less than half an hour to hold together the story about his expansion plans. Despite Michael's words of encouragement, it was longer than he would have liked.

Just before ten, Michael busied himself away from the tellers' counter. He didn't want Ron to give him an inadvertent nod of recognition. Michael saw Ron's back as he was ushered into Mason's office. Only ten minutes late, not twenty. He silently cursed. Ten to eleven, Mason's door opened, he stuck his head out and called for Michael. When he walked in, Ron was seated, looking happy and relaxed.

'Mr Smith, this is Michael Mitchell, our assistant manager. Michael, Mr Smith is a business customer of ours, he has a taxi firm that looks like it will be growing significantly in the near future. Ron's Taxis, you've probably seen the name. How many new cabs did you say, Mr Smith?'

'Forty-two in our first wave. Pleased to meet you, Mr Mitchell.' Ron smiled, enjoying the game.

'Likewise,' Michael replied, keeping a stony face to remind Ron to stay focused.

'Michael, I have to run, but could I ask you to go through some paperwork with Mr Smith? He has to fill in forms to change his company's name, and I've suggested he open a number two account to keep his merger and acquisition expenses separate from his ongoing running costs and revenue. That'll earn him interest and let him have a clearer picture of his day-to-day profits and cash flow. I'll leave you in capable hands, Mr Smith. Michael is excellent at taking care of these sorts of details.'

Michael could see Ron was enjoying Mason ordering him about. 'Very kind of you to say so, Ian,' Michael replied, hamming up the tone of servitude to remind Ron he too was playing a part. 'If you'll excuse me, I'll get the forms.'

When he returned, Mason had gone. Michael closed the door.

'Well?' he asked.

'Went like clockwork,' Ron replied. 'Not a single question you didn't give me the answer to. I played the part of the smart business guy. Enjoyed it, actually.' He grinned.

Michael gave him a curt nod of congratulation. 'Good. But don't think it will always be this easy. I'll be taking over the business side of the operation once we get started. Just so we're clear.'

As soon as the bank closed, Michael headed off to meet Ron at yet another pub to avoid being recognised.

'You did well today,' he told him.

Ron greeted his comment with an icy smile. 'Remind me, Michael,' he said. 'I hit the streets looking for new customers, and it's my balls on the line if we don't deliver. I've just shown I can front up to the banks if I have to. What exactly, might I ask, are you doing in all this?'

Michael wasn't sure if Ron was gently sparring with him after the euphoria of the morning or if he was moving to challenge his authority. He gave him the benefit of the doubt. 'My job is to design the schemes that can handle the existing cash and give room for expansion,' Michael said, softening his words with a benign smile. 'To keep a watching eye on whether our activities are attracting any unwelcome attention at the bank. So we're always one step ahead.'

Michael paused to stare at Ron for a few seconds. 'And I can do that with you, or with someone else. There are lots of criminals in Glasgow's mean city, so I'm spoiled for choice as to who I pick as my partner. You'd struggle to find someone like me. Just so we're clear.'

'Maybe I can do this without you; maybe I can't. But it seems to be working. I'm happy to stick to our deal. Fifty-fifty split of what we make. My money done for free. That's still our deal, right?'

'It is,' Michael replied. 'And there's one last thing: I'm invisible. Once we get started with other customers, you pay me my fees in cash, in a nice anonymous brown envelope each month. You don't ever know how I launder my own money. And no one ever gets to hear of my existence. You dreamt all this up yourself; you didn't need any help.'

'So if the shit hits the fan, I'm the only one going down? Are you sure it should be fifty-fifty?'

Michael knew he needed to nip these snipes in the bud. 'I think you're underestimating how valuable a product we've got here. There's a ton of money to be made if we don't squabble between ourselves. This is going to be big business. Did you see yesterday's *Glasgow Herald*? Jimmy Slavin sent down for three years, all because the police were on to him because of his bank accounts. Never got caught in the act in all those jobs he did. That's the future, Ron. The days of nobody caring where the money comes from are numbered. And the smart boys in your line of work are going to cotton on to that when Bar-L starts filling up with similar cases.'

'You think so? How much are we talking about?'

'I went to the library last weekend, went through the newspapers to look for all the big robberies in the west of Scotland over the last year. Tallied up the total, came to fifty million. Even allowing for exaggeration, if we got ten per cent of that, we'd be clearing a couple of hundred grand a year in fees. That's assuming every robbery gets reported. How much do you pay in after a typical job? Ten grand, max? You do the sums.'

Ron let out a low whistle. 'I'll say one thing about you, Michael. You're good with numbers. A couple of hundred big ones, you say? Maybe you're worth a punt after all.'

'Good. We've passed the first test, so now we can open for business. But slowly. When we do this, we do it right.'

'Slowly, slowly,' said Ron, without much enthusiasm. 'Okay, I agree. Not that it sounds like I've got much say in the matter.'

He left. The meeting at the bank had shown Michael's fears of instant discovery to be unfounded. Mason would have pulled the Ron's Taxis file to look at in the meeting, and he had obviously spotted nothing suspicious about the forged statements. Ron had never done anything like this before, but he was able to be convincing as a businessman with ambitious growth plans. Michael knew he would always have to be careful, but the powers that be did not take the responsibility of spotting fraudulent activity too seriously. This was going to be even easier than he had imagined.

Now it was off to Mary's house. He liked the irony that straight after taking the first big step into a life of crime he would be meeting Mary's policeman father for the first time. Mary had been beside herself with delight, seeing this as a momentous event in their relationship. And she was overjoyed that Michael had thought it equally important. Jacket and tie, a bottle of wine, flowers for the mother. This was to be a full-on charm offensive.

After the meal, when Mary and her mum disappeared into the kitchen to do the washing-up, Michael could start on his objective for the evening.

'Mary tells me you're in the police force, Mr Johnson,' Michael said, accepting the proffered cigarette. 'Must be a very satisfying job.'

'It is,' Mary's father replied. 'But not as exciting as it sounds, I'm afraid. I'm Fraud Squad. More akin to your line of work in many ways. Lots of paperwork, trying to account for how money is moving about.'

'Never thought of it like that,' Michael said. 'But then again, we don't lift too many stones to look underneath. At Royal Clydeside we respect our customers' privacy. Unless we see them getting into trouble, which happens all too often with students having to manage their financial affairs for the first time. I invite them into the branch, have a quiet word, see if I can help them get on top of things again.'

'Sound like a sensible plan. But I wish you banks would be more proactive in telling us about any funny smell coming from any of your business accounts. It would make our job a lot easier.'

Michael leant forward. 'I quite agree, sir. Personally speaking, I think it's not only good business practice but also one's civic duty to report any suspicions. We do get the occasional audit; we've got the head-office chaps coming in to do one in a few weeks. But speaking frankly, we don't get any training or advice on how to spot a bad apple. We just have to use common sense. I try to be vigilant about that sort of thing, but there's no encouragement from above about doing more, or what to be looking out for. Shocking really.'

'Refreshing attitude, Michael. Good to know we can rely on at least one bank manager to keep their eyes and ears open.'

'Oh, I don't think we have many master criminals in Byres Road.' Michael laughed, as Mary and her mother returned to join them. 'But I'll pick your brains as to what to look out for.'

'Would be delighted to help, young man,' Mary's father replied. 'Hopefully, you'll get a few more of your colleagues to take the same interest.'

Michael looked over at Mary and gave her a nod that the evening was going well. Very well. She had just received an indefinite extension to their relationship.

★ ★ ★

The audit managers Michael had mentioned arrived at the branch two weeks later. They spent the morning with Mason in his office; Michael not invited. They headed out for lunch and when they returned he was summoned to join them.

'This is Michael Mitchell, my assistant,' said Mason by way of introduction. Mason always referred to Michael as his deputy with customers, his assistant with bank staff. 'Michael, this is Mr Manning and his assistant, Audrey. I've spent the morning discussing our annual fraud-prevention audit, and now that we've sorted out what to do, I need you to give them every assistance. Everything should be clear, but if there's anything you need to check on, let me know.' He turned to Manning. 'You'll find Michael a dream to work with. Nothing he likes more than getting stuck into numbers.'

'Very kind, Ian,' Michael mumbled. 'So how can I be of help?'

'Oh, use the meeting room to discuss that, will you, Michael?' Mason said by way of a dismissal. 'It's a bit involved, dare I say tedious. Many thanks.'

Michael headed off to the meeting room with the auditors. Manning didn't proffer his first name.

'Can you get me the files of three business clients, please?' he asked, his tone rather offhand. 'Choose them at random, maybe try to get ones that have a lot of cash transactions. And we'll need a decent calculator. Audrey here will have a lot of calculations to make.' His assistant gave an awkward smile. 'And don't worry about what you've been told about being long and tedious. We'll be out of your hair in a couple of hours. I'd like to be on the train back to Edinburgh before rush hour.'

Michael lugged in the desktop calculator, plugged it in and went off to choose the files. He picked out the local barbershop and a second-hand car dealership on Great Western Road. And the newly renamed Alba Transport. He took a deep breath and went back to the meeting room.

'Think these will keep you busy,' he said. 'Our biggest client – a car dealership – and one of our cash-only customers, the barbers down the road. And a taxi firm who came in to meet Mr Mason recently, who are about to expand all over Scotland. Just changed their name, but that shouldn't confuse things too much.'

'Excellent. Let's get started,' said Manning. 'Audrey, you know what to do.'

Manning picked up the first file. 'Wonderful things, these calculators,' he said to Michael, with a nod towards Audrey. 'I see your office has the new Hewlett-Packard 9100A. Devilishly difficult to operate, with everything in Reverse Polish notation. Luckily, I've got a girl who knows all that stuff. Eh, Audrey?' Audrey glanced up to give a shy smile of acknowledgement.

Michael sat back and watched the two of them in action. Manning lit his pipe and flicked through the barber's bank accounts while Audrey concentrated on the calculations. She was a jolly-hockey-sticks sort of woman. Probably early thirties, but looked a lot older.

'Hmm, yes, hmm yes,' Manning said at regular intervals, writing down a sentence or two. Michael answered a few questions about the account, clarifying some file notes that weren't clear. When Manning picked up the Alba Transport file, Michael did his best to feign indifference as the 'hmms' were higher in pitch, and the sentences he was writing turned into paragraphs.

'Seem to make a pretty penny, these chaps.'

Michael glanced at the file as if to remind himself.

'Yes, if that's what it says.'

'And they're about to expand, you say?'

'Yes, I think so. That's what Mr Mason told me, at least. Big acquisition plans. I only met the proprietor for a few minutes because Mr Mason had to dash off for a meeting. They've opened a second account to deposit any excess cash in hand to earn a little interest, which has just one transaction so far. You can see it here.' He leant over to point to the transfer amount. 'Might become an important customer, so I presume Mr Mason wanted to show we try to do our best for them.'

'This chap runs a tight ship,' Manning said, puffing on his pipe. Michael found the acerbic smoke suffocating, nauseating. He was beginning to regret his earlier cockiness at volunteering his new operation for scrutiny.

Manning paused, then wrote some notes on his pad. 'Yes, remarkable. If he carries on like this, he'll do very well with his plans.'

'Hmm. Audrey, be a dear and do this one next, will you?' Manning said as he put down the file. 'Just popping off to the little boys' room, back in a minute.' He picked up the third file, the car dealership, laid it on top of his notes and left the room.

Michael was desperate to see what he had written, but that would mean moving the file. After a short while Manning returned and read through the third file quickly. A noticeable lack of hmms.

By three o'clock the audit was over and Michael, Manning and Audrey filed into Mason's office to go over the conclusions.

'Well, Ian,' said Manning, 'that's it over for another year. Everything checks out – your branch keeps excellent records. And Michael here is on top of all the detail. Made my job easy. I might even be able to catch the earlier train.'

'Saves me a lot of time, does Michael,' said Mason. 'Does a great job.'

Michael remained impassive, refusing to acknowledge Mason's condescending praise.

'You've got your Michael, I've got my Audrey. Wonderful girl, saves me from learning all this new-fangled computer stuff.' Mason and Manning laughed together, as if Audrey and Michael weren't in the room. Audrey gave Michael a sympathetic glance. It made him feel even angrier.

Manning turned to acknowledge them. 'If you'll excuse me, I'll get Mr Mason's signature on the compliance forms. Would you be a dear, Audrey, and wait outside? And good to meet you, Michael.'

Michael took that as a sign that he too had been dismissed.

He was heading back to his desk when he caught Audrey looking at him. The slightest of glances, but it was enough. He smiled back.

'How long does this take?' he asked Audrey.

'Five minutes, maybe ten. Unless they get talking, in which case I can be standing here forever.'

'We can't have that. Let's have a coffee and you can tell me about that calculator you were using. Never seen it used before, very impressive. Sits in our office gathering dust, I'm afraid. It's portable enough that you can carry it from room to room, and it's able to do even long division in an instant? Remarkable.'

Michael wasn't the least bit interested in calculators or Reverse Polish notation, but their conversation served its purpose. By the time Manning emerged from Mason's meeting room, he had Audrey's home telephone number and a promise to meet up in Edinburgh the following week. Another source of vital intelligence was on its way to being secured.

Michael watched as the pair left, Manning clutching his briefcase and the documents that meant, despite specific scrutiny, he regarded Alba Transport as an account beyond reproach.

So that was it. A once-a-year superficial glance at a fraction of the bank's customers. The response to every query unquestioned, unchallenged. A virtually non-existent taxi firm doing business on a scale that would mean they should be seen on every Glasgow street, and no one was batting an eyelid.

It was time to expand the operation.

chapter seven

Michael met Ron the next day at a park bench in the Botanic Gardens, on a rare sunny Glasgow lunchtime. A few people were picnicking on the lawns, pretending it was warm.

'We had our annual internal inspection at the bank and I had a couple of auditors from our head office take a good long, hard look at Alba Transport,' he told Ron. 'Didn't suspect a thing, they went on about what a well-run company it appeared to be. It's amazing what you can make people believe if you position it right.'

Ron's eyes narrowed. 'You had them look at my business? I thought the key to this was to keep a low profile.'

'It was the perfect test of whether this is going to work,' Michael replied. 'And if there had been any suspicions I would have been on the inside of the investigation, able to tip you off. It would have been a lot easier to pull the plug on the operation while it's still early days. Call it a necessary calculated risk.' Michael shrugged to signify the discussion was over.

Ron was having none of it.

'Yes,' he said. 'A risk that I might get caught. You shouldn't have done it, Michael. Not without telling me first.'

A couple walking by turned to see what the ruckus was.

'Keep your voice down,' Michael hissed. 'There was a risk for me as well, Ron. If anyone had checked the microfiche records, they would have found the current set of bank statements had been faked. Only someone in the branch could have done that.'

'It's not the way it should be, that's all I'm saying. We shouldn't have secrets.'

'No secrets? Then let me ask you this. What's the story about the ten grand you moved out of the transit account into a bank account I didn't recognise? Have you been freelancing?'

That put Ron on the defensive. 'I was paying back a favour. It's Billy Carlisle's money. A mate. We go back a long way. He came into a wodge of money and I said if he opened a bank account to stash it, I'd pay it in for him, so he'd have no worries about trying to bank the cash. Less our commission, of course. My turn to take a calculated risk, if you like. I can trust him to keep his mouth shut, but I wanted to know if punters would be up for our deal before I approach the real gangsters. To make sure I wasn't going to make an arse of myself asking some of Glasgow's hard men if they'd trust me with their money.'

'And you did this without asking me?' Michael shook his head. 'That doesn't happen again. I need to know about everything that's going through your bank account before it happens. You don't decide anything on that side of the operation.'

'Billy's okay. And it's my bank account.' Ron stabbed a finger at Michael. 'I don't like how you think you're in charge of everything, all of a sudden. It was a partnership you offered me, remember? I'm not your fucking skivvy.'

Michael's tone softened. 'You're right. You run the street operation; I don't want anything to do with that. But I run the banking side. I say when we do business, how much the process can cope with, and how we do it. And that means you don't pull another stunt like that without me giving the okay.'

A few seconds' silence, then Ron said, 'So, what happens next? Put an ad in tomorrow's *Glasgow Herald* saying we're open for business?'

'Not quite. I'm doing some research about how we go from cottage industry to major-league operation. With a conscientious, hard-working accountant who works in the bank's audit department. And I've got something going on with one of my student customers. Her father is high up in the Fraud Squad and doesn't mind confiding to his prospective son-in-law what the police are looking out for from dodgy banking. Between the two of them, I'm going to learn every scam in the book and every trick we can play to keep one step ahead.'

'Meanwhile, I'm to meet the city's criminals in dark alleys to convince them to trust us with their money? It sounds like I've got the raw end of the deal.'

'We each do what we're good at. I want to get as much information as quickly as possible, and this seems the best way to do it. We've had the audit, so we don't have to worry when Alba's turnover goes through the roof. You get on with making your contacts and let's make some money.' Michael offered his hand to signal the end of the meeting. It was the first time they had shaken hands.

★ ★ ★

It was a gradual start, but soon the cash started to pour in. The proposition was simple: a client handed over their money and got eighty per cent of it back as a cheque, which they were able to pay into a bank account of their choosing, no questions asked. This bank account was never to have any connection to their regular banking. That way, if any client were to end up in jail, the money would be safely waiting for them when they came out – as long as they kept denying its existence. And if they did decide to grass and the operation had to be closed down, they'd have the wrath of the rest of the clients who used the scheme descend on them, and on their friends and relatives on the outside. It was to be a private club for professional operators who wanted to keep cash hidden and who would spend it discreetly; hotheads and nutcases need not apply. Ron was the scheme's only visible face; Michael stayed hidden in the background.

With Audrey, Michael portrayed the image of a hard-working, but slightly dull bank employee, someone whose job was their life and whose conversation was limited almost exclusively to talking shop. Right from the start, he had told her about Mary, and that he wanted their relationship to be platonic. Things would be less complicated that way He vaguely mentioned to Mary that he saw a business colleague after work when he went through to Edinburgh on some banking errand, name and gender unspecified, and left it at that. Weighing up the risks and benefits of asking Audrey to sleep with him, or telling Mary more about her, had been a matter of calculation, like any other business assessment. Feelings didn't come into it.

His decision about Audrey turned out to be a smart one. If she was disappointed that he showed no inclination to make the relationship any more than a social, work-related acquaintanceship, she never showed it. It made it easier to keep their discussions about banking, rather than having to expend any effort on finding common emotional ground between them. Audrey turned out to be a gold mine of information about the ways people were using banks to hide their money: import-export operations, with an overseas accomplice creating inflated invoices and then banking the surplus to send back to the launderer; taking out an insurance policy and then instantly redeeming it and receiving a sanitised cheque; changing pounds into foreign currencies and back into pounds, starting off as cash and coming back as a cheque. Audrey's knowledge was encyclopaedic. And mainly theoretical. The number of times a customer had been identified and arrested for using any of these techniques in the two years she'd been an assistant auditor could be counted on the fingers of one hand.

He had to work hard to look interested in their other topics of conversation. Audrey was a keen member of the Woman's Institute and had a passion for needlework, neither of which Michael found it easy to feign interest about. She was a devotee of Sidney Devine, and was moved to tears every time she heard him sing 'I'm Nobody's Child'. Michael decided it was best not to get into discussions about Shostakovich and the works of Frederick Nietzsche.

After the meetings, which invariably took place at Audrey's favourite tea shop in the Royal Mile, Michael would make notes of everything she had told him, to be filed away for future use. For the moment the plan was to keep things simple, running the new operation as a sideline, using Ron's business as a cover. As long as he kept learning, he'd stay working at the bank, and he liked being around to pick up any whispers of suspicion. One day he would experiment with the new schemes that Audrey had told him all about. One day. In the meantime, he'd remain, to all appearances, a dutiful and diligent bank employee.

Mary's father was also full of useful and encouraging information. Sunday lunch was becoming a ritual, and Michael noticed with amusement that there was usually an extra family member invited along to size up the man in Mary's life who was making so much effort to get to know the family. All for a few brief, precious minutes with Mary's father when Michael invariably steered the conversation to whatever fraud cases were in the news. He was guarded at their first few meetings, but Michael explained that bank fraud was a particular interest of his; that he was hoping an opportunity would open up for him to move into that part of the bank's business. He complained about how frustrating it was that banks were being short-sighted in resisting efforts to becoming more proactive in fighting crime.

'Well, Michael, you'll be pleased to hear that the banks are coming around to your way of thinking,' Mary's father said one Sunday lunch. 'This is supposed to be completely hush-hush, but the Chief Constable had a meeting with all the Scottish banks' managing directors the other week. They met to discuss setting up a voluntary code of conduct to report financial crime. Stick to your guns, Michael. You'll be finding lots of opportunities to fight fraud soon enough.'

Michael was on instant alert. 'Excellent news, Mr Campbell,' he said. 'I'm pleasantly surprised. I've not heard anything about it, and we only had our internal audit people in the branch a few weeks ago. What is it we're going to do?'

The question was a little too direct. 'Sorry, Michael. I've already said more than I should have. It's meant to be known to only a few people at the banks. Take it as a nod as to the direction you should be taking when you're thinking of your next move at the bank.'

'Well, it's kind of you to take me into your confidence. I'm flattered. Don't worry, I don't want to know any more. I won't say a word.'

He was straight on the phone to Audrey as soon as he left. Sunday afternoon was his time for sorting things out at home, he told Mary, and catching up with any unfinished work from during the week. This explained why he always rushed off after his chats with her father, and why he didn't ask her back to the flat. In reality, it was when he did most of his money-laundering admin. Today, as always, there was a lot of pressing stuff to deal with, but this was something he needed to see Audrey about urgently.

'I'm going to be busy on Wednesday,' he told her from the first phone box he could find. 'But how about tomorrow instead? I can be on the train at five if I get away early from the office. Be in Edinburgh just after six.'

He was aching to find out if Audrey could fill in the blanks of what Campbell had told him, but waited until their evening together was almost over before bringing it up.

'Has your job changed, or something?' he asked as he settled up the bill. 'I'm hearing something about Royal Clydeside being involved with the other banks to give more help to the police to fight fraud. Are you involved?'

Audrey stopped munching her Tunnocks Teacake.

'My goodness, Michael, how on earth did you hear about that? Yes, Mr Manning told me something, but he swore me to absolute secrecy. Told me I needed to know because we'd be getting more staff, but that at the moment he and I were the only two outside of the board to be let in on it. How on earth did you find out?'

'Oh, I'd better not say. But you can probably guess. There's only one person at our branch who would know what's discussed in confidence at a board meeting.' Might as well drop a hint that Mason can't be trusted with secrets while I'm at it, Michael thought. 'So, what's going on? Sounds exciting.'

'Well, I shouldn't say …' She waited for Michael to agree with her, but he said nothing, leaving it to her to fill the uncomfortable silence. 'Oh, all right then. But promise not to breathe a word?'

Michael held a finger to his mouth, smiling as his stomach tied itself in knots.

'There was this big meeting, the managing directors of all the banks plus all the company secretaries. They've been getting some heat from the government to come up with an industry code of conduct to combat fraud and money laundering, so they got together to discuss what they could come up with, and how they might cooperate. It's never been done before, apparently.'

Michael maintained his fixed smile. 'Seems extraordinary. And what did they decide?' He tried to keep the stress out of his voice.

'Michael, I shouldn't be telling you this.'

Michael remained silent again until Audrey found herself having to speak to fill the uncomfortable void.

'It isn't much really,' she confessed. 'We're to check every business that turns over more than five-hundred-thousand pounds a year. If any of them have more than half their dealings in cash we go through their accounts with a fine-tooth comb, and can ask the other banks to check the details of any accounts they pay into. Mr Manning is all excited; he's going to get another five like me working for him. Though there's probably not more than a handful of the bank's customers that size who do so much in cash.'

Michael did a quick calculation in his head. Alba Transport was safe, but it wouldn't be for long at the rate it was growing.

'I hope it's good news for you too, Audrey. Glad you told me, you need to make sure you do well out of it, if you and Manning are going to grow into a fully fledged department. It's only biggish customers that are involved? I doubt it would affect many of my bank's customers.'

Audrey thought for a second. 'No, I don't think so. In fact, not that many customers across Scotland. But it makes us look as if we're doing something, I suppose. That's what's important.'

This changed everything. Michael needed to diversify, and do it fast; start up these new schemes before Alba

Transport became big enough to be picked up on the radar. That meant bringing forward the moment when he got into this full time. Ron would be pleased; he was getting more and more agitated at Michael's reluctance to quit his bank job and put the new schemes into action.

'About bloody time,' he said when Michael told him his decision. 'We could be doing a lot more business than you'll let me. I'm running out of excuses not to take some of the cash that's getting offered to us. Some big players are interested, and they're not used to people saying no.'

'One step at a time, Ron. These turnover and cash limits are key, and my contact might not have been willing to give me as much detail if I wasn't at the bank anymore. As long as there's stuff to find out, I need to stay where I am.' He shook his head. 'But don't worry, I want out as soon as possible. Once we're ready, I'll quit in a heartbeat. You don't know how much I want to get out of there.'

Then Ron came with the news that Billy Carlisle had been arrested for burglary. Michael was not impressed.

'I thought the deal was we only worked with professionals. He was the first one you trusted to use our operation and now he's behind bars?'

'Getting collared is an occupational hazard in this line of work. He was unlucky, it could have happened to anyone.' He glared at Michael to cover up his discomfort. 'Trust me, Billy's not a problem. He's not going to own up to the nest egg he's got salted away, and he'd never rat. And I shouldn't need to convince you. It's me that's at risk; I'm the one he'd grass on. You'd have a failed business venture, but I'd be the one to go down. I don't need to remind you of that.'

Michael could see Ron's mounting anxiety. He was right – Ron was the one who should be worried. But the cops were getting one step closer to them, and Michael didn't like it.

'Okay. We knew this would happen eventually. Another test of the system, I suppose. See what you can find out about what's happening to Billy.'

Michael couldn't understand why he felt so unsettled by Billy's arrest. His business model assumed the inevitability of some clients being arrested, and safeguards had been put in place to make sure the operation, and especially he, remained undetected. It was probably a good thing that the first test came from someone that Ron had personally vouched for. But it was moving from a theoretical scenario to stark reality. That's what made it so unsettling.

A few days later, the police arrived at the bank. Mason was at lunch, so Michael ushered them into a meeting room.

'What can I do to help?' he asked.

Michael held his breath as they spoke. 'We arrested a petty criminal, Billy Carlisle, two days ago,' said the senior officer. 'Stolen goods, so we had a warrant to search his home. It seems he has a bank account here. We want to check it for any sign of criminal activity. Can you let us see his last two years' bank statements?'

Michael could not believe his stupidity. Billy Carlisle was also a customer at his branch. And he didn't know. He only had himself to blame. Ron couldn't have been expected to know where Billy did his regular banking, and Billy himself would be unaware of the connection. This was one big coincidence. But a coincidence that could cost him dearly.

Michael returned with the file. 'I'm afraid our branch records only go back eighteen months. If you want anything further back, I'd have to have them retrieved from the microfiche in Edinburgh.'

'This should give us enough of a picture,' one of them said. He flicked through the file. 'You know, it's very odd. Carlisle doesn't seem to have any income from gainful employment, and he had lots of cash paid in for widely varying amounts all through last year. All that you'd expect to see from a villain. But four months ago, it all seems to have changed. Regular cash payments for round amounts, enough to cover his expenses. Like he has a regular source of income. He says he does piecework, casual labour, and this seems to back it up. Are you sure he doesn't have any other account here?'

'I'll do another check, but I'm pretty sure not,' Michael replied. 'Unless under another name. Do you maybe have an alias I could check under?'

'Not that we know about. Damn. Well, it looks like we've only got him for the job where he was caught red-handed. If he has been up to anything else recently, the slippery bugger has managed to hide it from us. And the trail will be cold on these cash transactions.' The detective smiled thinly. 'Never thought Billy Carlisle was smart enough to cover his trail like this.'

The police left empty-handed, and Michael could barely contain his elation. From a moment of the utmost dread, it had turned out to be a vindication of everything he had been working on. The containment strategy had worked, there was no paper trail linking Billy to the transit account or on to Ron. But most importantly, he had seen that people like Billy Carlisle kept their mouths shut when caught.

'Now we're ready,' he told Ron that evening. 'Billy has inadvertently been the perfect test of whether our system is bombproof. Somebody gets caught and the police find that, completely out of character, he has suddenly managed to hide all the money he's stolen and nobody thinks it could be part of a bigger operation. You've got people queuing up to give us their cash. I've had chapter and verse from the bank's auditors about what they look for in irregularities, and the Fraud Squad have told me how they go about an investigation. Nobody spots what we're doing even when I push the Alba Transport file under their noses. You say there's lots of demand for this, Ron. Give me a month after leaving the bank, and I'll take care of all the business you can get for me. Think you can handle it?'

Ron grinned. 'I'll have a bloody good try.'

Michael handed in his notice the next day. His colleagues all wished him well, but the look in their eyes told Michael how foolhardy they all thought he was being, starting his own business at the height of a recession. Their scepticism made him all the more determined to succeed.

He started the formalities of setting up a company and getting office space sorted out. It didn't take long to find the perfect property, a discreet end-of-terrace office just off George Square, with a useful back door leading onto a side street if he ever had to make a surreptitious exit. He paid the deposit and first six months' rent from the money he had managed to salt away already.

Now he was going to hit the big time.

chapter eight

Michael was two weeks into his notice when a young woman he didn't recognise came into the bank. She had an air of quiet confidence which fascinated and unsettled him at the same time, with fine aristocratic features as smooth as a porcelain figurine. She announced that she wished to open an account and lodge a little money, that she was starting back at university next month and needed an account in Glasgow as Coutts didn't have a branch there.

When Michael looked at her chequebook he did a double take. 'Lady Charlotte Aldford? Not so many people with titles at Glasgow University. St Andrews, maybe Edinburgh at a push.' Despite his best efforts, he found himself being impressed.

'Charlotte, please. My family have connections with Glasgow, apparently,' she explained. She dropped her voice to a whisper. 'I suspect we dabbled in slavery, but the official line is that we were tobacco barons. Made a lot of political donations at the turn of the century to have our past disappear and become respectable, which secured the first Earl of Aldford his title from a grateful David Lloyd George. Four generations later, I'm the result. My father was the Earl.'

'You're studying Fine Art at Glasgow?' Michael said, checking her application form. 'Well, there will be no problem in opening an account here, if you wish. Anything else I can help you with?'

'My financial affairs are rather complicated,' she replied. She looked down, avoiding Michael's eyes. 'The thing is, my father passed away rather suddenly a few months ago. I was in Europe with friends at the time, took a year out from uni. The house and estate is going to my younger brother, Timmy, with the rest of the inheritance being split three ways between the two of us and my mother. My parents separated about five years ago, but everyone is still on speaking terms. Very civilised.'

There was something she was not telling him.

'Sorry to hear about your father. Is it investment advice you want? That's certainly something I can arrange for you.'

'No, that's not why I'm here. Mine and Timmy's share of the estate has been put in trust until we're twenty-one – six months away in my case – and the trustees are real stick-in-the-muds about me squandering any of it. Keep me on a tight rein. They have Coutts send them a copy of my statements every month, which is why I can't go to them with my little problem.' Charlotte shuffled her feet and looked uncomfortable. 'I'm afraid I've been a bit extravagant on my European travels. The other girls were so lah-di-dah with their money, and I had to go along with all the excesses. Would have been mortifying to do otherwise.' She gave a theatrical shudder. 'I'm broke, I'm afraid. Need an overdraft until my next beneficiary payment. Is that too shocking?' She looked at Michael, blinking with embarrassment.

'Silly, I would say, rather than shocking. But sadly I'm not allowed to let you open an account with an overdraft on day one. Can't you explain things to the trustees, get them to see reason?'

Charlotte blushed. 'That would be too awful. Uncle Clarence is so beastly about these sorts of things. Isn't there anything you can do?'

'Tricky. I should mention that I'm leaving the bank in a few weeks to start my own business. Always been a dream of mine.' Michael said it as if he was confessing his deepest secret. She stared straight at him, her contrite expression softened by the hint of a mischievous grin.

He gave the impression of ignoring her flirtations. 'I have to make sure I leave things as my successor expects to find them, I'm afraid. But let me see what I can do. How much are we talking about?'

'Two hundred pounds until December. Piffling amount, really. So tiresome of me to get into this mess.'

'Pop back tomorrow and I'll try my best. I might have to sail close to the wind to push it through, but leave it with me.'

After she left, Michael's pen hovered over the application form. He could change the date to make it look like she'd been a customer for three months – that way she could get her overdraft right away. Then he shook his head. Risks were everywhere as he embarked on a life of crime, and this was an unnecessary one. All to get to know someone with a title before their name.

He paused.

Not only a title. Money. And connections. And beauty.

Some risks were worth it. He made the change. He wouldn't be at the bank much longer, and it would be unlikely anyone would spot that the paperwork didn't match up while he was still there. To make the subterfuge less obvious, he went through some other customer files, removing key documents here and there.

Michael put her through a grilling when she came back the next day, ostensibly for purposes of pushing through the overdraft but really to find out all about her: hobbies, interests, where she hung out, what she was planning in the months ahead. Everything he could use to make sure this wasn't the last time they would meet. And he liked seeing her squirm under pressure. Lady Charlotte was not used to holding out a begging bowl.

At the end of the interrogation, he gave her the good news.

'I'll get the overdraft arranged today, Charlotte. Leave it with me.'

Her look of appreciation had a grateful quality that he found curiously erotic.

'The bank has a firm line that students can't open bank accounts with an overdraft. I've slightly gone out on a wing, made it look like you've been a customer for three months. I hope you're not too shocked.'

Charlotte looked worried. 'I hope I'm not getting you into trouble, Mr Mitchell. I didn't realise it would be this involved.'

Michael laughed off her concerns. 'Not at all, just a little white lie. No one will even notice.' He stood up. 'Well, Charlotte, it's been very nice to meet you and I'm glad I could help out. Be careful with your money in future.' He placed his hand on her back as he guided her out of the meeting room.

As soon as she left, Michael noted down all the details about lifestyle and habits that he had gleaned. Anything he could use to impress her when they next met. Now it was just a question of finding how to achieve that.

He checked her new account every day and was amused to find that one of the first cheques she'd written since getting the overdraft was to the People's Theatre box office. So much for the promised austerity drive until the overdraft was paid off. There, written on the back, was the date of the performance so the theatre could make sure they sent her the correct tickets. Bingo.

Michael bought two tickets for the same performance and turned up early. He was glad he'd left in plenty of time; the theatre was well off the beaten track on the South Side of Glasgow, a small oasis of highbrow theatre in an urban desert. Chekhov's *Cherry Orchard* reimagined as Scottish gentry returning to their Highland estate. He smiled at the irony.

Michael flicked through the programme, checked out the announcements of next year's productions. John Osborne's *Look Back in Anger*, Joe Orton's *Loot*, Edward Albee's *Who's Afraid of Virginia Woolf?* He quickly memorised snippets of the synopses to show he knew his theatre.

When Charlotte arrived, Michael was pleased to see the second ticket was for a female friend. She spotted him, gave a gasp of recognition, and came straight over. 'It's Mr Mitchell, isn't it?' she said. 'Charlotte. Charlotte Aldford. You're my bank manager.'

'Miss Aldford! Of course!' Michael replied. 'You must forgive me; I have so many student customers. You're studying mathematics, right?'

'No, not quite. Fine Art.'

Michael pretended to look embarrassed. He could see that Charlotte found it endearing.

'You like theatre?' he said, making his question sound like a clumsy attempt to change the subject.

'Love it,' replied Charlotte. 'I'm here with my flatmate Diana.' She waved over to a gamine young woman with pixie-cut hair on the other side of the room. Diana waved back and stayed put. She had read Charlotte's body language.

'And you?' Charlotte said. She looked over his shoulder. 'With someone?'

'Ah, no. Should have been, but sometimes these things don't work out. On my own, unfortunately. A spare seat for my jacket.'

They went to find their respective seats, and during the interval Michael saw that Charlotte was on her own at the bar, Diana having presumably been told to make herself scarce. He seized the moment.

'Charlotte, I hope you don't think this is inappropriate. I've got a spare ticket for Scottish Opera at the Theatre Royal next Thursday. The consequences of a failed relationship do linger, I'm afraid. Would you like to be my companion? If that's not too forward, coming from your bank manager.'

Charlotte smiled. 'I'd love to. What a strange coincidence, meeting you like this. I felt a little … I don't know … when I left the bank after meeting you.' The interval bell rang. 'Gosh, that was quick,' she said, looking around. 'I can't think where Diana has disappeared to.'

'Well, I'll see you on the steps at the front entrance at seven. Here's my home phone number in case you change your mind.' He scribbled it on a bank business card.

Charlotte looked at it and then at Michael. 'Oh, I can't believe I've met you again.' She gave a coquettish giggle at her display of excitement. 'See you on Thursday.'

Michael looked at her as she headed back into the theatre. He thought he could detect a skip in her step.

★ ★ ★

It was the perfect date. *Idomeneo* by Mozart. And going to the opera was no sham. Ever since Michael first heard a collection of arias on a *Music for Pleasure* LP as a teenager, he'd fallen in love with the passion and grandeur of *opera seria*. He impressed Charlotte with his knowledge of the libretto and they rounded off the evening with an espresso at a little Italian café tucked down a side street. As the evening drew to a close, he took Charlotte's hand.

'I've enjoyed tonight, Charlotte.' Michael looked down at the table in a convincing display of bashfulness. 'I know this might sound strange, seeing as we are from different worlds and I met you as your bank manager. But would you consider us seeing each other again?'

Charlotte squeezed his hand. 'I'd love to, Michael. How we met doesn't matter to me in the slightest. It's me that should be worried. Most men seem so intimidated by my background. You're different.'

Michael drove her home. A first-floor flat in a sandstone tenement in Hyndland, no doubt purchased from the trust fund. Substantial, but not too grand to be daunting to her fellow students. No lights were on; Diana was either asleep or staying elsewhere. The air crackled with expectation. As they went into a long, lingering kiss,

Charlotte breathed faint murmurings of encouragement. But Michael gently, gracefully, backed off. He gave her a peck on the lips to signal the end of the embrace. As he leant back, the light of a street lamp caught Charlotte's face. She gave him a look, first of surprise, then disappointment and finally, he felt sure, of longing.

Michael gave her a final kiss, small and tender. Charlotte gave a regretful smile.

He was proud of his restraint. Sent all the right signals.

★ ★ ★

Their next meeting was as stallholders at a Second Chance jumble sale. Michael hadn't had the time to keep involved with them when setting up the money-laundering operation, but now that he was leaving the bank he wanted to get connected again. After making sure Mary wasn't going to be there, he invited Charlotte to help out. The charity had proved beneficial once before in meeting Kenny McGowan, and he was forming some ideas how it could be useful again in future.

Charlotte had never been to a jumble sale, much less been involved with one, and she seemed to love it.

'So, how do we know how much to sell things for?' she asked as they set up trestle tables and sorted out the jumble.

'Use your best judgement,' Michael replied. 'For example, that table, two pounds. Maybe thirty pence each for this pile of LPs. And expect to haggle. Everyone wants to get a bargain.'

He'd chosen to go to the sale to show his caring side, and it turned out to be perfect. Charlotte glanced through the LPs and pulled out the O'Jays, Van McCoy and Gloria Gaynor.

'Can I buy these for myself?' she asked. 'Or is that against the rules?'

'Be my guest,' Michael replied. 'That'll be ninety new pence please.' He looked at the O'Jays' *Backstabbers* album. 'Never heard of them. Any good?'

'Disco. The best. One night at Tiffany's and you'll be hooked.' Michael shook his head and laughed at the ridiculousness of the notion of him grooving on the dance floor.

Charlotte plunged into negotiations about the cost of things she hadn't got a clue about with effortless self-confidence, and wandered around during quieter moments to chat to some of the Second Chance volunteers like she was Princess Anne on a royal visit. Michael had seen her as no more than a passport into a world he always thought he would be excluded from, but to his surprise he found himself liking her. A lot.

They cleared everything up around five o'clock, the sale raising the princely sum of £117.28 for the charity, and headed to the snug bar at Sloans in the city centre, a cosy, hidden-away little extension to a traditional salt-of-the-earth Glasgow pub. The crowded, claustrophobic nook heightened the chemistry of the moment. Charlotte downed her Moscow Mule in seconds, and when Michael stood up and silently took her hand, she gave him a look of complicity, aching with desire.

They were back at Michael's flat twenty minutes later, straight into the bedroom the moment the door was closed. Michael slid his hand up her thigh, gasping when he found she was wearing nothing under her halter-neck minidress, then remembering the enigmatic look she had given him when she returned from the ladies just after they arrived at Sloans. His hand found her already-moist sex; his fingers slipped inside her. Charlotte started pulling at his zipper and Michael was momentarily startled by her intensity. His trousers were around his knees when he thrust inside her, still fully clothed, neither of them wanting to wait a second more than was necessary. She took and met each thrust, then matched each with hers. For the first time in his life, Michael found himself lost in an ecstasy of soaring, agonising perfection. He felt his strength increasing, the heat of the passion rising. There was no gravity any longer. It was like he was floating on air.

Charlotte leapt on top of him, straddling his body, putting her arms on either side, pressing her palms into the mattress to steady herself. Then she sat up, swept her dress over her head and unclipped her bra, leaving herself naked except for her knee-length leather boots. With an expression of determined concentration, she pushed her hands onto his shoulder blades, her body strong, her breasts like smooth stone. She was the one in charge now, uncontrolled, set free; a wild freedom, like horses galloping along a moonlit beach. After two more thrusts, she collapsed, went limp, then toughened and readied herself again. Her eyes were glassy, indistinct, like they had filled with smoke.

'Fuck me,' she yelled, the words sounding incongruous in her cut-glass aristocratic accent. 'Fuck me, Michael. Fuck me.'

Michael pinched her nipples, gently at first, then harder and harder.

'I'm coming,' she cried. 'I'm coming; I'm— u … u … uh.' Her body jerked and shuddered to silence her, as Michael also lost control. He gasped in wonder, without restraint, as he released himself inside her. When he finished, he pulled back a little and caught her look, a sly grin that signalled the winding down of her ardour.

'Why, Mr Mitchell,' Charlotte said, her eyes sparkling. 'I don't believe I ever thanked you properly before now, for being so kind as to arrange that overdraft for me.'

'My pleasure,' Michael replied, as he pulled out from inside her. 'I can assure you.'

Charlotte burst out laughing and Michael joined in, giggling like a schoolboy, not recognising the person she had turned him into. Then, slowly, the old Michael returned.

Mary. He needed her. He needed her father to keep him informed of developments in the Fraud Squad. To give that up would be irresponsible, illogical, irrational. This had to be a one-off. He couldn't take the risk that Mary would find out about Charlotte, that all his scheming would have been in vain.

Charlotte had started nibbling at his earlobe, and he found himself responding.

Michael had been driven to succeed all his life, never doing anything that would get in the way of achieving his goals. Perhaps it was time to enjoy life for a change.

chapter nine

Friday afternoon, Michael said goodbye to his life as a bank employee. The moment he had dreamt of, ever since that first meeting with Ron.

'And I hope we haven't seen the last of you, Michael,' Mason said, as he concluded his farewell speech. 'Be sure to consider Royal Clydeside as a worthy repository for your business millions.' He glanced around, inviting the rest of the assembled group to join his sarcastic chuckle and received a few nervous, sycophantic laughs in response.

Michael joined in to show he got the joke. The ritual would soon be over, and he was glad he'd declined the offer from some of his colleagues for a night out on the town as a more informal way to say goodbye. This life would soon be in the past, and he wanted his new one to start as quickly as possible. Every second spent as the someone he used to be would have felt like forever.

The weekend was spent tidying up loose ends and preparing for the future. He ended the relationship with Mary over a Gibson Street curry, Michael breaking the news to her with an impressive display of regret that he felt the age gap between them too wide, and that with his new business he wouldn't have the time to give her the attention she deserved. She was devastated, and Michael felt a pang of guilt that he had treated her so badly. Just because the world had been unfair to him, that was no excuse to be unfair to someone who had done him no wrong. He had been cynical enough, however, to have spent the last few visits to the family home wangling an invitation to join her father's Round Table organisation, but grateful for Mary's sake that she didn't make the connection when he ended the relationship a few days after his application for membership was accepted.

He gave Audrey a similar story. She could still be useful, although perhaps less willing to volunteer the bank's secrets on money-laundering detection to someone now on the outside. Starting his own business was his big opportunity, Michael told her. He'd be working all hours, with next to no free time. A vague promise to meet up if he was ever in Edinburgh, but no invite to see him when she was in Glasgow. He headed back to Glasgow as soon as he could. To spend the rest of the weekend with Charlotte: the future.

Michael revelled in the free time he now had, no longer having to work nine to five at the bank. He was meticulous in the detail of moving the money through the transit accounts and back to their customers – there was no one else he trusted to deal with the minutiae of the operation. But that still left plenty of time to plan ahead, to start severing Alba Transport's ties to Royal Clydeside by switching to another bank so he could take over the running from Ron. And best of all, to use the stockpile of cash he was accumulating to reinvent himself as a man of means, taste and refinement, well-connected in Scottish society.

He finally became the person he had always wanted to be. His suits became sharper; he had a box at Scottish Opera; went to opening nights of Kelvingrove art exhibitions; was seen at every black-tie charity event. And Charlotte provided the contacts to help him build the foundation of his new social life. There were weekend canters at the Renfrew stables where he was learning to ride, shooting lessons in Bearsden to prepare him for the stalking season. And Charlotte was not the only recipient of his affection; he acquired a pair of Dobermann Pinschers whom he whimsically called Lucifer and Satan, full of puppy mischief but silenced into instant obedience whenever he commanded it.

Then there was the design and decoration of the new house he'd started renting – a vast Charles Church detached house on the outskirts of Glasgow. Michael developed a passion for contemporary art and frequented auction houses looking for the perfect pieces to fill the walls of his home. He started collecting antique swords and pistols for his hallway; revelled in the delights of opera on his few nights alone with a state-of-the-art Linn turntable; and indulged his love of cooking, carried over from his days of austerity, in a bespoke Poggenpohl kitchen.

The humiliations of his rejections for promotion and his harsh, unloving upbringing seemed a lifetime away. Five years playing by the rules with Royal Clydeside, and all he had achieved was the modest status of an assistant bank manager. Six months playing by his own rules and he was rich beyond his wildest dreams.

His new-found success made meeting with Charlotte's family easier. Charlotte insisted that Michael accompany her to a christening, meeting her extended family for the first time. He would have preferred a little longer to ensure his transformation was complete in case she had to endure any backlash that she was getting involved with someone too plebeian for their tastes, but the event was a big success. His well-practised charm went down well with the dowager aunts, and his oleaginous flattery towards the family patriarchs led to him being invited to join the Aldford menfolk for cigars and brandy afterwards.

Michael listened attentively as the discussion turned to the financial markets and the turmoil being caused by the industrial unrest sweeping the nation.

'This Heath chap was supposed to face up to the unions,' grunted Charles Aldford, the family grandee, 'but all he seems to do is sail about on his yacht while the rubbish piles up in the streets. I don't think he's got the bottom to put a bit of stick about, bring them to their senses.'

'We never should have had a grammar-school boy leading the party,' agreed someone Charlotte had introduced to Michael as Uncle Clarence. 'The miners are holding us to ransom. Did you see that notice in today's paper? SOS. Switch Off Something. Electric heating banned in places of entertainment and one can only heat a single room in one's own home. Hundred pound fine if you ignore it. We're heading for the dark ages.'

'Well, I for one am not taking any chances,' said Charles. 'I told my broker to sell all my stocks and shares, every man jack of them. I'm putting everything into gold bars until all this nonsense is over. Times like these, you want something you can rely on.'

'We've got a financial chap here,' replied Clarence, giving Michael a nod. 'Where would you be putting your money, young man?'

Michael seized his chance. 'Well, sir,' he said, looking straight at Charles, 'I can't fault you for your decisiveness. These are difficult times and the markets agree with you. But you'll be selling your shares at rock bottom and buying gold at a record high. That might give you peace of mind in the short term, but this miners' strike must come to an end eventually, even if it takes another general election to do it. Then the markets will recover. Now's the time to buy, not sell.'

'By Jove! Michael, isn't it?' Charles replied. 'Well, well. That's what my broker told me. Tosh, I said to him. Maybe I was hasty. You should listen to this chap, Clarence, if the younger Aldfords are to have anything left of their trust.' The room erupted in laughter.

Charlotte gave Michael the feedback the next day. 'You went down well. I'm proud of you. Congratulations.'

Michael looked relieved. 'It was a surprise to me, I don't mind saying. I expected to be put in my place.'

'You look like a responsible, smartly-dressed grown up. You run your own business and work in finance. I thought that was a white lie I should tell. Better than saying I'm dating my ex-bank manager.'

'I think I know more about what's smart, money-wise, than the people in your family who make the financial decisions. They don't seem clued into the real world.' Michael paused for a second. 'You should get someone to run a slide rule over your trust fund. I worry that Uncle Clarence might not be investing it wisely.'

'Oh, he doesn't let me get involved in all that,' said Charlotte airily. 'Vulgar to talk about money.'

Vulgar, thought Michael. That was why none of them seemed to care. A thought for a new business idea was growing in his mind.

★ ★ ★

Michael looked on with satisfaction as the fitters installed the plush new office furniture he'd ordered. When he had opened the office a few weeks earlier, it was a basic operation. He and Ron had a room each, Michael's dominated by a large safe where they kept cash after it arrived from their clients and before Ron despatched it. By the entrance, there was a third desk where Mildred, the receptionist and secretary, sat. Mildred's husband was two years into a ten-year stretch for armed robbery, and Ron had vouched for her as an old-school gangster's wife who would see nothing and say nothing about what was going on.

The set-up was simple. Michael worked in the office during the day; operating, developing and refining the laundering techniques. Ron would turn up mid-afternoon, and the two of them would go through what money was going where. Ron would prepare the envelopes and lock them into his briefcase, which he padlocked to his wrist. Then he would leave to do the rounds, paying the money into their various bank accounts. Michael had never thought there was any point in making the office look fancy; no one would ever see it.

Now that was going to change. A black leather Eames chair sat behind a seven-foot Drexel cherrywood desk in his office. There were simpler G-Plan desks and chairs for Ron and Mildred. A Bauhaus sofa was installed along one wall underneath a giant Allen Jones painting. Blue-glazed ceramic lamps on matching side tables completed the look. A fully-stocked drinks cabinet was in the corner, every bottle unopened. The office would not have looked out of place in a Madison Avenue advertising agency.

Ron looked completely nonplussed when he came in for the afternoon meeting.

'What the fuck, Michael?' he said, as he looked around. 'Sorry, Mildred.'

Mildred nodded her forgiveness.

'I said I was going to do the place up,' Michael replied. 'What do you think?'

'I think you've gone insane. All this stuff better be coming out of your pocket. What the hell is going on?'

They went into his office and Michael closed the door.

'We're going to get more involved in international banking and some fairly complex financial instruments as the business keeps growing. I need an office that looks the part – I'll be dealing with Swiss banks and trading in stocks and bonds. Looking like an entrepreneur has been okay till now, but the stuff I'm going to be getting into is too sophisticated for your typical Glasgow businessman. There's going to be a second business alongside Alba Transport. Mitchell and Partners. An upmarket financial consultancy, giving investment advice to a select few high-profile clients. With all the window dressing to make it look like a big concern, but only one or two clients so it doesn't eat up my time.'

'Isn't that risky, being so visible?' Ron looked concerned. 'Maybe we shouldn't be drawing too much attention to ourselves.'

'The more respectable we look, the less likely we are to be asked questions,' Michael replied. 'Charlotte moves in these circles. I've seen how her trust fund's being managed, and it's obvious people who've never had to worry about money haven't got a clue how to make it work for them. I'm going to see if I can get some of her family to open a few doors for me, get a couple of clients as a cover for what we're doing the rest of the time.'

'Financial services to the criminal classes and the landed gentry.' Ron shook his head. 'No one can accuse you of half-measures, Michael. Talk about hiding in plain sight. When's all this going to happen?'

'Now. And I'll tell you why. Look at this.'

Michael showed Ron the system he had designed, set up to show thirty people paying money into over a hundred different bank accounts. 'This is where we need to go next. We need an army of little people to run around opening accounts for us. We need to have a wider variety of signatures and addresses on new bank accounts.'

Ron peered at the first foolscap page of the document, everything written out, waiting for the first numbers to be added in. The blank neutrality of his expression showed he had no clue what it meant, but he gave a short nod to signal that, whatever it was, it looked impressive.

'And who exactly are our little helpers? And how do we keep them from screwing up everything we've got going on?'

'I do some work with a charity, Second Chance. As the name suggests, it gives people some support to do something better with their lives.' Michael caught Ron's look, obviously never having thought of Michael as a do-gooding charity type. 'Ron, there's a lot you don't know about me. It was all part of the image I had when I worked at the bank. I know a lot of people coming to Second Chance who could be trusted to help us, with the right motivation.'

Ron arched a quizzical eyebrow. 'What, vandals and glue sniffers?'

'No, the ones I think are reliable. I've got a fan club there. Leave it to me.'

'And what will these model citizens do?'

'Pay money in when and where we tell them, in dribs and drabs, and if they keep their mouths shut and their fingers away from the cash, they get a nice retainer for helping out.'

'A little army of smurfs, working for Grandpa Smurf?' Ron chuckled.

'Smurfs? What are they?' It was Michael's turn to be bemused.

'Characters from a Belgian comic. I've got a cousin who's big into all these international ones you get nowadays. I'm a *Broons* and *Oor Wullie* man myself.'

'Well, it's a good name. Let's call them smurfs. If anyone ever overhears us, they'll have no idea what we're talking about.'

He closed the ledger and slipped it back into his briefcase, locking it shut. 'There's another thing we need to do. None of these transactions is particularly complicated, but there's going to be a whole lot more of them. I'm going to need better systems and more manpower to track things as they get bigger and more complicated. We can't have a repeat of last month.'

Ron looked embarrassed. As things had become increasingly complex, he'd struggled to keep tabs on all the small parcels of money moving through the operation. Several hundreds of pounds had fallen through the cracks, and it had taken Michael hours to painstakingly track down where they had got lost in the system. Someone more suspicious might have thought that Ron had done it deliberately, but Michael gave Ron the benefit of the doubt. The time he'd spent sorting it out had been worth it. He'd shown Ron he trusted him and that, so long as it was a genuine screw-up, there'd be no recriminations if things went wrong occasionally.

'It's all going to be based around better financial control,' Michael said, 'so key to this is getting a tame accountant. I've talked to Kenny McGowan about it. His bookkeeper has been in semi-retirement since he went on the straight and narrow, working in a high street accountancy firm, but he misses the big bucks he used to make when he was on Kenny's payroll. Eric Jenkins. Ever heard of him?'

Ron shook his head.

'That's what I wanted to hear. I wanted to talk to you first, but I'm going to try to get him on board. Once he's sorted, you won't have so much paperwork to do. Leave you more time to be … what did you call it? Grampa Smurf. Happy?'

'Ecstatic. But if you're going to bring someone new on board, you'll not mind if I do the same. I don't think having

111

an army of smurfs is going to be plain sailing. I can't be everywhere and have the muscle to keep them in line. I want to deal with our customers, and we bring in a heavy to keep the smurfs in line. And I need to have protection myself, when I'm carrying the amount of cash we're handling. You get your accountant; I get my heavy man. Deal?'

'Can't complain, if you think we need to. Did you have anyone in mind?'

'Yeah. Ever heard of Big Jockie?'

Michael blanched. 'I must be getting too familiar with the criminal underworld. Of course I have. Isn't he the colossal thug who was the enforcer for that gangster that went down recently? The guy you hear all the horror stories about?'

'The same. With his boss banged up for twenty years, he's at a loose end. He'd be perfect as our enforcer.'

'I don't want him, Ron. He's too scary for me.'

'No, he's perfect. The threat of Big Jockie keeps people in line without him ever having to do anything. Reputation is a wonderful thing.'

Michael was unconvinced. 'If we hire Big Jockie, one day we're going to use him. That's not the sort of business I want to run.'

'Then what happens when one of the smurfs absconds with the money he's handling, and when we catch him he just gets a rap on the knuckles? You're smart, Michael, but not street smart. We need a deterrent that people are really shit-scared about.'

Michael shook his head. 'I'm sorry, Ron. No violence.'

'I run the street operation, remember? You keep to the moral high ground on your side of the operation, if that's your fancy. But don't tell me how to run mine.'

In the end, Michael relented. But first, he said, he wanted to meet Big Jockie, to understand just what sort of hard man he really was before it was agreed to bring him on board. It was a sop to his conscience, he knew that. Ron was right; eventually something in the operation was going to require some heavy tactics, and, if his reputation was anything to go by, Big Jockie would be ideal for that. One day, Michael suspected, there would indeed be blood on his hands. But he'd do everything possible to make sure that day took as long as possible to arrive.

* * *

Michael asked McGowan to make the introduction to Eric Jenkins, and they met at the Caledonian, the gentlemen's club that had recently accepted Michael as a member. In the oak-panelled smoking room, he sat Jenkins down at a corner table, his squat frame shifting nervously in the well-worn leather Chesterfield chair. He looked like someone who had been fifty years old his entire life.

After ordering a single malt for Jenkins and a club soda for himself, Michael got straight to the point. 'Thanks for seeing me at such short notice, Mr Jenkins. Eric. May I call you Eric?'

Jenkins blinked rapidly and took a sip of the whisky. Then another. 'Of course,' he said eventually, as if some momentous commitment had been wrestled out of him.

Michael leant forward and smiled to try to put him at his ease. 'The thing is, Eric…' He looked around and lowered his voice. 'The thing is, I need an accountant who's not afraid of running the management accounts of a consultancy firm that has complex, and, some would say, relatively opaque fiduciary processes. You were recommended by our mutual friend who's enjoying his retirement, but he's not involved. I manage financial services for a wide variety of clients and need someone to do the accounts for them.'

'If I might ask …' Jenkins paused to take another sip of his whisky. He blinked again, and Michael noticed a bead of sweat on his brow. 'If you don't mind, that is. What sort of services? What sort of clients?'

'Small to medium-sized entrepreneurs. Not big organisations, but people who nonetheless have specific financial needs that benefit from our specialised fiscal expertise. And you will stay at arm's length from the operation, and never be involved with the clients themselves. I'm told you're not someone who likes to enquire too much about the operational end of businesses. That's a quality I admire.'

'I try not to make a nuisance of myself.' Jenkins gave a strangled half-chuckle. Michael realised this was an attempt at humour.

'Not making a nuisance. Good, good. I like that.' Michael chuckled away to try to relieve the tension. 'Let me scope out the parameters of the role. Current turnover of four hundred thousand a year, give or take. High growth forecast. We move money in and around the banking system in a multitude of small-scale transactions. Each transaction is relatively straightforward, but the accounting challenge is to manage a huge number of them. And keep tabs on a substantial number of freelance operatives we are bringing on board to implement our strategy. Think you can handle that?'

'Oh yes. Numbers are fine. As long as it's just numbers. Sometimes I see more of my employers' operations than I feel comfortable with. I prefer being behind the scenes. Minding my own business.'

'You'll find I'm the same. I have a business partner who deals with our clients; at the sharp end, shall we say. You come highly recommended, Eric, especially for the discretion you mentioned. You would run an accountancy practice; I'd be your sole client. A financial manager would cost me ten thousand a year; I'm willing to triple that given the unorthodox nature of our business and the fact you wouldn't be an employee. How does that sound?'

For the first time, Jenkins cracked a smile.

'Sounds very agreeable, Mr Mitchell. Sorry, Michael.'

'Let's meet again, and I'll take you through the specifics. And you can meet my business partner, Ron Smith.'

As Jenkins was leaving, Michael saw Ron arrive. He'd save the introductions for the next time. Ron beckoned him to come outside, where he introduced the biggest man Michael had ever seen. But it wasn't his size, it was the rage in his eyes that was the most overwhelming feature. A bestial savagery that could erupt at any second.

The meeting with Big Jockie was perfunctory in the extreme. His very presence would be enough to ensure that no smurf would ever get greedy or indiscreet. After a few monosyllabic exchanges, Michael nodded to Ron that all was agreed and went back inside the club, leaving Ron to sort out the details. Money was what bought Big Jockie's loyalty and power. His cost to the operation would be painful in the short term, but smurf compliance was the key to the success of what they were setting up.

In a few minutes Ron was back in the club. He slumped down in a chair opposite Michael.

'Have you ever seen someone so scary? I know it was my idea, but now I'm not so sure. Wouldn't like to get on the wrong side of that bugger. I was scared shitless the whole time I was with him.'

'How did you leave it with him?'

'He wants a grand a month as a retainer. For that he'll sort out anyone that needs sorting on the assumption that it's not too often. Ten grand a month if we want him to be exclusive to us. I said I'd get back to him first thing in the morning. But I've changed my mind. Let's find someone cheaper, preferably someone who seems to be part of the human race. That fucker could snap someone's neck with his fingertips, and I don't want the neck in question to be mine.'

'I'm not so sure, Ron,' Michael said softly. 'I think he could be perfect.'

Ron stared in astonishment. 'Last time we talked, you were giving me a whole lot of namby-pamby shit about how you don't want any hard stuff. "*I'm sorry, Ron. No violence.*" Now you want somebody who would give the Kray brothers nightmares to go on the payroll?'

'I don't want violence. And Big Jockie is the best way to make sure of that. With any regular hard man, there would always be some smurf willing to chance his arm. Introduce them to Big Jockie and we'll have complete obedience.'

'Well, I want to sleep soundly at night, not having to worry if I've inadvertently pissed off that psycho. If you want him on the payroll, you bloody deal with him.'

'I will. I was going to propose just that.'

Ron's mouth slackened. 'Now you want to run the street operation as well? Fuck me, Michael, what do they put in the club sodas in this place? Five minutes in Big Jockie's company and suddenly you're Al Capone.'

Michael smiled. 'Don't worry. I'm not talking about muscling in on your side of the operation. If we use Big Jockie, it has to be in a way that's structured and disciplined. I should call him, say we'll go for the exclusive deal, with one condition. If we ever have to use him, he gets his instructions from me, and he does what I ask him to do to the letter. No getting carried away by the sight of blood, no improvising. That way if we ever have to resort to violence, it will be controlled, rational and proportionate. I'll see to that.'

Ron laughed. 'It's not a game of chess we're playing. I don't think you understand how things work on the streets. And ten grand a month is a bit rich, considering he'll be sitting on his hands ninety-nine per cent of the time. It'll set back our profits to what they were three months ago.'

'I don't want anything to happen by accident to someone Big Jockie has to punish. That means he needs to be closely monitored. Having him work freelance is how accidents happen. When we first met you'd have been over the moon to make the money we were making three months ago. Smurf security and obedience are critical to our business operation. If it costs a hundred and twenty grand to do it right, then that's what it costs.'

'As long as it's your door he'll come knocking on in the middle of the night, that's fine with me. Okay, I'll tell him. There's no figuring you out, Michael. One minute you don't want violence, the next you're in charge of meting it out. But as long as you don't interfere with my street operation, I'll go along with it.'

Michael sat back in the leather seat, the murmur of the Scottish business elite drifting around him. In the space of an hour, he'd set up both sides of his new operation: the civility and business-speak of Jenkins and the raw terror of Big Jockie. His insides felt queasy about what that brute would do if it ever became necessary to bring someone in line or eliminate a problem.

The business was now more than numbers on a piece of paper. It had a dark side that Michael wasn't particularly proud of. He told himself it would be visited as rarely as possible.

chapter ten

For the first time in his life, Michael had fallen in love. Simple, pure, unadulterated euphoria for life. And Charlotte was the cause.

What had started as an infatuation with her background had broadened into something much deeper. After the successful meeting with her family, Charlotte began to introduce Michael to her world, her friends, the things she liked to do. A dinner party had been the start, four of Charlotte's friends coming round to her flat, squeezed around an antique table handed down from the family; Michael spent hours in the kitchen beforehand preparing prawn cocktail with avocado, beef Wellington and crêpe Suzette. 'I can't believe it,' Charlotte had said when he volunteered. 'A man who likes cooking.'

Michael had developed and honed his skills in another life, working in hotel kitchens in every corner of Scotland. He was wary of being teased by the other guests, even more so of having to reveal his past to people born into privilege. As the hour of the dinner party approached, Michael was having feelings of self-doubt.

Charlotte's promise to keep quiet about his culinary skills lasted all of ten minutes into the first course.

'This is Michael's special recipe for Marie Rose sauce,' she informed the guests as she served the prawn cocktail in martini glasses on a bed of shredded lettuce. 'With a secret ingredient he won't even tell me about. From when he was a chef at one of Scotland's finest hotels.'

Michael was mortified, but tried to laugh it off. 'If I tell Charlotte all of my secrets, I'll have nothing left to impress her with. Really, Charlotte, don't put people off their dinner by telling them I cooked it.'

'What, you cooked everything?' said Sybil, one of Charlotte's horse-riding friends. She looked over her glasses to her boyfriend. 'It's time I saw you with an apron, Henry. I don't suppose you have a brother, do you, Michael?'

Michael laughed and shook his head.

'Pity. All the men I meet ever seem to do is talk rugby and get plastered. And Charlotte tells me you're an opera buff? How fascinating.'

Michael found himself holding court, as he described a rose-tinted version of his formative years. Rather than his upbringing being something to be embarrassed about, to people who had never experienced hardship or obstacles it was both exotic and inspiring. For the first time, he found that his past was nothing to be ashamed of.

'I've never seen you like that,' Charlotte said afterwards. 'So open, I mean. That joke about keeping secrets from me to appear mysterious. It's true, you know. I found more out about you tonight than I've learnt in all the time we've been together.'

'I felt relaxed in their company,' Michael admitted. 'You're right; I am usually a bit guarded. But every one of your friends tonight can trace their ancestry back at least a couple of centuries. There's nothing we ordinary mortals can do to match up to that, so for once I celebrated my past, rather than disowning it.'

'You're so silly.' Charlotte laughed. 'This is 1974. No one cares where people come from anymore, what school they went to. Did you see how impressed everyone was when you told them about going back to night school to become a banker, and then when the bosses were so beastly to you, having the courage to walk away and set up your own business? And look how successful it's been. That's a lot more impressive than having some draughty castle in the middle of nowhere that your family have owned for generations. You've inspired me, Michael. I need to do something more with my life, not take advantage of everything that's been handed to me on a plate.'

'Something more' turned out to be volunteering with Second Chance. Charlotte met with Jason, the guy who had introduced Michael to Kenny McGowan. He suggested that she help out at the Friday-night soup kitchen. Under the pretext of free food, it gave the charity a chance to connect with recently released young offenders who were trying to put their criminal past behind them.

Michael and Charlotte turned up at seven in the evening. Marrow bones and mutton flank were already bobbing about in two huge tureens of boiling water, and pearl barley, split peas and lentils were being added to make Scotch broth. They helped with chopping the carrots and onions, and once they'd tipped them into the soup they got busy laying out the trestle tables with the bowls, spoons and plates of bread and butter for the eight o'clock opening.

'Means they get a bowl of something warm and nutritious to see them through the night,' explained Jason. 'Be prepared for the rush when we open the doors.'

The doors opened bang on eight, and a jumble of people poured inside – wizened alcoholics, grungy tramps, pinch-faced, jittery women. All waited patiently in line, and Charlotte strained to understand what was being said to her in broad Glaswegian accents, constantly turning to Michael to supply a translation. They didn't get a chance to talk properly until the last of the soup was ladled out just after nine.

'I feel I've done something real for the first time in my life,' Charlotte confessed to Michael. She laughed. 'And discovered a few new words, not all of them repeatable! I must admit I was nervous to meet people who lived like this, intrigued to see what they'd be like. But they weren't scary, they were just people who've made some wrong choices in life. I think more of my friends should be persuaded to do things like this.'

She was more enthusiastic than Michael would have liked. It had been easy to spot who to recruit as smurfs – the ones who were on the brink of a life of destitution but had enough saving graces that meant they could follow a simple set of orders without screwing up. The dysfunctional, the psychotic, the ones who led irretrievably chaotic lifestyles, could easily be identified according to how they responded to Second Chance's overtures to help them find a better life. It was the perfect recruiting ground for Ron to find as many smurfs as he needed, but Charlotte needed to be steered away from too much direct involvement with the people the charity was helping, to minimise the risk she might stumble on what was going on.

In the meantime, meeting Charlotte's friends was only the start of the new world Michael was being introduced to. He had always been dismissive of popular music, and the free-love culture and guitar histrionics of the 1960s and early 70s had left him cold. Barry White and soul divas were the limits of his excursions into music that wasn't classical or jazz. Charlotte turned up at Michael's flat one evening, clutching a plastic bag in her hand like it was a holy relic.

'Wait till you hear this,' she told Michael. 'The new Three Degrees album, bought as an import from Bruce's Records. They haven't even started playing it on the radio yet. It'll blow your mind.'

Michael sat on his black leather sofa, watching as Charlotte started dancing, the slinky Philadelphia sound filling the room. As 'When Will I See You Again?' started to play, she pulled him to his feet.

'C'mon, baby, let's groove!' she said, slipping her hand around his waist and shimmying to the beat of the music. Despite himself, Michael started to sway along with her. When it finished, Charlotte gave him a congratulatory kiss.

'You've got natural rhythm under that ice-man exterior,' she told him. 'You've got to hang loose, Michael. You belong on the dance floor.'

With only mild protestations, he was persuaded to head off to Tiffany's in Sauchiehall Street the following Saturday night. Charlotte promised him he wouldn't regret it.

They pulled up in a taxi and looked at the long line of partygoers waiting patiently in the rain, the men in leisure suits and ruffle shirts, women in jumpsuits or spandex tube-tops, huddling under umbrellas. The sight was enough for Michael to decide that this wasn't going to be the fun experience he had been led to expect.

'I'm not hanging about in the rain with these people,' he said to Charlotte. 'It's not too late to head off to the jazz club at the Albany. They don't make you wait in the rain.'

'You mean this queue?' Charlotte replied. 'Don't be silly, that's not for us.' She walked up to the bouncers at the door. 'Charlotte Aldford,' she informed them. 'Here with Michael Mitchell.'

The bouncer checked a typed list on a clipboard. 'Of course, Miss Aldford. Through you go.'

Michael and Charlotte were ushered into the disco foyer, to yells and catcalls from the bedraggled punters waiting in line. Charlotte tried not to look too smug; Michael maintained a dignified aloofness.

'Jeremy should be in here somewhere.'

Michael looked at her blankly.

'My cousin. He practically lives here.'

Michael went to the bar to order a Moscow Mule for Charlotte and a club soda for himself, while Charlotte scanned the thronging masses.

'There he is. Cooee, Jeremy!' she yelled over the stomping beat. A snake-hipped man in loon pants and a lilac blouson waved back a greeting. She turned to Michael. 'Let's go over. Don't bother with the drinks.'

Michael found out why. Jeremy and his friends were in a roped-off booth, the VIP area. A bottle of Moët &

Chandon was in an ice bucket, and three of Jeremy's acolytes were topping up their glasses as they entered.

'Charlotte, darling. Who's your friend?' Jeremy gave Michael an admiring once-over.

'Taken, darling, taken,' replied Charlotte. 'Anyway, I don't think he's your type.'

Michael sat at the edge of the semi-circular velvet bench, trying not to look uncomfortable.

'I think maybe we should sit somewhere else,' he whispered to Charlotte. 'This isn't my scene.'

'Jeremy's not a fruit, if that's what you're thinking,' Charlotte replied. 'It's just his way. And his style is a big hit with the ladies.'

Charlotte was right. A procession of Glasgow lovelies swayed up to the red rope, flirting and bantering with the group of men. Two giggling girls from Shettleston made the cut and were soon kissing Jeremy and one of his friends. The other two headed down to the dance floor to seek out some action.

The logistics of the booth meant that Michael could turn his back on the canoodling couples and give his full attention to the dance floor. The sight was so bizarre that he couldn't help but give a bemused grin. 'I think I've lived a sheltered life,' he said to Charlotte. 'I never knew that Sodom and Gomorrah were right on my doorstep.'

★ ★ ★

The only flaw in the new world of which Michael was now part was that you needed money to participate, and lots of it. Charlotte presumed Michael's income came from his financial consultancy, but with four members of the Aldford family and a smattering of other upper-class clients that Michael's new-found contacts had put him in touch with, the commission he was making on handling their investments was responsible for only five per cent of his earnings. And took fifty per cent of his time. Smurfs and money laundering were an inevitable part of his life now, and one day he was sure that Charlotte would discover that.

Charlotte was also having another effect on him. Michael began to toy with the idea of doing some genuine good with Second Chance, of being purely altruistic for a change, rather than exploitative and manipulative. Second Chance's big ambition was to open a social and leisure centre in Castlemilk, a vast council estate on the South Side of Glasgow which was notorious for the lack of any amenities for the residents. Street after street of identical pebble-dashed terraced houses, with nary a pub, café or even a supermarket in sight. The leisure centre was a year behind schedule and, at a trustee meeting, there had been a discussion about whether it should be abandoned, given the lack of support from businesses and the public alike.

When Michael mentioned this to Charlotte, he was impressed by her reaction.

'I've got the contacts, you've got the business brain,' she announced. 'Let's take charge and make this happen. Teamwork. We can do it.'

The previous leader of the fundraising effort gratefully handed over the reins of responsibility and Michael and Charlotte got to work. Charlotte organised a charity dinner at the family estate, Michael sat down and planned how they were going to raise the other funds. Kenny McGowan agreed to be the guest of honour, amused to be extolling the virtues of Nietzsche to a room full of upper-class socialites. Ron was bemused by Michael's new passion, but with the smurfing operation running smoothly and the laundering schemes continuing to expand to deal with increasing demand, his complaints were no more than sarcastic ribbing that Michael was having his brain turned to mush by all the posh totty he was getting.

It took two months to achieve the financial targets, and the dream of a Second Chance leisure centre in Castlemilk could finally be realised. Michael posed for a photo with Glasgow's Lord Provost, handing over a giant cheque for £50,000. The article praised him as a new breed of Scottish entrepreneur, showing that there was room at the top for anyone who had the ability and determination to succeed. He was touted as a product of an egalitarian new world order that was reinvigorating the business community with a dynamism that hadn't been seen since the glory days, when Glasgow had been the second city of the Empire. Michael was becoming the symbol of this renaissance.

Offers came flooding in. There was talk of him becoming chairman of Second Chance, once the current chairman decided to call it a day. A seat on the board was offered as a way of preparing him for the role. He was tempted, but the higher his public profile, the greater the risk that his criminal activity might be exposed. His work with Ron would be a means to an end, Michael decided, a way of giving him financial security; he would put that world behind him as soon as the income from his investments was sufficient to provide the lifestyle he wanted. A million pounds in capital would suffice, two to be on the safe side, and at the current rate of growth he would be there in two years.

Two years of keeping the truth from Charlotte. Then his new life could truly begin.

chapter eleven

Michael's money-laundering operation grew in complexity. After three months, he had six separate schemes in place; Jenkins had set up an elaborate ledger system to track the small individual sums being paid in by the smurfs, and there was a byzantine network of shell companies to move money about. There were even a few more legitimate clients, Michael advising them how best to invest their cash tax-efficiently.

Ron's criminal clients knew only about Ron; Michael's investment clients knew only about Michael. For the first time in his life, he felt fulfilled, enjoying the ever-increasing money he was making, but also getting a curious intellectual satisfaction from the elegance and meticulousness of how he was amassing his fortune. Yes, it might be illegal, but it felt more like he was spending his days playing an intricate game of three-dimensional chess, always thinking one move ahead to make things bigger and better.

It couldn't last. When Ron called to say they had to meet urgently, Michael knew something was up. The fact that it was Ron wanting the meeting rather than Big Jockie was reassuring. An emergency Big Jockie meeting would mean that a smurf had exposed them to police attention;

with Ron, it would probably only mean an awkward customer issue to sort out.

Ron arrived at Michael's house, casting an anxious glance over his shoulder and talking too quickly.

'Michael, we've got a problem,' he said, without preamble. 'Ivan Young has got wind of our operation and has taken offence that there's activity on his patch and he isn't involved. He wants to meet up. Pretty sure it's to tell us if we want to keep going, at least on the South Side, he has to be in charge.'

Michael paused to light a cigarette.

'Are you hearing me, Michael? Ivan Young. Crazy Ivan. He's a fucking nutter. You don't mess with him; if he wants to run our business, we've got to let him. Otherwise, we're dead meat.'

'What's happened? Have you spoken to him?'

'Not directly. One of his heavies stopped me in the street, said Ivan was told about our operation by one of the guys involved in the bank job in Merchant City. Ivan was behind the heist, and the driver had been part of a job we got the money from a couple of months ago. The guy saw how our operation to handle the money went like clockwork, and recommended us to Ivan. Not his fault, he thought he was using his initiative.' Ron seemed to be trying to convince himself. 'Had to happen sooner or later, I suppose.'

Michael leant back into his leather armchair. The gentle tick of a grandfather clock filled the room.

'We don't have time to worry about whose fault it was,' he said eventually. 'This Ivan character. What's his problem with our operation?'

'His problem is that we exist. He put out some feelers, found out how much we're into, and went ballistic that nobody had told him. I've to meet him, and not just me. They figured out I'm not in this on my own. You've to come along too.'

'Ron, you know I'm not going to do that.' Michael took a deep breath. 'This is your area. Deal with it.'

'Don't you think I want to? Look, Ivan knows we've got a big operation, and that it's becoming more and more sophisticated. No way can I convince him I'm doing this all by myself. He knows someone like you exists. If I don't produce you, I won't be around much longer. It's up to you, Michael. If we're going to keep this operation going, we've got to meet with Ivan and give him what he wants.'

Michael felt the sense of injustice rise up inside him again, that someone could come along and muscle into something that he had worked so hard and risked so much to achieve. He thought he was keeping his feelings hidden, displaying a veneer of calmness, of being in control. But his two Dobermanns chose that moment to muscle into the room, and instantly picked up on his mood. They weren't puppies anymore, and growled a low, threatening snarl towards Ron, this intruder upsetting their master. Michael rubbed the backs of their necks.

'Satan, Lucifer. Go!' The dogs skulked off to their baskets, Satan giving one last reproachful look towards Ron as he left.

'They should know you by now,' Michael said. He got up and closed the door. 'Look, I know I'm an amateur when it comes to these things, but there must be some way to reason with this guy. I'm not going to hand over everything we've worked so hard to achieve, just because some mindless thug threatens us.'

Ron didn't speak, just stared into the distance. His defeatist attitude made Michael all the more determined.

'Look, he must know the operation would never be able to survive if he was running it,' Michael insisted. 'The criminals who use our services are much too suspicious of each other to trust one of their own to handle the proceeds of their crimes. The thing is, it only works if it's run by people who are not pulling jobs themselves. You need to make Ivan see sense.'

Nothing Michael could say would shift Ron's fatalism.

'I can't do that, Michael.' His voice had the flat tone of defeat, with an edge of real fear. 'I need you to come with me. I know what we said about you never being exposed to the sharp end, but we don't have a choice. An operation under Ivan is better than no operation at all.'

He saw the defiant look in Michael's eyes.

'Please?'

Michael had never seen Ron like this. It should have been a warning of how dangerous the situation was. How the smart, sensible, businesslike thing to do was swallow his pride and give in. But instead, Michael surprised himself by the delicious icy chill that spread over his body as he made his decision. He had proved to himself that he had the mind to succeed in the life he had chosen for himself. Now he had to prove he had the stomach. It was time to fight for what was rightly his.

'Okay, I'll meet him,' was all he said. 'Let me do all the talking. I'll convince him to let us be. And if I don't

...' He paused for a second. 'If I don't, I'll deal with the consequences. You won't have to worry.'

Ron looked at him as if he was seeing the real Michael for the first time.

★ ★ ★

Michael insisted on meeting at The Buttery restaurant, reckoning a classy setting might help keep the conversation civilised. He and Ron turned up on time, sat at a corner table, both staring into space, not saying a word to each other. Ivan arrived half an hour late, without apology, and with an ape in a suit as a companion. He was not what Michael was expecting. Dressed in a tan leisure suit over a brown turtle-neck sweater, bouffant hair spilling over his collar, Ivan looked more like a mid-Atlantic crooner than a Glasgow street fighter. He glanced around.

'You've got a few airs and graces, pal,' he said. 'You didn't need to go to all this bother. We'll have this sorted out before *garçon* has taken our orders.'

Ivan sat down, the ape by his side. He glanced at the solid gold Rolex on his wrist. 'Maybe even faster than that. I'll no' be staying long. You two can enjoy a nice candlelit dinner together when I'm gone.'

'I'm glad you've got in touch, Ivan,' said Michael. 'I've been waiting to prove I had an operation worthy of your attention and now I think we've got there. I think we can be good for each other.'

Ivan gave a thin smile, then a slight shake of the head. 'Aye, we'll be good for each other. First of all, I'll no' kneecap you pair o' wide boys for starting this caper without my say-so.' He leant back as if to congratulate himself on his restraint. 'Just to prove what a reasonable guy I am.'

Looking perfectly relaxed, he pointed a finger at Michael's face.

'You're going to tell me exactly how this wee scam of yours works, and how much you are making. And I'll tell you what; I'll let you keep fifty per cent for having the gumption to come up with this. Oh, with my boys checking all your numbers and holding your hand as you get used to working for me, so there are no misunderstandings.' He spread his hands apart to signal that the deal was completed. 'So, if that's all agreed, I think I'll order a bottle of their best champagne as a carry-out.'

Ivan stared at Michael with a defiant look in his eye.

'And thanks for picking up the tab to say sorry for the disrespect.' He grinned. 'See? That was easy. *Un morceau de gâteau* as they say here.'

'That's one way to do things,' Michael replied.

Ivan stared at him with undisguised fury at his impertinence.

Michael continued. 'Look, hear me out, okay? Some of your … can I call them your competitors? … are keen to use our services, but they'd lose face if it was your operation. So, what if you give us your blessing, and we help you out by laundering your money free of charge? There're a lot of costs to the operation, so you avoid all of those. You get this deal, nobody else does. We keep it our secret. You get to keep every penny of your money; I get to keep my business. A win-win business proposition. What do you say?'

Ivan grasped Michael's wrist and pulled it across the table towards him.

'I say you do what I tell you. If you don't, then don't blame me if I stop being reasonable. You've got balls, Mister City Slicker; I'll give you that. But you've also got brains. Use them. You've got forty-eight hours to give me your answer. And it better be that you're working for me, no' another one of your fucking business propositions. Capeesh?'

He left.

Ron had kept silent during the discussion. When Ivan was safely out of earshot, he finally spoke. 'That sounded like a final warning to me. You don't get a second chance with Ivan. I told you.'

'That's not what I heard,' Michael replied. 'He could have strong-armed us into agreeing, restaurant or no restaurant. Said that if we wanted to be alive in the morning, we needed to agree on the spot. He was sussing us out, to find out how strong we were, whether anyone was protecting us. Behind all that bluster, he's not as strong as he pretends to be.'

Ron shook his head in disbelief. 'Michael, you're out of your league here. If you don't want to find yourself floating down the Clyde, say yes to Crazy Ivan. We can still do well on fifty per cent of the business, even if we lose a few clients when word gets out he's taking over.'

'We're not going to do that, Ron,' Michael said softly. 'Look, I can see you're uncomfortable. Let's do this: get word to Ivan that I'm the one saying no, that I need time to think about it. We keep away from our usual haunts. Then I go to see him when I'm ready, on my own, taking all the risk. See if I can make him see reason. If I don't, I have to deal with the consequences. But if I do, I get the rewards. You want to give him fifty per cent of the operation, so we'd only have twenty-five per cent each. If there's no Crazy Ivan, you keep thirty-five per cent; I get the other sixty-five. If I fail, you still get thirty-five per cent; I accept fifteen. I take all the risk, and under both scenarios, you get more than is on the table at the moment.'

Michael gave the satisfied smile of an entrepreneur who had just solved a knotty business problem.

Ron was not convinced. 'No one crosses Ivan and lives to tell the tale. You're not street-savvy enough to get that, Michael. But let me tell you, we don't have a choice.'

Michael's smile faded and died on his lips.

'We do have a choice, Ron. It's a case of whether we want to make it, that's all. Do whatever you need to do to make sure Ivan knows this is my idea. But it's what we're going to do.'

Despite his confident words, Michael knew that he needed to act quickly. Any delay and Ivan would start destroying the operation one job at a time, and when it was damaged beyond the point of no return and there was no reason to keep them alive, he and Ron would suffer the final retribution.

There was only one thing for it. He had to meet with Kenny McGowan again.

chapter twelve

They met in the same bar as before. McGowan listened carefully as Michael outlined how his business had grown since their first meeting and the threat that Ivan posed. He asked Michael to describe every detail of the conversation.

'Did he really say *capeesh*?'

Michael nodded, and they both smiled.

McGowan fixed Michael with a piercing stare as he delivered his verdict. 'You're a man I'd like to see succeed, my friend,' he said. 'You've got a smart operation going on there, you've got ambition and you're in a hurry. But what matters to me is you're doing this with your head, no' with a chib. Aye, you need Big Jockie around to help keep your troops in order, but I can see he's a last resort, no' a first one. I like that.'

Michael felt a childlike flush of pride, like he'd been praised by a favourite teacher.

'I hate violence,' he said. 'He's my Polaris missile. Threatened, but never used.'

'Good, good. You can't win respect with fists. And you've got good instincts; you see what's going on. You were right to notice that Ivan gave you time to think about his ultimatum, to realise that was a sign of insecurity. He wants to know if you've got a bunch of Glasgow heavies in your pocket, ready to strike if he attacks. But when you meet him next, Ivan will have seen that's no' happened, so he's going to be a lot more confident. He might look like Neil Diamond's long-lost brother with all that nancyboy get-up; but believe me, he's one evil bastard. You'll no' get to walk away again unless you've got a smart way to fight him. The trick is to have him lose, but make him think he's won. No matter how smart your plan is, if he doesn't like it, he'd rather have everything destroyed than see someone stand up to him and succeed. Even if it costs him a lot and he gets nothing out of it.'

'I understand,' Michael said. 'I need to demonstrate strength without it looking like strength.' He waited a long minute. 'Here's my thinking. I'm going to show him I can switch off this operation, and that I'm prepared to keep it switched off and disappear forever, rather than accept his demands. But I need him to want the operation to start up again, even if it's not under his control – he has to know that he needs what I'm offering. And he's got to feel that's his decision, not something I've forced him to do.'

McGowan looked sceptical. 'And how are you going to do that? Hypnosis?'

'No, psychology. Dangle the carrot again of agreeing to launder all his money for free, as long as he leaves me alone. It'll save him a fortune; even Crazy Ivan will be able to work that out. But I also need a stick, a stick that I can't be seen to wield. The word's got to get out to the top echelons of the criminal fraternity that the party's over; there's to be no more money-laundering service in Glasgow. Maybe start a rumour the guys behind it have shut up shop because they're scared of someone who is trying to muscle into their organisation. The big boys need to hear about it and get around a table and agree that my operation is off limits to interference. We already have most of them on the books. Ivan will be at that table, and he can either risk the wrath of every gang boss in Glasgow if they find out he's the one behind the threat, or he can smile quietly to himself that he's getting a service for free that everyone else is paying through the nose for. He might convince himself he's come out of this the winner and decide to leave us alone.'

'Smart plan, but it'll no' work. You need to get to a lot of top men and get to them quickly, and then have them make the moves you're looking for. Ron doesn't have that sort of clout, Michael. He'll never get to all these chiefs in time.'

'Not Ron, Kenny. You.'

McGowan gave an exasperated snort and stood up to leave.

'You're getting on my tits, pal. I'm fucking retired, Michael. How many more times do I have to tell you that? And I'm no' your messenger boy. It's a good enough plan, Michael. But you need to do it yourself.'

Michael sensed that McGowan was tempted.

'Look, I'm not asking you to do anything illegal. Hear me out. You make a few phone calls; they avert the all-out bloodshed that would be inevitable when the recriminations start flying around about who's screwed up an operation every gang in Glasgow is benefitting from. You're an elder statesman making a discreet, low-key intervention to avoid carnage. You stop a needless and unnecessary gang war. Only you can do that.'

McGowan sat down. 'You're a persuasive wee bugger, Michael.' He smiled, and Michael tried not to show his elation. 'Okay,' he said. 'If I'm going to save your skin, the least you can do is buy me another pint.'

★ ★ ★

Michael called Ron, saying he had a plan and needed to tell him what it was. When they met, Michael's tone was understated; calm and strong.

'Look, I know we don't have the muscle to stand up to him. And we can't watch our backs twenty-four hours a day. We've got to strike back in a way that doesn't try to fight force with force.'

Ron pleaded again with Michael to give in, hand everything over to Ivan and accept their new role in the organisation.

Michael shrugged off his concerns. 'Our clients are becoming used to using our services,' he insisted, 'and they like that we take their cash disposal problems off their hands. You need to get to every one of our customers before the end of the day. You'll find there's a rumour going around that there is a security threat to the operation. Tell them it's true, we're closing everything down with immediate effect until the threat is lifted. Then you and I do a disappearing act, and I get word to Ivan that we stay gone until he says we can restart the operation with his blessing. He'll pick up the word on the street that whoever's causing us problems has got to stop. He'll know the whole of the Glasgow underworld will hate him if word gets out that he's the cause of it all. We don't threaten him with anything; we leave him to figure it out for himself.'

'How do you know about any rumour? What's going on, Michael – is there something you're not telling me?'

'Listen, you're right that things need to change after this. But our deal is I take all the risk, for a bigger share of the rewards if I'm successful. The less you know, the better it is for you if it goes wrong. You need to trust me on this. We agreed I could try my plan. And if I do it, it has to be done my way.'

'Michael, you don't get it, do you? There's no reasoning with the likes of Ivan. If you go to him with that proposition, you won't walk away from the meeting alive.'

'It's just business, Ron. A strategic solution to an obstacle that needs to be overcome. With the might of the Glasgow underworld behind us, he won't dare try to terminate our operation.'

'I'll bring flowers to your funeral. But at least don't meet him on your own. Take along Big Jockie.'

'That will look like I'm scared of him, unsure of the strength of my position. No, I'll meet him face to face. In a very public place, in case he gets a little hot-tempered. It's the only way to make this work. I didn't go down this road to be some criminal's lackey. We've got twenty-four hours before Ivan's deadline expires. In that time, you've got to make the calls and shut down what's left of our operation. Then you disappear and stay gone until I tell you otherwise. Only I will know where you are; you tell no one. Understand?'

Michael met with Charlotte that evening. At her insistence they headed to the Scotia Bar, down by the

Clyde, to see Cado Belle, a new Glasgow blue-eyed soul-funk band, perform their debut concert. It wasn't the ideal location to explain away his sudden departure, so he suggested they go for an after-show drink at the Central Hotel nearby.

Charlotte was still buzzing after the concert. 'Was Maggie Reilly's singing not amazing? And the rest of the band, so tight. Especially the sax. Forget your glam rock and heavy metal nonsense. This is the music of the future.'

'Wonderful,' agreed Michael. 'You do have an ear for great new sounds.'

Normally he would have indulged Charlotte's enthusiasm for a lot longer, but tonight he had other priorities on his mind.

'My turn,' he said, 'to suggest something exciting for us to do. The financial-planning business tends to get a bit quiet in the run-up to Christmas. I thought I'd get away for a day or two, recharge the batteries, come up with some ideas for the new year. There's a hotel in the Highlands I thought would be perfect. What do you think? Want to come along?'

'I'm not sure, to be honest. It's mid-November, Michael. Not exactly long country walks weather. Couldn't we do it another time? Plus, I've got my prelims coming up, and—'

'I thought you'd like it. I don't get much chance for time off and I've booked a week. That was a bit impetuous, I suppose. Are you sure you don't want to come?'

Charlotte reddened slightly. 'Honestly? Not really. I should be studying. Would you think it ghastly of me not to come along? I will if you want me too. I feel such a heel.'

Michael tried to hide his relief. Having Charlotte along would have made it tricky to extend his stay if it took longer than expected to get the message to Ivan. He was planning to stay disappeared until the pressure mounted from the other Glasgow crime bosses for the operation to be restarted.

He left the next morning, with only Lucifer and Satan for company. Before going, he mailed off a cheque to the charity Kenny McGowan supported that campaigned for penal reform, big enough to ensure that McGowan got to hear about it. McGowan hadn't asked for any payment for his services in helping Michael out, and Michael wasn't sure if he should have offered. This way, McGowan would know he was willing if asked.

Michael spent two weeks at the hotel, keeping himself to himself, walking the dogs on the moor every day, filling his lungs with the mountain air and contemplating the next stage in his life. He called Charlotte every day, from a village payphone so that the pips went after two minutes and he could wind up the call. The only other person he called was Kenny McGowan, who told him that a gangland summit had been called to discuss the cessation of his operation and what could be done about it. And that his donation was noted and appreciated, no further payment required.

Back in Glasgow, Michael finally contacted Ivan. As he expected, the man was furious at his disappearance. Michael turned Ivan's anger back on himself, insisting they should meet in as public a place as possible, with the promise that everything would be sorted out once and for all. That appeased him a little. Ron wasn't mentioned.

The meeting was set for Monday morning, under the Salvador Dali painting at the Kelvingrove Art Gallery and Museum. Michael arrived early and spent the time wandering around the exibits. There was hardly anyone there, and as he strolled around the vast, high-ceiling spaces, his footsteps on the marble floor echoing around the halls, he felt a certain foreboding about the hours and days ahead.

As the time for the meeting approached, Michael slowly climbed the staircase to the first floor, pausing after every step, as he prepared to meet his fate. He walked round the balcony encircling the hall, glancing down to see if there was any sign of Ivan. Finally, he found the meeting spot, stood in front of Dali's *Christ of St John of the Cross* and gazed at its God's-eye view of Jesus's powerful dignity. It gave him the inner strength he needed.

Ivan arrived with two muscle-bound minders in pinstriped suits. He saw Michael had come alone and, after checking there was no one with him, gestured for the two men to move out of earshot. They walked in opposite directions, blocking Michael's only two routes of escape.

'I've decided you can have the operation,' Michael said without any preamble. 'You win.'

Ivan gave a relaxed smile. 'I knew somebody with your brains would make the smart decision. I'll no' take the hump at your wee disappearing act. This time. But from now on you don't take a piss without checking with me first.' He grabbed a piece of Michael's cheek in his fingers and squeezed it. 'Just so we're clear.'

Michael's cheek was still stinging as he spoke. 'No. I said you can have the operation, but not me. I'm packing it in. I'm too much of a coward to get this close to your business, Ivan. I like a simple life. It's Ron who deals with customers, and we have Big Jockie keeping our helpers under control. You don't need me. I'm going back to the straight and narrow.'

Ivan gave Michael a look of demented astonishment. 'No fucking way, Michael. Ron and Big Jockie don't have your savvy to run an operation like this. You come along as well.'

'I'm being honest with you, Ivan.' Michael's insides were churning, but he kept his voice level and calm. He gave his ear a scratch. 'I could say okay, and do a runner, but I'm telling it to you straight. I closed down the operation after our last chat, and I'm finished with it. You can speak to Ron about starting it up whenever you want to after I'm gone.'

'Aye, I heard you've closed up shop. The word on the street is that everyone's going ballistic, wanting to know who the fuck has caused the wheels to come off. If I take over your operation and everyone finds out that's me, I'll be persona non-fucking-grata around here. No, you stay put, pal, and you get things back up and running pronto.'

'We both know that if I say yes now, I'm out the minute you figure out how to work things without me. So, I've nothing to lose if I say no. If I don't have your support, you'll get me sooner or later. This way, it's on my terms.'

'Take a look around you, pal,' said Ivan, barely above a whisper. 'Enjoy your last few moments on God's earth. It won't be for very long. You've signed your death warrant. And it's going to be a very unpleasant way to go.'

'You don't think I thought of that?' Michael replied. He gestured to the other side of the balcony. 'You might not have noticed, but someone was standing across from us when you arrived. He has been taking photos of us all through our chat, slipped away when I scratched my ear a few minutes ago. He's well out of the museum by now, off to develop the photos. They'll be included in a package along with a full statement of what's been going on here, naming you as my killer. If I disappear again, an envelope will be mailed to the police and the editor of every newspaper in Scotland. As well as some of my customers. You might be able to take me out, but I'll take you with me.'

Ivan's face reddened. The two minders noticed and took a step towards them. Michael looked Ivan in the eye, a look that said there was more to come. Ivan waved them away.

'I've got a way out of this. Let me run the operation on my own, no interference. And think of that deal I offered you. You still get the deal that your money is laundered for free, giving you the edge over every other criminal in Glasgow. You let the street know that you've tracked down the guy behind the operation and convinced him to start up again, giving him your personal guarantee that you'll provide the reassurances he needed on his security and any additional muscle whenever he might need it. It'll make you untouchable by any of the other gangs. We both win. The alternative is me spending the rest of my days waiting for your two art lovers over there to catch up with me, and you incurring the wrath of every Glasgow crook because you screwed up the best money-laundering racket the city's ever seen. Some people might not be too happy with that.'

'Don't you fucking threaten me, you little punk.'

'I'm not. Just the opposite. Because you have my respect, and yes, because I'm scared. I'll take my chances, I've got no choice. Any other option leads to me one day getting caught by the cops or being done in by your boys. The only way I want to be in this business is if I'm in control of my own destiny. That means being invisible, and it means not being part of anyone's organisation. I'm not disrespecting you, Ivan. It's the only way I know how to make this work for me.'

'Nobody says no to me. You should know that.'

'That doesn't change. All of this is between us. Think of the kudos when you pull the rabbit out of the hat. Everyone's a winner. You put the word out you've solved the problem and, bingo, the next day I say we're open for business again. Think about it.'

Ivan didn't move a muscle, and he didn't take his eyes off Michael.

Michael spoke again. 'Are we agreed?'

'I'm thinking about it.'

Michael turned to look at a painting, not trusting himself to keep his icy composure under Ivan's relentless stare.

'I'm going to let this play out,' Ivan said at last. 'If it works, fan-fucking-tastic. If it doesn't work, my friends here come and see you. They'll take you somewhere nice in the car and they will rearrange your anatomy one bit at a time, starting with your big mouth.'

Ivan stood up and walked away without looking back, and his minders fell in behind.

Michael ran the back of his hand across his forehead. He sat there for several minutes. He had kept his operation, but he was sure there would be a price to pay further down the line.

chapter thirteen

Charlotte was a lot more suspicious about Michael's disappearing act to the Scottish Highlands than he thought she would be.

'Is there something going on? I thought you'd be gone for a couple of days and it turned into a fortnight. You disappear off to goodness knows where, you never have enough change for a decent phone conversation, and then you're back in Glasgow for days before you get in touch. Tell me the truth. Are you seeing someone?'

They were standing in Michael's living room. Charlotte hadn't taken her coat off since she arrived.

'Of course not,' Michael said. 'I needed a break, and it was the perfect time to take it. I did invite you, remember? But you're right, I should have called you the moment I got back. It won't happen again, I promise. Can I take your coat?'

She stepped away from him. 'I think you need to be more open with me, Michael. I don't mean to pry, but a lot is going on in your life that you're not telling me. We shouldn't have any secrets.'

'I'm sorry I didn't call. Now, will you forgive me?' He stepped forward and gave her a little kiss of contrition.

She bit down on her lower lip. She obviously had more to say.

'It's embarrassing, Michael. I haven't got a clue what you really do for a living. I'm always being teased by my friends that I've become a gangster's moll. It was funny at first, but now the joke's wearing a little thin. And your fancy office, all the stuff that keeps arriving at your house? Where's the money coming from to pay for that? Tell me, Michael. What's going on?'

'If you want to know, I'll tell you,' Michael replied. 'If you're sure you want me to.'

Charlotte gave a few rapid, jerky nods. 'Yes, Michael, I want to know.' She took off her coat and sat down, folding it across her lap.

Michael sat across from her, looking her directly in the eye. Charlotte's elbows were resting on her coat and her hands were clasped under her chin. An unconscious gesture of prayer, he thought. Her eyes were a mixture of despair and expectation. He could see she yearned to know the truth, but was afraid of what that truth might be.

'I help people keep more of their money.' There was a flat tone in his voice, to make his confession as anticlimactic as possible. 'That means helping them invest it better and, for some of them, paying less tax than they did before. Nothing illegal, but some of my clients like to sail close to the wind.' Michael shrugged. 'There, so now you know. I don't rob banks and I don't steal from little old ladies, but I do deal with some shady characters. Do you still love me?'

'Of course I do, darling. Don't be silly.' Charlotte looked relieved and embarrassed at the same time. 'And I suppose a lot of people are impressed by appearances. Is that why you need to have a fancy office?'

'A business expense, Charlotte, a necessary one. As you say, people can be superficial.'

Charlotte's smile turned into a frown. 'But I still don't see why that meant you had to disappear so suddenly. Are you in trouble or something?'

'Just the opposite. I wanted to stop a problem from happening. Some people simply want advice on how to legitimately pay less tax. Like your Uncle Clarence, for example. There are others who are less scrupulous and want me to be … more creative, shall we say. And occasionally, I have a client who is too greedy and wants me to do something I'm not comfortable with. That's what happened the other week, and this chap wouldn't take no for an answer. I kept out of his way for a couple of weeks, until he decided to go elsewhere to get someone to do his dodgy stuff. As soon as he stopped hassling me, I was able to get back to normal. That's the reason for my little disappearing act.'

'But Michael, that's awful. Did he threaten you? You should go straight to the police if that happens again. I won't stand for someone being so beastly to you.'

'It's not that simple. It's all a matter of degree. If word got out that I got one of my clients into trouble, others might think I'd do the same thing to them. It's a small world. I didn't want to start any rumours. It was easier to do it this way, without ruffling any feathers.'

'You're too nice to people, Michael, that's your trouble. Whoever this chap is, he deserves to have a few feathers ruffled, and a whole lot more besides.' She laughed. 'But I know I'll never stop you trying to look after people, no matter how much they deserve to get into trouble. Sorry for being silly. Will you forgive me?' She went over and hugged him.

Despite himself, Michael felt a dull pang of guilt.

★ ★ ★

The money kept rolling in, and Michael kept lavishing it on his new life. He would buy thoughtful gifts when he spent weekends at one of Charlotte's friends' houses in the country or some remote shooting lodge. He would pick up the bill for a meal, without any qualms about the cost. Above all, he acquired the things that sent the right signals: the exclusive watch, the Savile Row jackets. All part of a secret code that identified who he had become. Michael had tasted the deep pain of rejection; now he savoured only approbation and esteem.

It was easy to see who had worked to join this exclusive club and who had been born into it. Charlotte was not the only one who went on about how hard up she was: every one of her blue-blooded friends thought the same way. Michael would have loved nothing more than for some of them to have been in his shoes when he was younger: the grinding boredom of real poverty, the constant worry that you could fall into some abyss at a moment's notice. With an allowance slipping into their bank account every month, they had gone through life in a reverie of self-indulgence. Not having to worry about the next bill was something Michael would never take for granted.

Their rose-tinted view of poverty, he found amusing. He supposed that, deep down, it was about guilt for some of them. Charlotte was never happier than when she was joining some protest march about apartheid or human rights, popping a fiver into a collection box for striking miners, or swooning over the anti-establishment posturing of rock stars. And getting involved in the Second Chance charity. Michael would have preferred her to display her social conscience somewhere less close to home, but he couldn't budge her.

The arrivistes into Charlotte's social circles fell into three categories. There were the ones, like Michael, who bought or charmed their way on board. There were charismatic con artists and hangers-on, displaying an effortless disaffection with the whole scene while all the time scheming to keep their place at the table, always with an eye for the main chance to sweep some of society's riches their way. And there were the genuinely gifted artists, writers and philosophers, their talent matched only by their poverty; people in this category were sponsored, even championed, by the wealthy elite.

It was the last group that Michael enjoyed talking to the most. He filled his mind with new ideas, new tastes in art, new books to expand his horizons. Inspired by that first meeting with Kenny McGowan, he started to read more Nietzsche, collected first editions of rare books, became more educated about what was good and what was indifferent in the art world.

★ ★ ★

Nietzsche said that if you have a 'why' to live, you can bear any 'how'. Michael was about to be tested on that. It seemed that for one smurf, the terror of Big Jockie was not enough to resist the temptation to run off with the money with which he had been entrusted. Within twenty-four hours, Ron was able to tell Michael that the smurf had been found. Now Michael needed to let Big Jockie know what to do about it.

Michael sat alone in his study, silently contemplating what action to take. He wanted nothing that carried the risk of permanent injury, no lasting effects. He remembered the injuries someone from his schooldays acquired in a street fight – broken jaw from punches, cracked ribs from kicks. Painful and debilitating, but after a few weeks the boy was back at school. That would be his instruction to Big Jockie. A second transgression would result in a more permanent disability. He didn't want to think about a third time.

After calling Big Jockie, Michael pondered the kind of person he had just become. This had been his baptism into the world of crime, he realised, and it was right for him to have decided to order the punishment of the smurf himself. The men in the world he had chosen would never shy away from using violence when it was necessary – sometimes even when it wasn't. To hesitate, to show weakness or a lack of resolve, might one day prove fatal. And it would certainly be the coward's way to leave such things to Ron. He was about to pay the blood price for his life of crime.

What does not kill me, makes me stronger. By being decisive when called upon to do so, he was sending a message that disobedience and betrayal would not be tolerated. This would be the way to make sure it didn't need to happen again.

That turned out to be naive. Some smurfs just couldn't be relied on to think logically, to behave rationally. No matter how clear the message that any disloyalty would be summarily dealt with, that they would invariably be caught and punished, there was always some impetuous, hot-headed, unthinking young kid who would be unable to resist the temptation of a single, reckless moment. As the number of smurfs increased, Big Jockie started to be called upon more and more often; and Michael realised that all his intellectual philosophising about the power of deterrence, about the logic of violence, wasn't having the impact he had hoped for.

It was a sickening feeling. He wanted success, but not at this price. He decided to change tack, told Ron simply to fire any smurf who misbehaved and to step up recruitment to cover replacements as well as growth. After the first smurf was fired without retribution, another transgressed a fortnight later. The next one was the following week. Then another. Then another.

Ron had had enough.

'The operation's going down the toilet,' he told Michael. 'And it's your bleeding-heart conscience to blame. I admit I was wrong to say don't hire Big Jockie – that fucker had the smurfs terrified. Now it looks like he's been put out to grass. Word's getting out that screwing us over doesn't carry the same penalties anymore. I can't hire fast enough to make up for the piss artists that are fired, never mind handle more business.'

Michael cursed his earlier weakness. Nothing is achieved without danger, Nietzsche had said. He vowed never again to let sentiment blind his decision making.

The phone calls to Big Jockie resumed. Soon they began to become so much a part of his business routine that it wasn't the violence that bothered him; it was the impact the beatings were having on business efficiency.

'We need to be smarter at keeping the smurfs in line,' Michael told Ron. 'We have to wait too long for a smurf to start working for us again after he's learnt his lesson. And it's far too indiscreet. There has to be a better way.'

'You don't want to get too sophisticated with that lot,' Ron replied. 'Fear of Big Jockie keeps them in check, and anyone who Big Jockie works over is a walking advert for what happens if you step out of line. Nice and simple. Let's keep it that way.'

'The street operation is your call,' Michael replied. 'But this is different. There's too much in the papers these days about the violence on Glasgow's streets. All it takes is some interfering do-gooder, and we could find ourselves getting some unwanted attention. It has to become more inconspicuous. Smurfs filling up A&E at hospitals all over Glasgow is too high-profile. We need something that's effective but invisible.'

Michael was shocked with himself that the solution came to him while he was attending an anti-Pinochet rally in George Square with Charlotte. Speaker after speaker denounced the brutality of the Chilean dictator's regime, detailing the torture that was meted out to Allende supporters. If Michael wanted a lesson on how to run a system of terror, all the information he needed was in the graphic details of the leaflets handed out at the rallies. He scrutinised them, and Charlotte delighted in his new-found enthusiasm for the fight against totalitarian regimes.

It wasn't that overnight he'd turned into a monster, he told himself. What he was looking for was very specific. Not life-threatening; no permanent injuries. But something severe and agonising that could be deployed in a controlled, disciplined way to achieve exactly the result required. Michael wanted less violence, not more. One short, sharp, shock, not the uncontrolled frenzy of Big Jockie's fists.

He found what he was looking for in a liquidation sale in the West End. It was a wind-up generator that Ron christened the Electric Warrior, after the T. Rex album. With a minor adaptation, the faster the handle was turned, the higher the voltage. The higher the voltage, the greater the agony. Legs and torso were first, the flesh and muscle absorbing the current and lessening the pain. Then feet, penis, anus – each one provided an excruciating and intolerable increment. If anyone needed more of a lesson, they were given a soaking with a hose. Water would make it worse the second time around.

It was perfect. Big Jockie could mete out the punishment, and the smurf would be fully recovered the same day, not a mark on them. The punishment would fit the crime: a few shocks to the body as a taste of what a full session would be like; for a more serious or repeat offender, a level of severity that was appropriate. No more having to rely on what mood Big Jockie was in. If violence was a necessary evil in the operation, at least this way it could be done with bloodless efficiency.

If the smurfs behaved, none of it would be necessary, Michael kept telling himself. If they transgressed, they had only themselves to blame.

The Electric Warrior brought order and discipline to the job of keeping the foot soldiers under control. It was precise, proportionate and persuasive. Michael devised a three-square grid containing an array of offences and their consequences, which he shared with Ron. The left square represented a 'mild' lesson. If you had to be punished a second time you moved to square two. The third square was reserved for anything that threatened the security of the operation, and contained precise instructions for delivering a level of pain that was unendurable. The Electric Warrior became a business process designed to increase productivity and eliminate inefficiency. Michael had no doubt that Ivan would one day plan some retaliation for being thwarted in his plan to take him over, and he wanted the smurfs to be left in no doubt that whatever pressures they were put under, no matter what temptations came their way, they would never dare give in to his demands.

But when the first attack on the organisation came, it wasn't from Ivan but from a low-level crook. Mickie Ferguson somehow found out which smurfs would be carrying money, where and when. He hit six of them in twenty-four hours, netting ten thousand pounds. When Michael met with Ron, they were both clear that they had to deal with it, and deal with it ruthlessly. Nobody should be under the illusion that the money the smurfs were carrying was easy pickings.

'I suppose it had to happen eventually,' Michael said. 'You're sure he's working alone, not in cahoots with these smurfs?'

'Pretty sure,' Ron replied. 'We've leaned on each of the ones who were robbed, and their stories stack up.

They're not all from Second Chance; there's some of my boys there too. I reckon Mickie has been keeping his ear to the ground, picking up enough gossip to identify these six as regular carriers. He must have decided to knock off all six in the same day before we had a chance to change the routines or put in more security.'

'And definitely nothing to do with Ivan? You sure about that?'

'Sure,' he replied.

'Okay,' Michael said. 'First thing is to find Mickie Ferguson. That has to be done now. We need to deal with this firmly and quickly. Send a message that this is unacceptable.'

'A bounty will flush the wee fucker out,' replied Ron. 'There's no loyalty amongst these Easterhouse bampots. Let me put the word out that the first person to point us in his direction has a ton coming to him. I guarantee we'll be frying Mickie Ferguson's arse by Friday.'

Michael looked out the window.

'No,' he said softly. 'What we do now will set a precedent as to how we deal with this in future. I don't want anyone benefitting from our problems, even if they are helping us. I want you to bring in two people who know him. Take them to a quiet spot, maybe the woods outside Barrhead. Toss a coin and whoever loses, Big Jockie uses the Electric Warrior on him, level two. Let the other guy watch. When he's seen enough tell him he's got twenty-four hours to find Mickie or he'll get the same, for twice as long. We can play that game with more of his pals until Mickie turns up.'

Ron shook his head. 'That will all take time. In any case, I'm pretty sure Mickie won't have broadcast where he was going – even to his friends. My plan's faster and easier. If we go about torturing folk who know Mickie for no good reason, anyone who *could* help us will run for the hills.'

'This is not about Mickie Ferguson, Ron. This is about establishing a code of honour. Every criminal in Glasgow has got to see that anyone who tries to muscle in on our organisation is dealt with, and if it's someone you know, you get punished, not rewarded. It doesn't matter whether you were involved or not. Somebody does wrong; everybody gets hurt. That way, the whole world will know that attacking us and doing a runner means there will be a dozen people nursing a grievance that they'll want to do something about. Nobody who crosses us and tries to get away with it will ever be able to show their face in Glasgow again.'

'It makes something simple more complicated. These low-lives couldn't spell codes of honour, never mind abide by them. But, listen – I'm not suggesting a soft option here. Once I find him, I'll make sure Mickie suffers for the aggro he's given us.'

'That's another thing,' Michael replied. 'When the time comes, I think I need to step out the shadows for a moment, tell Mickie the good news face to face. Build a reputation for myself. It's our first betrayal, and I want the word to be that the person ultimately behind this operation is so ruthless, nobody who crosses him will ever get away with it.' Michael half-smiled. 'I think I can act the part well enough to terrify Mickie Ferguson, what do you think?'

Ron didn't look convinced. 'I think it's an okay idea. But – don't take offence, Michael – you've not been at the sharp end before. I hope you have the stomach. I think when you see what we're really dealing with ... Let's just say it will be an eye-opener.'

Ron was right. Michael had put off coming to terms with the world he had got himself into for too long – the brutal reality of what was required to succeed in an arena ruled by fear and intimidation. It was an induction he was not looking forward to, but he needed to go through it. He maintained a grim, but otherwise unreadable, expression. Ron was to know nothing of his inner doubts and anxieties.

It took three days and three crooks – three sessions with the Electric Warrior – to flush out Mickie Ferguson.

'We've got him in a basement,' Ron reported. 'Waiting for your go-ahead to make him regret the day he was born.'

'Send Big Jockie round, tell him to stay in the room with him, but not to lay a finger on him. I'll meet you outside. Bring along his three unfortunate friends and we'll all head in together. An hour or two in Big Jockie's company before we arrive will put him in the right frame of mind for the pep talk I'm going to give him.'

★ ★ ★

Michael let the others enter the room ahead of him. He had told Ron precisely the set-up he wanted – complete silence, a bright light on Mickie's face, otherwise darkness. When he stepped inside, he stayed behind the lamp so it was just his disembodied voice that Mickie heard. Mickie sat on an upright chair, his hands behind his back and his ankles taped to the legs of the chair. Big Jockie stood behind him, his gargantuan bulk dwarfing the seated figure. Michael smelt the acrid odour of urine, noticed the dark stain on Mickie's trousers. He steeled himself to deliver the speech he had prepared.

'You need to understand I run my business on trust and respect.' The words were measured, radiating menace. 'And so, I need to make sure that no one takes advantage of that.'

Mickie struggled in the chair, and as it started to rock Big Jockie held it still. Michael found it chilling to see that it required only a small iota of his strength. Mickie collapsed back into the chair, shaking, his face contorted with terror and despair.

Michael stepped forward so that he stood between Mickie and the lamp. He wanted to show that he feared nothing, that he had complete confidence that showing his face would represent no risk whatsoever.

'So, unfortunately, you've given me a problem.' His voice was as gentle as a lover's caress. 'As you were the first person to cross us, it took a considerable amount of persuasion before your friends … opened up to us. More than I would have liked. I'm afraid they had to endure quite a lot of suffering.'

Michael moved back, and his voice became more detached, more businesslike.

'So, my little friend. If we had to offer these poor unfortunates some encouragement to help, just because they had the misfortune to know you, Big Jockie has to offer a great deal more to you. Everything has to be proportionate. You do see that's fair, don't you?'

Mickie's groans were primal in their intensity. Michael nodded to Big Jockie. 'Okay,' he said, with an air of casual indifference.

Big Jockie's beating began. Michael kept his features dispassionate, but inside his stomach was churning. Not just from revulsion at the violence, but from sheer anger that he'd had to resort to it. Every descent to brutality was a failure to secure loyalty by strength of will. But when he had to use it, he would use it with exactitude, logic, and a carefully calibrated level of intensity. Michael had found the perfect instrument to do that. Big Jockie could snap someone's neck like a matchstick, but he didn't get carried away. He delivered exactly what was asked of him.

Ron drove Michael home after it was over.

As Michael stepped out of the car he leaned in and said to Ron, 'Hopefully, it will be some time before we have to do this again.'

With that, he headed into the house. With the door closed behind him, he could finally let the mask slip. Exhausted, he slid down the wall and sat motionless on the floor. Satan and Lucifer appeared, their canine curiosity piqued. As Michael listlessly patted them, Lucifer gave a little whimper, as though sensing some unspoken wretchedness in his master. It was enough to snap him out of his black mood. He would never be the cause of sympathy. Getting to his feet, he headed into his study to collect his thoughts.

As he sat brooding, it became clearer and clearer to Michael what he needed to do. His success so far had been due, not only to the elegance and sophistication of his money-laundering operation, but also to its underpinning by raw, brutal violence. He had accepted the intellectual necessity of this when dealing with it in the abstract, but seeing it for himself for the first time had brought home to him what he was doing and what he had become. However hard he tried to rationalise the violence on the basis that it would only be inflicted on those who brought it upon themselves, he couldn't deny that he was responsible for actions that repulsed him. And he felt vulnerable for a second reason. A fear had been growing inside him ever since that first breach of security that brought Crazy Ivan to his door. His whole enterprise was built on a motley army of unreliables: every half-brained, hot-headed, impetuous recruit presented a potentially fatal security risk that could bring the entire operation down in a moment's irresponsibility.

Michael looked around the room. Every accoutrement and accessory was testament to his refinement and good taste. To a lifestyle that cost a fortune to maintain. Everything he had achieved was tainted by blood, ready to be brought down by variables that were outside his control. And all because he needed smurfs to run the operation. There had to be a better way.

chapter fourteen

It was Charlotte who was the beneficiary of Michael's feelings about the punishment carried out on his orders. It continued to eat away at him. He had to find some way to reconcile himself with the horror he had unleashed.

The answer was a charitable foundation, a new, philanthropic arm to his business empire. It would aim to help disadvantaged young people in Glasgow to change their lives and get into work, education, training or volunteering, to make sure every young person had the chance to succeed. Michael told Charlotte his idea over dinner a few days later and was pleased to see how much she liked it. Then he told her the second part of the plan.

'I'd like you to run it, Charlotte,' he told her. 'Once you sit your final exams. Not the operational, logistical stuff; I'm recruiting a charity professional for that. I need someone to identify the self-help programmes we can support, someone to define the goals we need to achieve. Want to try?'

She protested that she didn't have the experience, but only half-heartedly. When she finally said yes, Michael was elated. He could prove to himself that some good could come from the evil with which he was involved, and finally start to dispel the disgust he was feeling about the life he led.

But he would only fully be free when he no longer needed the smurfs.

Michael told Ron his new plan a few days later.

'I've been looking at the business since the Mickie Ferguson incident,' he said. 'We managed to stamp down on that problem, but there are always going to be more. There's a strategic flaw in our business model, and that's the fundamental unreliability of the way we put the funds through the system. The smurfs. They're a security risk, a) because they can't be trusted, and b) because they're easy pickings for any gangster who wants to try his luck. The operation will always be at risk as long as we have to use them.'

'You think? I say let Big Jockie deal with keeping them under control. There's intimidation on the street, but all we have to do is make sure the smurfs are more scared of us than the other guy. You think too much, Michael, that's your problem. This is a simple business. You don't have to make it complicated.'

'The business needs to be run more intelligently, Ron. Smurfs were great to get us started, but we're outgrowing them. I'm going to start working with Jenkins on a new way to launder money. One that's safer, more efficient and, in the long term, more profitable. We're going to start buying businesses – like your taxi firm – that can handle cash without drawing attention to themselves. I want a portfolio of companies so we can move money about in large business transactions, not lots of little ones with smurfs walking around with piles of cash in their pockets. Within a year, smurfing will be a thing of the past.'

'It sounds impressive, but where's the money coming from? You might have some cash salted away, but this sounds like a mighty expensive exercise, and all this charity bullshit must be costing you big time. Even your piggy bank isn't big enough to pay for this kind of expansion.'

'You're right. It's a big investment. But the potential it gives us is huge. The set-up costs will be recouped in a year, two at the most if things go slowly. You just keep bringing in the business. I want to get it done as soon as possible.'

Michael went over the numbers with Jenkins. The strategy was clear. They would start acquiring businesses slowly, expanding and taking on new ones as they built up enough reserves. They could close down the smurfs in three years if the money-laundering operation continued to grow at its current rate. Or they could do it in a year if they borrowed £250,000. Michael smiled at the irony of the situation. His plan was robust and well-funded, the projections and cash flow analysis demonstrating a viable and attractive business case. Even with the most prudent assumptions, it would be a loan application that any bank in its right mind would not hesitate to support. The only flaw was that it was illegal. A small detail. It would be too big a risk to have to endure the sort of scrutiny that would be required to secure a loan. It looked like he had no choice but to take the slow road to his destination.

When the solution dawned on him, he kicked himself for not thinking of it sooner. Michael was having dinner with Charlotte at their favourite restaurant, on a hill overlooking the Kingston Bridge, the sinuous snake of the new M8 motorway carving a swathe of car lights through the city centre below.

'I had a big meeting with my accountant today,' he told her after the meal. 'Been discussing my expansion plans. Like to hear about them?'

'Of course, darling,' she replied. 'Expansion? Sounds wonderful.'

'As you know, the basics of my business are that I give wealthy people investment and tax advice. How to build long-term resilience into actively managed portfolios, that sort of thing.'

Charlotte looked at him blankly.

'Well, having such a broad-based overview has given me some ideas about not only investment opportunities, but also the type of business that is going to take off in years to come. I'm thinking I should have some real brick-and-mortar companies under my control, not just make a living from advice and consultancy.'

'Brick and mortar sounds good,' said Charlotte, trying to keep up. 'Like what, exactly?'

'Travel agents, for one,' Michael replied. 'People are flocking to places like Benidorm and Magaluf. In a few years, it will be as common to have a holiday on the Costa Brava as it is to go to Blackpool at the moment. And estate agency, that's another boom area. Until recently, most of the buying and selling in Scotland has been done by solicitors, but estate agents are popping up all over the place. I think that's the way things are going.'

'I read,' Charlotte said, 'that house prices are set to go through the roof in the next few years. Hard to imagine, but in ten years they say you won't be able to buy a semi in Glasgow for anything under ten thousand pounds.'

'But people will aspire to. And if I've got an agency that takes three per cent of every sale, and house prices go up by twenty per cent a year, I'm making money even before the business starts growing.'

'Does this mean you'll be doing less of the iffy tax-dodging stuff?'

'Exactly,' Michael replied. 'You'll be a boring businessman's adoring partner in future, rather than a gangster's moll. I hope you're not too disappointed.'

'Much less glamorous, you're right.' Charlotte laughed. 'It all sounds very exciting, Michael. But without being too vulgar, do you have the money? Sounds like it might cost a lot.'

'It will. And until I've been in business for two years, the banks say I'm not eligible for a business loan. I'll have to cut back, maybe put the foundation on hold for a while, save like mad and buy a tiny operation to get started. That's one of the reasons I wanted to tell you tonight. The foundation will still be important, but we might not be able to see through all the plans you've come up with. Frustrating, but that's the way it is.'

'You do know I come into my inheritance next month?'

'I think you mentioned that. But what's that got to do with—?' Michael allowed just enough time to let the penny drop. 'Oh no, Charlotte, you shouldn't even be thinking those thoughts.'

'You know I would if you wanted me to.' Charlotte leaned over and squeezed his hand. 'Whatever you decide to do, I'm sure you'll succeed at it.'

'It doesn't seem right. People would think I was taking advantage of you.'

'No, I mean it, Michael. No one needs to know.'

'It is tempting,' Michael said. 'But if we did think about it, it would have to be done properly. I'd insist it would be a loan; secure it on my business and pay you the going rate of interest. And you'd have to get a lawyer – I'd want to make sure you had someone protecting your interests. But it's a very kind offer, Charlotte. Let me think about it.'

Michael waited a week before raising it again.

'Charlotte, your idea about lending to the business. Do you have a family lawyer you could talk to about it? I wouldn't want you to do anything irresponsible, but if a lawyer was to draw up a loan contract, make sure you were fully protected, see that your money would make more interest than it would if you invested it, it seems crazy not to at least look at it.'

'We don't need lawyers, darling. I trust you. Tell me what you want to do, and I'll do it.'

Michael knew it would be folly to agree. Any arrangement had to be beyond reproach. If word got out that he'd exploited Charlotte's naivety, his days in her circles would be over in an instant. The lawyer wasn't there to protect Charlotte, he was there to protect Michael. He insisted that she needed a lawyer to handle the contracts and deeds and she finally relented.

The family lawyer drew up the documentation and invited Charlotte and Michael to his office. He was effusive with Charlotte, kissing her on both cheeks and taking her coat. Michael, on the other hand, he greeted with a grunt and waved into a chair. Clearly, Michael was the gold digger and Charlotte the latest in a long line of valued Aldford family clients. Michael did his best to alleviate his misgivings, agreeing to everything he asked for, even volunteering to pay a bit more interest to make sure the deal was as favourable as possible to Charlotte. Two weeks after her twenty-first birthday, £250,000 from Charlotte's trust fund was paid over to Michael as a fully secured loan, to be paid back in twenty-four monthly instalments with interest at five per cent above base.

Michael had the funds he needed to expand. He promised himself it would be a decision Charlotte would never regret.

1975

chapter fifteen

It took three months before Avalon Travel was open for business, the name chosen because it had no significance whatsoever: classy, but anonymous. The girlfriend of an acquaintance of Ron's worked as a receptionist and Michael chose two of the smurfs who were the most switched-on to be the office manager and assistant. He hired a travel professional on a six-month contract to start things up and teach his team the ropes – they'd be gone before they noticed anything suspicious. The operation had every appearance of being genuine, while behind the scenes Michael's accountant, Jenkins, was putting ten times the legitimate revenue through the books.

A buffer bank account was used to hide Avalon Travel's corporate set-up from clients. The scheme was deceptively simple. Along with a few genuine bookings from people who walked past the shopfront and popped in to find out more, all Michael's criminal clients' monies were paid into the company account as cash, seemingly from customers who didn't want to pay by cheque when booking their summer holiday. The money was transferred to an offshore account in the name of a fictional package operator, from there to a Swiss bank account, and finally back to a Scottish bank account with no connection to

Avalon. This money was now inside the banking system, clean as a whistle, and could be paid back to the criminal clients who had given them their money in the first place.

The estate agency was even easier to operate. Most criminal clients' money would be identified as cash deposits to acquire property, and the rest would be disguised as rent paid by fictitious customers to fictitious landlords. An existing company was purchased to make it look convincing, Jenkins blending the laundered money in with the genuine business.

Michael's operation was able to continue growing using only the capacity of his new businesses; no more smurfs were recruited. It was bigger, faster and more controlled. It all looked so believable, Michael even invited Charlotte to the office to see how her money was being used. His pride in what he had achieved, his eagerness to impress her with the success of his business, blinded him to the risk he was taking.

It was his first mistake.

Ron and Michael had been having a meeting with Big Jockie at the travel agents, a rare occurrence, to talk about the latest smurf defection, when Charlotte turned up unannounced. Ron, Big Jockie and Michael were in the manager's office, the door slightly ajar. Charlotte had been shopping nearby, she told the receptionist, and wanted to drop off some bags until she was ready to return home. Michael heard her ask if he was free, the receptionist's floundering only making matters worse.

He had no option but to make the introductions.

'This is Jockie McPherson. He handles the admin side of the operation. And of course you know Ron.'

Charlotte stood in the doorway, her eyes blazing with horror and suspicion. Ron gave a half-hearted wave of acknowledgement. Big Jockie remained silent, his face devoid of all expression.

'I'm sorry to disturb,' she said, her voice strangled with emotion. 'I've got to be going now. Really, I have.' Before Michael could react, she turned and fled.

She was in tears that evening.

'That man works for you?' she said. 'Michael, how can you stand there and say he runs your flipping admin? I always thought Ron looked a dubious character, but I tried to tell myself not to be such a snob. But that other man? He looks pure evil. How is someone like that a part of your organisation?'

Michael tried his best to convince her, told her she was being silly, not to judge people by their appearance, but she was having none of it.

'And I want to know something else. A lot of people we help at Second Chance are dropping out. What's that about? I try to ignore rumours but what I hear is that they are getting recruited for some criminal enterprise by a dodgy-looking bloke who promises them a great life if they go to work for him. Then they find he's got a great brute of a man who terrorises them into doing whatever's asked of them. From the description, the guy doing the recruiting sounds a lot like Ron. And now I think I know who the other one is. What are you mixed up in, Michael? Is Ron a criminal? Who is Jockie McPherson and what does he do? Tell me. Please?'

'It's all nonsense, what you're hearing, Charlotte. Who's telling you these stories? You know the foundation and Second Chance mean more to me than anything. That's why I work so hard to try to be successful. Not for my own good, but so I can help others.'

Charlotte burst into tears. 'I want to believe you, Michael, I really do. My money's helping you grow, isn't it? That means I'm mixed up in this too. I'm not stupid. You don't need people like that man working for you if you're running a travel agents. I'm scared, Michael. What are you up to?'

'You've got to trust me, Charlotte. They're not criminals and neither am I. I've told you that already. You need to believe me. Yes, McPherson's a brute of a man. We even have a nickname for him, Big Jockie. But I'm giving someone a chance. He has a violent past, and he's trying to put that behind him. He struggled to find a respectable job, and I wanted to help him make a fresh start. I see the best in people, Charlotte. Is that really such a bad thing?'

Charlotte said evenly, 'Exactly what sort of work does he do, Michael? If I walked into a travel agents and saw him, I'd run a mile. Or do you want me to believe he sits with a slide rule all day, calculating commissions? I don't like it, Michael.'

'He runs errands for me, a sort of trouble-shooter. Helps Ron with the logistics of our tax-consultancy business. I find him useful to have around, that's all.'

Michael could see that she was listening, wanting to believe him, but not really convinced.

'Look, Charlotte, there's something I've been waiting to talk to you about, but I wanted to make sure all the expansion plans were in place and the new businesses were doing well before I broached it. But I'd like to expand the Avalon Foundation to be twice, maybe three times as big once we get into next year and I've paid back your loan. I know we discussed you running the show once you've graduated, but we're talking about something much bigger now and everything will need to be on a proper corporate footing. I'd like you to be the managing director, chose your own team to work for you. It's a big responsibility but I know you're up to it. It would be a great start to your career. What do you say?'

'Are you serious? Last time we spoke it was a part-time job and giving ten thousand a year to charity. You want to increase that?'

'I do. I want you to have sole charge of the foundation's direction. We'll be able to help so many more people. Now, does all that sound like the actions of a blood-thirsty criminal?'

Whether Charlotte was convinced was a moot point, but the whole incident had shown Michael that no matter how careful he was, there was always a chance his activities could attract unwanted attention. He needed to be sure that if that ever happened, he would be made aware before it became an issue.

Kenny McGowan's words kept coming back to him. Get inside information, he had told Michael, if you want to be sure that you're not in danger. He'd convinced himself that he'd ticked that box by cosying up to Mary's policeman father when he started out. But he was kidding himself if he thought the occasional slightly awkward exchange whenever he bumped into him at a Rotary Club event constituted an inside track as to what Glasgow's Fraud Squad was up to. He had to do this properly, find someone in the force who was on the take and get them on his payroll. But it needed to be handled with the utmost sensitivity; choose the wrong target and everything could come crashing down.

Ron started dropping a few hints to his more sophisticated clients that he was looking to improve his police intelligence, fishing for the name of someone he could approach. But he was met with a wall of silence; no one wanted to talk. Just as he was about to give up, one of his customers, Charlie O'Connor, was arrested for allegedly running a numbers racket on the South Side. Ron told Michael about it so that Jenkins could put the procedures in place to make sure their operation wouldn't go the same way.

The next day, Michael read in the paper that O'Connor had been released on bail. He was surprised. The guy was a career criminal and from what he had learnt so far about how the criminal justice system worked, someone like O'Connor getting bail was unlikely, to say the least. He got Ron to find out more, and was told that the operation was uncovered based on a tip-off from a disgruntled punter and that all the gambling records and betting slips had been seized.

'He'd better enjoy his time on the outside while it lasts,' Ron told Michael. 'The cops have more than enough to put him away. But not to worry, we go way back. He won't breathe a word about our operation.'

A few days later, there were further developments. The most serious charges of fraud and running an illegal gambling operation were dropped, the reason given being lack of evidence. That only left tax evasion, which carried a hefty fine but generally not a custodial sentence. Despite Ron's belief that jail time was a certainty, it looked like Charlie O'Connor wouldn't be behind bars after all.

'There's only one explanation,' Michael said to Ron. 'O'Connor's had some help. First, he gets bail; then the incriminating evidence is watered down. Find out who did this for him. That's the guy we want working for us.'

'I know O'Connor well, but he wouldn't give me that,' Ron replied. 'Even if he's got a bent copper looking out for him, the last thing he'll do is volunteer his identity. He's a bit of a pillock, but he's not that daft. He'd a need lot more persuasion than I'd be able to give him. Big Jockie-style persuasion.'

'And this guy's a friend of yours?'

Ron laughed. 'Not a friend. An acquaintance. Actually, not even that. He's just somebody who's been around a while.' He laughed again. 'A wee visit from Big Jockie might get him cooperating. Want me to try?'

Michael shook his head. 'He's a client of ours. He's done nothing wrong, just the opposite. You said he'd keep his mouth shut through all this, and that's turned out to be true. If he plays by the rules, he can't be punished. There has to be another way.'

'He'll not be a client much longer. He'd be mad to start up his operation again, and the fines and legal costs will clear out all the money we're holding for him. And that's not counting what he's bunging his bent copper.'

'Okay, that's our angle. O'Connor's strapped for cash, and it's in everyone's interest he doesn't do anything foolhardy in the short term. You approach him, make him a business proposition. He introduces you to whoever's been looking out for him. If that person wants to talk to us, O'Connor has no money worries for the next six months or so.'

Ron shook his head. 'I run the street operation, find the clients, manage the smurfs,' he told Michael. 'I don't go meeting with cops. I'll put the offer to O'Connor. But I don't do the hiring. If you want a cop on board, you need to do the asking.'

'This is your world, Ron. Not mine. It's your operation the cop would be listening out for. That's why you need to meet him.'

'I say we don't take the risk. Everything is fine at the moment; I do everything I can to keep our operation from showing up on the police radar. I don't think we should be looking for trouble. If trouble comes along, let's deal with it then.'

Nothing Michael said could convince him. The only concession was that Ron would put the proposition to O'Connor and report back to Michael on the outcome. Michael got the news a few days later.

'First he told me to fuck off, denied that anyone had helped him, but when I told him the cash we were prepared to pay for his help he got interested. You're right, he's looking at a hefty fine. He was even considering getting right back into the game the minute he paid his fines. Mug.'

'So, what happens next?'

'He'll contact the guy who helped him out, tell him he knows someone who has a proposition for him, without giving anything away. He'll say his friend is not into heavy stuff and only needs a pair of eyes and ears in the force, that's all. Then we wait to see what the response is.'

A week later, Michael found himself in a Rutherglen Wimpy, waiting for Detective Sergeant Grant to turn up. As he waited, Michael realised Ron had been right to be concerned. At any moment he feared the scream of police sirens, a tap on his shoulder, a dead-pan voice telling him he was under arrest. It took all his strength to fight off his paranoia and wait for Grant's arrival. The man would be mad to turn him in, Michael thought, take the risk his life of corruption would be exposed. It didn't make the waiting any easier.

When Grant arrived, it was anticlimactic. He asked Michael what he wanted to be kept informed about, and listened stony-faced as Michael told him.

'I make money disappear,' Michael said. 'So, I need to know if there is ever a task force set up to investigate money laundering, if some punk ever tells the police he has someone doing this for him, or if my name ever gets mentioned. And for that, I'm prepared to pay.'

'I don't like your type,' Grant told him. 'Your pretensions to be a businessman. But you were smart about how you got in touch. Discreet, low key. That I like.' He took a paper napkin out of the dispenser on the table and wrote something on it. 'This is how much.' Grant handed Michael the napkin.

A thousand pounds a month; what he had been expecting.

'That's a big number,' he said.

'If you say no, the next time you ask it'll be bigger,' Grant replied. 'I like to keep things simple.' He took the napkin back. 'Do we have a deal?'

Michael nodded.

Grant smiled. 'Well, son, we have an arrangement. A thousand pounds a month, even if I've nothing to report. I get to use your services for free when I want to. And I get the right to say no if you ask me to look somewhere that I think is too risky to poke my nose into. I only ever speak with you, and when I don't want to do something, I don't do it.'

As Grant got up to leave, Michael gave him the most cursory of handshakes. He sat alone in the café afterwards, bridling at Grant's arrogance and supercilious manner. With that sort of attitude, he could imagine Grant pushing for more cash if there ever was an investigation. And if that came to pass, it would be when Michael needed him the most.

Michael thought back to Kenny McGowan's advice on strategy. Always have a plan B. He got Ron to check Grant out, to see what his weaknesses were. It didn't take long. One of Ron's contacts operated a brothel just off Blythswood Square, an upmarket operation catering for the more discerning customer. He'd confided to Ron that one of his punters was a middle-ranking married detective, Davie Grant, who had a weakness for the ladies, but one that was only usually reciprocated on a professional basis.

Michael's plan started to take shape when he was told of an unusual property that had come on the books. A block of tenement flats had been refurbished in an up-and-coming part of Maryhill. The communal stair toilet had been rendered defunct by the installation of a bath and WC in every flat; fireplaces had been blocked up and replaced by central heating. But one flat was different. It was next to the old shared toilet included in the particulars;

but rather than incorporating it into the flat, the builders had left it alone, so it was billed as a 'useful external storage'. Michael went to have a look. Sure enough, the toilet was on the other side of the bedroom wall. Knock a hole in the wall, install a two-way mirror and you'd have a perfect set-up for surveillance and blackmail. He worked out how cheaply he could buy the flat and got his manager at the estate agency to convince the seller it was the best offer he'd get. Once it was his, he had it furnished and had the mirror installed, and a microphone set into a power socket on the bedroom skirting board. It would be perfect for taking out a nice insurance policy against any troublemakers.

Ron booked a session with one of the girls in the brothel, and after enjoying her services he talked her into doing a little freelance work with the detective. Grant found himself the recipient of some flattering attention at his favourite watering hole and required little persuasion to head off to his new admirer's flat for some special attention. After three visits Michael had all the photos and sound recordings he needed, and DS Grant's nights of passion ended abruptly.

Michael congratulated himself on his foresight. The flat could be a useful honeytrap again in the future. Definitely an asset to hang on to.

★ ★ ★

In the meantime, he had a new thing to worry about, a campaign of intimidation from Ivan. Another smurf had been bragging down at his local boozer about the easy money to be made paying in cash to the smurfing bank accounts, only to be cornered by a group of Ivan's thugs a few nights later.

'I despair at how moronic these guys can be,' Ron complained to Michael. 'I tell them, over and over again, about how dangerous it is to let anyone know they're part of this, and yet after a few drinks there's always somebody who can't keep their mouth shut. And paying them more makes it worse. The more money they get, the more they spend and the more they can't resist telling their mates about the easy life they've stumbled into.'

'I suppose it helps us weed out the loose cannons. That's something we can thank Ivan for. This intimidation can't go on forever. He'll eventually see there's no benefit in continually hassling us and as we switch more of the laundering through the new business, there will be fewer people in the street handling cash. Another good reason for getting out of smurfing.'

Ron looked more worried than pleased by the prospect.

'There is a downside to having fewer smurfs. It means there's going to be a lot less enforcing for Big Jockie to do. I think that's going to be a problem.'

Michael was surprised. 'In what way? He gets paid regardless.'

'That's what's bothering me. If Big Jockie's sitting around doing nothing, it's going to be difficult to stop him freelancing on the side. Maybe he even starts putting out feelers to find if there is someone more in need of his talents. If he's not working for us full time, maybe he shouldn't be working for us at all. Do we still need him, once the smurfs are gone?'

Michael thought for a moment. 'I think we do. He's an asset that you never know when you're going to need. I'd feel too exposed in this business if it was just the two of us, what with Ivan's intimidation or anything else that comes along. I don't want to lose him.'

'Well, there is a way to keep him busy. And make some more money while we're at it.'

'And that is?'

'Get into the loan shark business. Loads of people are feeling the pinch with the current level of unemployment. We give somebody a hundred, two hundred to see them through until their next giro and they pay us a quarter of what they owe us every week until they pay off the loan. We get a couple of smurfs to do the collecting, and we use Big Jockie as back-up if they need any persuasion to make the payment.'

Michael shook his head. 'I'm not getting into that business, Ron. I don't trade in human misery. You should come along to a Second Chance meeting and see how desperate some of these people are. I want to use my money to ease people's suffering, not make it worse.'

Ron burst into spontaneous laughter. 'Who the hell do you think you are, Jess Yates? That bird you're hanging around with is making you soft in the head. Second Chance is our smurf recruitment agency, in case you've forgotten. I've been thinking that all this Avalon Foundation stuff was completely over the top, drawing too much attention to us, but I've never said anything. You're not telling me it's for real, are you?'

'Of course it is. There's nothing wrong with making your money one way, and living your life another. Yes, I started off using Second Chance, but that changed when I saw the good it could do. I could have done with a second chance when I was younger. Now I'm giving people opportunities I never had.'

'I don't get it, Michael. I don't know about you, but I'm in this to make money. And Big Jockie sitting around with time on his hands is an accident waiting to happen. If you don't want to use him for what he's good at, at least let me. Otherwise, we might find he's no longer around when we need him.'

'No. I'm not having you use him to beat up people who've got themselves into problems. I couldn't live with myself.'

Ron sighed. 'Okay, let's look at it from your point of view. You want to keep Big Jockie, but there will be nothing for him to do when we get rid of the smurfs. You want him to hang around on the off-chance that he might come in handy if some aggro comes our way? That's not ... what would you say? ... that's not maximising a business resource. If you don't keep Big Jockie busy, he'll go elsewhere. He's a psycho, for fuck's sake. He likes his work. He's not going to sit at home playing Scrabble until you decide you need him.'

'Then use him for something else. Just not this.' Michael sensed he was losing the argument.

'Like what? Contract killing, armed robbery? Do they make more sense in this cloud-cuckoo land you're telling me about? Big Jockie beats people up for a living. You tell me how we can use that skill in a way that makes you feel you're helping a noble cause.'

Michael stared at the floor for a few seconds.

'Okay,' he said. 'You win. Set up your loan-sharking, I want nothing to do with it. But I want you to stick to some basic rules. Nobody connected with Second Chance gets lent money, only the druggies, alkies, gamblers; people who only have themselves to blame. No single mothers trying to make ends meet, no steelworkers who've been thrown on the dole. Make your dirty money, but at least have some principles doing it.'

'That'll be me. A principled moneylender. Code of ethics and everything.'

Michael knew he was being ridiculed. 'Okay. But this is only so we can keep Big Jockie. If it wasn't for that, I'd say no. You tell Big Jockie. You sort it out with him. I don't want to be involved.'

They parted, Michael fuming that for once Ron had got the better of him. Ron running his own operation, strictly controlled and with Michael neither being involved nor benefitting, was the least bad solution to the Big Jockie problem. But it didn't make Michael feel any better.

chapter sixteen

'I'm leaving you, Michael.'

Charlotte trembled as she spoke.

'You've been lying to me from day one about what you do. I've come for my things, then I never want to see you again.'

She was standing on his doorstep having turned up unannounced, shivering in the rain.

'What are you talking about?' Michael said. 'Is this still your worries about the company I keep? It's not what I expect from you, Charlotte. Let's talk this over as adults.'

'No, Michael. I tried to make myself believe you. Now I see what a fool I've been. I've found out what that gorilla does for you. You lend money, don't you? To people who can't afford to pay it back. Don't deny it. One of the guys at Second Chance, Alex, someone who's trying hard to give up the drink and make a go of his life – he got beaten up because he borrowed money he couldn't afford to pay back. Got beaten up by someone who sounds a lot like that thug in your office. You've got Ron recruiting gullible fools to do God knows what, and you've got a sadistic animal doing your dirty work when you trade on people's misery. And to think I loved you. Michael. You've broken my heart.'

'Charlotte, I have no idea what you're talking about,' Michael protested.

It sickened him that he knew every word was true. Ron had agreed too readily to the moral boundaries he had imposed on the loan-sharking operation. He had agreed as you would to humour a child, and then had blithely ignored his instructions. He would deal with Ron later. Charlotte was his priority right now.

Charlotte had prepared herself for his denial.

'Michael, please don't take me for a fool. I know it must be these two hoodlums who work for you. Every detail of the description matches them perfectly. I could never work out why you cared so much about charity; it doesn't seem like you at all. Now I know. You want to exploit people. It's sick. You're sick. And I want nothing more to do with you.'

'Charlotte, if I promise to be honest with you, will you promise to hear me out?'

She shook her head vehemently. 'No, Michael. I told myself you'd try to talk me out of leaving. I'm not going to listen. I've brought a suitcase for my things, and I want you to leave me to pack up and go. If you don't, I'm calling the police.'

'Please, Charlotte. Give me two minutes to explain. If you still feel the same, I can't stop you from going. But two minutes. I promise after that you'll know the truth. Don't throw away everything we've built together. I'm not just talking about us; I'm talking about all the people we've helped. Surely you owe it to them to hear me out?'

The wind gusted, bringing with it a burst of heavier rain. It mixed with the tears running down her face.

'Look, you'll catch your death standing there. Come in and let's talk.'

Charlotte stepped into the hallway, looking around with an expression of genuine fear, as if some assailant were about to burst out of the shadows. She swallowed hard.

'Okay, two minutes. I'm listening.'

'Some of my customers are more than just unscrupulous businessmen trying to cut their tax bills. I can't prove it, but I'm convinced some of them are out-and-out criminals. I have Big Jockie around as a sort of bodyguard-come-enforcer, to be on the safe side. Probably being silly, but it makes me feel safe. And you're right, Ron's from a world where he knows where to find these sorts of customers and can talk to them in their language. I never meet them, I do the numbers and provide the advice. I remember Ron asking about Second Chance and I told him all about it, but it didn't occur to me he had an ulterior motive.'

He could see hesitation in her eyes.

'So yes, I might have a few clients who operate on the wrong side of the law. But so would a bank, or indeed many other businesses. That doesn't make me a criminal. And I swear I knew nothing about Jockie McPherson beating up Second Chance people. If I find out that's true, I'll get rid of both of them.'

'No, Michael, that doesn't stack up. Nobody working for you would do anything without you knowing. And legitimate businessmen don't need bodyguards. I'm not buying it.'

'Look, think about this logically for a moment. Let's assume that I am capable of doing the things you're accusing me of. Why on earth would I? I don't need the money. You'd be bound to find out if it involved Second Chance. I love you, Charlotte, I want to spend the rest of my life with you. Why would I risk all that to beat people up to collect their weekly giros?'

'I don't know. Because you're evil? Because you enjoy it?' She shook her head. 'I can't work it out. But I'm not stupid. You work with thugs. You make a lot of money. These thugs are beating up poor defenceless, vulnerable people. You can't make me believe you are innocent in all this. I'm here for my things, and then I'm getting you out of my life.'

Michael sunk in a chair, filled with genuine despair.

'And then what?' he said. 'Are you going to the police? There's not a shred of evidence I'm involved, but the slightest whiff of a scandal will bring down the foundation, destroy everything we've worked on together. Is that what you want?'

Charlotte backed away from him, wide-eyed with fear.

'Don't threaten me, Michael. I'll scream, I promise I will, if you take one step towards me.'

Michael shook his head and stayed in the chair.

'I'm not making any threats,' he said quietly. 'There's the phone if you want to make a call. Come back with someone to look after you as you pack, if that's what you'd like. Or go upstairs and get your things now. It's up to you.'

'I promised myself not to let you sway me. I don't know what's really going on. But I do know I can't trust you anymore.'

'That's your choice. But promise me this. Walk out on me, if you want to, but keep your suspicions to yourself. And give me a chance to deal with this Second Chance problem. I promise you I don't know anything about it, but I suspect you might be right. If you are, I'll put a stop to it right away. If you find out it's still going on, that means I'm lying to you. If it stops, it means I'm telling you the truth. Then all this stays our secret. We don't want either of us linked to any scandal.'

'I don't know what game you're playing, Michael. You're involved in something bad. I don't know what.' She paused for twenty, maybe thirty seconds. 'But I'll agree to give you a chance to clear things up. Not because I believe you, but because it might help the poor unfortunates you're exploiting. But if I hear one more story about someone getting into trouble because they've taken out a loan from those thug friends of yours, I'm calling the police straight away. So, don't worry, I won't tell anyone. For the moment. This can be our dirty little secret. Now can I go?'

After Charlotte collected her stuff and left, Michael called Ron over to the house.

'It's betrayal, Ron, pure and simple,' he said. 'Against my better judgement, I agreed you could operate a loan-sharking operation, with one proviso, and one proviso only. Stay clear of Second Chance. And you reneged on the deal. It's cost me my relationship with Charlotte, and could have brought down the whole operation if she'd gone to the police. There's no forgiving you for this.'

Ron was unrepentant. 'You need to get real, Michael. Yeah, I went along with all your moral-boundary,

Nietzsche-spouting bullshit, but that was just to avoid argument. Yeah, I said I'd leave Second Chance alone, and shit, I might even have meant it when I said it. But things move on. Some pals of the smurfs needed some dosh, and I was happy to oblige. It's fuck-all to do with you.'

'It's everything to do with me. This is my operation and, forgetting my scruples for the moment, it was a bad business decision. You've risked everything, because you couldn't resist a fast buck.'

'Now that's where I agree with you, pal. This Charlotte bird sounds like trouble. If you've finished shagging her, we might have to figure out how we keep her quiet for good.'

Michael drew in a series of slow, steady breaths.

'Listen, Ron. You might be blasé about ignoring me over Second Chance, but if you harm so much as a hair on Charlotte's head, then everything between us is over. I mean it. The operation closes down, I don't care how much it costs me, and I'll never forgive you. I'll deal with Charlotte. She'll get over this; we'll get back together. Until then, let me deal with her.'

Ron had the sense to back off. 'Okay, maybe I shouldn't have taken a shit in our own backyard. I'll lay of the Second Chance punters; you take care of Charlotte your way. And we can shake hands and put this behind us. No hard feelings?'

Michael shook hands and attempted a smile of reconciliation. As he looked Ron in the eye, he promised himself that one day there would be retribution for this. He might need Ron now, but that wouldn't always be the case. The minute he became expendable, his time was up.

In the days ahead, he tried to convince himself that there might be some positives from Charlotte leaving him. Having someone so close had always been a risk. He cleaned out his reserves to pay off her loan, and when she said she wasn't going to work for the Avalon Foundation when she graduated, he didn't protest too much. For the moment, the foundation's days were over.

The end of his relationship with Charlotte marked a significant change in Michael's lifestyle. He wasn't going to make the mistake of getting close to someone again. He got his own VIP booth at Tiffany's, called up some of the acquaintances Charlotte had introduced him to. He made himself the centre of the Glasgow club scene, and an invite to join his inner circle was a privilege offered to only a select few.

And there were women. At the heart of disco culture was sex: no-strings-attached, casual, hedonistic sex. He had his routine tuned to perfection. Send someone over and ask whoever caught his eye if they'd like to join him for a drink. The offer of free champagne invariably resulted in success. Everyone was out for a good time, everyone wanted to look good, and everybody grooved like there was no tomorrow. It was a world where nothing was expected of you after a night of the most intense intimacies.

Once his cash had built up again, Michael started a spending frenzy, to further put the pain of his rejection behind him. His taste in fine art was growing more expensive all the time, and he would travel to London to find the galleries that sold the quality of paintings he was looking for. The purchase that gave him the greatest pleasure was a version of the René Magritte painting, a print of which he had acquired at Woolworths years earlier, the one with the businessmen with apples covering their faces. He loved that he could now afford it, and he loved its symbolism. It perfectly captured who he now was, and his lifestyle. As he gave it pride of place in the living room of his new suburban mansion, he reflected on how far he had come in just a few years.

The conversation he had with the gallery owner who sold him the Magritte sparked off another idea for expansion. He was increasing the amount of money going through his existing companies as quickly as he dared, but it still wasn't enough to keep up with the growth of the money coming in from clients. The gallery owner had asked him if he was paying by cheque or cash.

'Cash?' said Michael. 'Surely not for that amount.'

'You'd be surprised,' the gallery owner replied. 'For some of my customers, their taste in fine art happily converges with their need to unload large amounts of cash which they seem to have for some reason. It's not my job to ask where the money comes from. Let's say I've had a few nervous walks to the bank to deposit some of the funds I've received in the past. Live and let live, I say.'

So, the idea for the Avalon Art Gallery was born, perfect for dealing with any big one-off cash deposits his criminal clients wanted to make. It would be the most top-end art gallery in Scotland, which would mean he'd only need to sell a few paintings for it to look legitimate. The only issue was to find someone compliant and more clued-up about art than the folk Ron had found to run the other Avalon businesses, but he'd cross that bridge when he came to it.

High-priced works of art, a library filled with rare first editions, a house bristling with the latest technology – everything about Michael oozed success. Success could buy him everything. Everything, that was, except for Charlotte.

chapter seventeen

Michael stared at the monthly report from DS Grant that had turned up in the mail.

'Report' was probably too grandiose a word. A single A4 page, typed up in a heavy-handed style with so much Tipp-Ex it resembled a contour map of the Alps, no doubt on a typewriter Grant had hidden away in his home. At least this was a full page. The first couple of months had been only a few lines: news of crimes where the police had been finding it difficult to trace the proceeds when they'd apprehended the perpetrator. But no one had made the link that they were all connected. Michael was paying a lot and getting very little back, but he took that as a good sign that his attempt to remain invisible was working.

The news in the report about Jake Strachan was different. He was a medium-sized client who specialised in robbing post offices. Steady income, nothing too flashy. But now he was planning a bank robbery and had brought in some accomplices, one of whom was a police informer. Grant had tipped Michael off because Strachan had been taken in for questioning and all the post office proceeds had mysteriously disappeared. Grant had guessed he was an Avalon client, and guessed right. Now he was alerting Michael that Jake would be walking into a trap when he tried to pull the bank job – giving him an opportunity to save his skin.

Michael decided on a different plan. There was a meeting with Ron and Jenkins the next day to run through client status and money movements, and Michael used it to check how robust the barriers were surrounding Strachan's money. When he mentioned the name, Ron was immediately on the alert.

'What makes him so special that he needs checking up on?' he asked Michael, his eyes narrowing.

'Just a random check, that's all. What's the concern?'

'Me and wee Jake go back a long way. If there's anything I should know about him, tell me. You don't usually get into this detail at these meetings. So, Michael?'

'So, nothing,' Michael replied. 'There's nothing you need to know about him. Sounds like you know him well enough already. Eric, what's the status on his account?'

Jenkins rifled through the papers in his briefcase. 'I wasn't expecting to go into this, but … ah, yes, here!' He produced a sheaf of papers with a flourish. 'We're holding almost fifteen thousand pounds of his money in his transit account. He's not made any withdrawals since he started using our services. Probably one of the safest clients we've got.'

'Good, good,' Michael said, giving Jenkins a crisp nod. 'Sorry for that distraction, but I was just curious. Let's get on with what we're here for. Ron, how are the smurfs behaving themselves?'

Ron went through the rest of the meeting eyeing Michael with barely concealed distrust. As he was leaving, he brought up the question of Strachan again.

'Michael, you don't ask questions without a reason. What's with the sudden interest in Jake Strachan?'

'I told you, random check,' Michael replied. Jenkins was busying himself on the other side of the room and Michael dropped his voice to a whisper. 'I like to make sure that Eric's on top of things by asking him a few unexpected questions from time to time. That's all.'

Ron raised an eyebrow. 'Maybe I should ask you a few unexpected questions from time to time too. To check nothing is going on I should know about.'

'Ron, there's never anything going on that you should know about that I don't tell you,' Michael replied. He called over to Jenkins. 'Eric, leave me that copy of the client report, would you? Some bedtime reading.' He ignored Ron's probing gaze as he left.

A week later Strachan was caught red-handed. Ron turned up at Michael's house that evening, apoplectic with anger.

'You knew, didn't you? Jake Strachan was caught bang to rights today, stitched up at a robbery. You knew it was going to happen and you did nothing to stop it.'

'Calm down, Ron,' Michael replied. He paused for a long second. 'Strachan's arrest was on the news this evening. Even if I did know about him being under suspicion, there was nothing I could have done about it. Losing a client is less important than taking the risk of questions being asked how Strachan would have known to cancel the job.'

'I could have found a way to save his skin without raising any suspicions. Five years, he's going to get – he's still on probation from his last spell inside. He's got a family, for fuck's sake. I asked you directly about him and you lied to me.'

'Saving Strachan's skin would have been an act of weakness, Ron. We run a business, not a safety blanket for criminals who can't look after themselves. If you want to talk about this, we can do it in the morning, in the office. I don't take kindly to you coming to my home to confront me.'

Ron continued to rant and Michael continued to stonewall every fresh tirade. He told himself that Ron was letting sentiment get in the way of business logic. But deep down, there was another thought, festering away and giving him the delicious taste of revenge. Ron had killed off the only relationship Michael had ever cared about; now, Michael's inaction has cost one of Ron's closest friend's his liberty. There was a degree of poetic justice in that, but his feeling of satisfaction spurred on another thought. It might be time, he told himself, to deal with Ron himself.

Simply firing him was too risky. The way to deal with Ron was to increase the operation massively in scale without his involvement, reducing him to a small cog in the machine that could be distanced from the core of the operation; any role he did retain being insignificant in the grand scheme of things. It would mean extending nationwide. If he could be this successful north of the border, Michael told himself, the potential for expansion throughout the UK was unimaginable. But for that, he needed Kenny McGowan's help again.

Michael invited McGowan round, gave him a tour of the house. The gun and sword collection now stretched the full length of the hallway walls and McGowan particularly liked the bird room, a large, octagonal salon painted in subtle shades of white, with a large Victorian birdcage in the centre, full of multicoloured finches. McGowan stared at them, fascinated by their beauty, and it occurred to Michael that there was something about caged birds that struck a chord with ex-cons. Even the hardest of hard men had a soft side.

Michael cooked McGowan a steak, flambéed in cognac, and endured his acerbic teasing about what a ponce he was, doing the cooking. He told McGowan he found it relaxing; also, that McGowan should feel honoured – mostly he cooked only for himself. Michael topped up McGowan's glass with the best Chateau Petrus and sipped tonic water himself throughout the meal.

'Don't anybody tell me crime doesn't pay,' said McGowan, chuckling as he looked around the room. 'You've come a long way from sprinkling fairy dust over Ron's Taxis to make all his problems disappear.'

'Worked hard for it, Kenny,' Michael replied. 'And I'm not a criminal in the real sense of the word. I provide a service, that's all.'

'If that's what you think, I'll no' burst your bubble,' McGowan replied. 'So, you've got plans to move south with your operation? You'll no' be the first to head off in search of glory from this wee country of ours.'

'I'd like to find partners who have the connections to the sort of clients who use our services. They have to be savvy and discreet at the same time. My plan is to have the operation based around a single entity that I can use to move money about as quickly as possible. Ideally, something big enough to cover the entire country.'

'There are a couple of gangsters that I *allegedly* had some dealings with, in the dark days of my youth, you understand. Dick and Eddie. I'll no' tell you their second names until I check if they're interested. Dick's semi-retired now, lives in a villa in Spain with a lass half his age. He'd be your man for the business idea if you can come up with the right sort of proposition. And there's nobody who knows the criminal underworld better than Eddie. He fences jewellery, only high-end stuff. If any of the big boys get their hands on something they have difficulty shifting themselves, they go to him. He must have contacts in every corner of the land.'

With the help of McGowan, and another big donation to his charity, a poolside meeting at Dick's villa in Spain was arranged. Michael went alone, making sure that Ron had no inkling of what was going on. Dick introduced him to Eddie, who'd arrived on an earlier flight. They couldn't have been more different. Dick enjoyed the good life, his face as leathery as a crocodile after years of Mediterranean sun. Eddie had all the charm of a dead halibut, with zero small talk, and announced he was going to find some shade until the meeting began.

Dick took Michael on a tour of his sprawling, white-walled villa, perched on a hillside overlooking the high-rise hotels of Marbella. He introduced Michael to Sharon: big hair, back-combed to within an inch of its life, skin-tight metallic leggings and lime-green tube top. 'Michael's visiting us from Glasgow,' he told her. 'Ever been to Glasgow, love?'

'Never been to Scotland,' she replied, standing next to Dick with her arm on his shoulder. Michael thought of Sid James and Barbara Windsor and tried not to smile. 'Take me there one day, will you, Dick? We can go looking for the Loch Ness monster.'

Dick patted her on her behind to send her on her way.

'Love it here,' he told Michael. 'Everyone's happy. Back in Blighty, every second person is a miserable fucker, walking about with a face tripping them. Like Eddie here.'

Michael glanced over to Eddie. He was sitting bolt upright on a wooden high-backed chair, staring into space, like a robot switched to Off. Dick walked over to the pool, the mosaic of a large-bosomed mermaid shimmering through the crystal-clear water.

'You'll have to excuse Eddie,' Dick said. 'Gets tense when he comes out here. The heat doesn't agree with him, and he hates the food. I served him calamari the last time he was here, told him it was chicken. He had a hissy fit when he found out the truth.'

Michael took a sip of his tonic water and changed the subject. 'So, you're in the furniture business now, I hear. Doing well?'

Dick laughed. 'Haven't a clue. It's not the furniture that pays for all of this; it's what's inside it. It's how Los Zetas move things about. Heard of them?'

'Em ... a little.' Michael felt the need to impress.

Dick stared at him, waiting for him to admit his ignorance. Thirty seconds passed. Finally, Eddie's shout broke the silence. 'Are you two ready to start this meeting? This heat's like having a hairdryer in me kisser. I want out of here.'

'Los Zetas. The Spanish mafia,' Dick said as they walked over to join Eddie. 'But you knew that already.'

There was a glint in his eye. 'Bring lots of white powder over to Europe, from their dago cousins in South America. Need someone to forward it on to grateful customers in countries where the sun don't shine so much. I handle England. Hence my interest in furniture. Big stuff, furniture. Lots of drawers.'

They sat down next to Eddie, who'd already finished off the carafe of water on the table.

'So, Mr Mitchell. Let's hear your proposition. You've got an impressive little operation going on up in Glasgow. You're a man whose reputation precedes him.'

'As you say, we've been introduced to each other by a mutual friend, so I know we can all be open with each other here,' Michael began. 'I plan to buy a national furniture chain, Mallards. They're up for sale and although they only have twelve branches, these are located in all the main cities we'd want to operate in. Dick, you have the business partners in Spain who would supply Mallards with their furniture. That will give us an invoicing point overseas that will allow me to expatriate my clients' money. Eddie, you've got contacts in every corner of the UK. You'd be in charge of putting in place someone in every city to do the same job as I've done in Glasgow. Our clients' cash would be mixed in with that of the stores in all the main cities, and for every one pound of real furniture invoiced from Spain, another twenty would look like it was being paid to the Spanish manufacturer. In reality, it would be syphoned through a number of offshore accounts before being paid back to our clients. Dick, from what you told me earlier, your partners will be happy supplying us with invoices in pesetas so we can move money offshore and then back to our clients' holding accounts. You get a second revenue stream from shipping furniture to the UK, without doing any more work. I've done the numbers. At the end of the first year, we could be looking at a million in laundering fees.'

Now that they were talking business, it was Eddie who made the running. He was a stickler for details, wanting to know the exact amount of revenue going through the current Glasgow operation, who Michael had running it, how it all worked. The grilling was intense, but also structured and methodical. Michael found himself relishing the challenge of being able to answer Eddie's questions, to show how well he ran his business. After dealing with the oafish Ivan, Michael found it stimulating to be challenged by someone who was as meticulous in his planning as he was, just as clear in his thinking, every question as sharp and precise as a scalpel's edge.

When it came to agreeing how the proceeds should be split, Eddie left the negotiation to Dick, as if getting involved in mercenary haggling was beneath his dignity. Dick's contribution was in marked contrast to Eddie's interrogation, the discussion rambling, circuitous, taking forever to reach the obvious conclusion that the profits should be split evenly between the three of them. Michael felt this split was being overly generous to Dick; his part of the operation seemed to involved little effort. If it hadn't been for McGowan's parting words, that Dick had hidden strengths and should be part of the operation at all costs, Michael would have been tempted to cut him out of the full deal until he could see that he was worth it. But this was a new world for him, and until he knew more it was best to listen to the voice of experience.

By the end of his trip, the plan was agreed. Eddie would be installed as the head of all UK operations, except Ron's patch which would be the whole of Scotland. If he didn't like it, tough. The two Mallards stores in Glasgow and Edinburgh would test out the new operation before they rolled it out nationally.

A follow-up meeting in Glasgow was arranged in three months to check on progress. It looked like Michael's growth was unstoppable.

chapter eighteen

In the meantime, there was Ivan to contend with again. Smurfs were still being intimidated by his goons. Stupid, petty acts of violence, dark threats of more to come if they kept smurfing. Rumours were spreading that the police were on to them. It was all combining to make some smurfs reluctant to keep going.

'Why the hell is he doing it?' Ron gritted his teeth in exasperation. 'This must be costing him money as well. What does he get out of it? I could understand someone trying to rob the smurfs of the money they're handling, but he's victimising them for the sake of it.'

'He's trying to send me a message that he won't go away, that he'll be a thorn in my side until I agree to let him control the business. And he's smart, that's why he's not stealing the money. He doesn't want to anger the other bosses. This way, it's my problem, not theirs. He's going to keep nipping away at us until I give him what he wants.'

'So, what about shutting up shop again, getting the others to lean on him? It worked a dream last time.'

'Sadly, it's not an option anymore. I talked to Jenkins about it. I've got too many overheads now to stop the money coming in.'

It was frustrating. Michael needed the smurf operation to stay in place for six months, a year at the most, then all his clients' business could be moved through Mallards and the other shell businesses. But with every day that Ivan's intimidation went on, there was more chance that one of the smurfs might decide they'd had enough and run to the police for protection, or that Ivan's tactics would lead to someone uncovering the operation.

Now, more than ever, he needed as much cash coming into the business as possible. The Mallards deal was coming to a head, but it was a big number he had to pay out to buy a national furniture chain. A bank loan was out of the question, too much scrutiny. No rich girlfriend this time. He needed every penny from the operation to make Mallards happen as soon as possible. Ivan's little war of attrition had come at the worst possible time.

'I can't increase the money going through the Avalon businesses more than I already have,' Michael told Ron. 'I don't want to jeopardise these operations by making them look suspicious. They're the future. I want to get out of smurfing. I don't have a choice. I'm going to meet with Ivan and find out what it takes to get him off our backs.'

'You know what his answer will be. He wants the operation for himself. He's already told you that.'

'Then we need to give it to him,' Michael replied. Ron looked shocked. 'Don't worry; I'm not talking about you and me coming under his control. I'm on the verge of a big deal that will give us all the capacity we need, without the smurfs. But it could be months before it's finalised, even longer before it's fully up and running. I need to buy time with Ivan. After that, he can do what he likes with the smurfs. I won't care. Let him have the operation if he wants it.'

'This is news to me. And this brave new world you're heading into. Am I part of it?'

'Of course, Ron. The business is going to change and grow, but you'll be a part of it for as long as you want to be.' Michael kept his face expressionless. 'We started it together.'

'Then what are these big plans you have? Shouldn't I be involved? You said no secrets, remember?'

'No secrets, Ron. Once I've got things finalised, I'll let you know. Once I've got things finalised. You get word to Ivan that I want to meet him, and concentrate on holding the smurfs together for a few more months. Recruit as few new ones as possible. Leave sorting out Ivan and the future to me. And beef up the protection for the smurfs so there are not so many sitting ducks.'

Ron looked less than happy. 'If we're going to hire some muscle, let's use it to give Ivan a taste of his own medicine. That's the only language a psycho like him understands.'

'No, I don't want to do anything to antagonise him. You focus on keeping the smurfs safe. We leave him alone. Is that clear?'

'I've said it before, Michael. You lead too sheltered a life.' Ron's voice was edged with anger. 'This business you've chosen isn't about sitting in a glitzy office with a ledger and a slide rule, doing some fancy tricks moving money around. It isn't about trying to do gentlemanly deals, especially with the likes of Crazy Ivan. The real business is getting your hands dirty, out there on the streets, where you don't go. Where I'm going to be thought of as a ponce if I don't give Ivan a kicking. Not hiding under the table, getting babysitters for the smurfs.'

Michael kept his voice calm. 'We deal with this the way I want to deal with it. When I'm ready to tell you why, you'll see the reason. If you don't want to do that, you can go back to running Ron's Taxis. There are plenty of others out there who would be all too happy to step into your shoes.'

Ron left, slamming the door behind him. Michael was concerned. Ron was not going to like the new operation and could easily become incensed. And incensed people do stupid things. Maybe not as stupid as Crazy Ivan, but still with the potential to be disruptive. Ron would have to be made to understand that he needed Michael more than Michael needed him.

★ ★ ★

When Michael heard through DS Grant that Ron had been picked up and was being questioned about a robbery he had nothing to do with, he made enquiries; and the word was that his arrest was the result of a tip-off. It could only be another bit of Ivan harassment.

His first instinct was to call Joe Beltrami. Beltrami was gaining legendary status in the Glasgow underworld as a criminal defence lawyer, and no one was better equipped to get Ron out of jail. Michael spoke to Beltrami on the phone, the lawyer's gravelly voice sounding like a Caledonian Johnny Cash. Mistaken identity, Michael told him, instigated by a business rival with malicious intent. The next phone call was from Ron, a few hours later, telling Michael he'd been let go when it became obvious the whole thing was spurious. Beltrami had worked his magic, brow-beating the arresting officer over the ludicrousness of the accusations before a report had even gone to the Procurator Fiscal, but that didn't soften Ron's mood. Michael sensed he was on the point of cracking. He'd wanted to wait until everything was a done deal before bringing Ron on board with the new operation, but he couldn't delay any longer. Michael told him to come around the next day and he'd tell him everything.

Ron turned up just before nine.

'If you've got a plan to deal with this mad bastard, I need to hear it,' he told Michael. 'I had a cast-iron alibi for that job; otherwise, I wouldn't be here talking to you now. Beltrami or no Beltrami, I'd still be locked up at Her Majesty's pleasure.'

Michael ushered Ron inside and they went into his study. He waited for the clock to stop chiming before he began to talk.

'I've been working on a plan to make our current operation obsolete, and give us the scale to meet the demand for our services, no matter how high, and not limited to Scotland. The smurfs will be gone and replaced by a streamlined business process. You'll no longer have to worry about being exposed by their indiscretions. There will be no more hassles to keep them in line. And we're all going to make a lot more money.'

'Sounds like Christmas has come early. But if it's all so wonderful, why am I only hearing about it now?'

'I'm dealing with some new people to make this happen. If word got out, I wanted to be sure it came from them, not from this side of the operation. I need to know I can trust them before things go any further.'

'Yeah, like you trust me … What new people?'

'We're going into the furniture retail business. Outlets all over the country and big-ticket purchases to make it easy to mix clients' money in with the takings. I needed somebody to supply the furniture who can also process our clients' money abroad, and I needed somebody who can take our current money operation into the rest of the UK. So, I've got new partners I'm bringing on board.' He told Ron about Dick and Eddie.

Ron said he had met Eddie in the past and knew Dick by reputation.

'The plan is, within a year, we have all of our clients' money going through apparently legitimate businesses,' Michael said. 'The bulk through Mallards, with the others being used for special situations, large one-offs, contingency planning, that sort of thing. We get the whole thing automated. Jenkins runs the finance side, Eddie's in charge of the new English customers; you handle Scotland. Once it's up and running we close down the smurfs and the operation is off the street, completely invisible. There will be nothing left that Ivan can muscle in on.'

Ron was grudgingly impressed. 'It'll be sweet if you can pull it off, Michael. But don't count Ivan out of the picture that easily. He's obsessed about running the smurfs; he's not going away without a fight.'

'I've thought of that. I think we should start getting out of smurfing in Glasgow sooner rather than later, and use Glasgow to build and refine the Mallards processes before we start the national operation. The smurfs have outgrown their usefulness. They're risky and time-consuming. I want to put them up for sale.'

Ron laughed. 'You're not Tiny Rowland, Michael. This isn't Lonrho. You can't buy and sell these sorts of businesses. In case you've forgotten, we're talking about a bunch of neds stuffing brown envelopes into bank drop boxes.'

'I'm aware of that. We need to find the right kind of buyer. I'm thinking of approaching Ivan, offering him the business, rather than him trying to muscle his way into it. He can have yesterday's operation, use it for petty crime money, stuff that's too small and too much hassle for us to bother with, and leave the big stuff to us. He won't know that part. I'll tell him that I'm going straight and that you're moving on to pastures new and he can have the business if he leaves us alone while we're setting up our new lives. And he can tell the world that he finally achieved victory over the smurf-masters, if that makes him happy. I don't care.'

Ron shook his head and grinned. 'That's some play, I'll give you that. Do you think he'll go for it? And what do I do next? No fucking way am I going to work for him.'

'You and I aren't part of the deal. I can make Ivan see that. And we've got big-time muscle behind us now if he tries to insist otherwise, in the shape of Dick and Eddie. This way we get the smurfs off our hands quickly and Ivan gets the operation he's been wanting all along. Everybody wins.'

'Except Ivan, even if he doesn't know it. You do know the operation will never last five minutes under his control, don't you? He's too hot-headed. No one will trust him with their money and he'll end up beating the smurfs into a pulp for every screw-up. And if we mop up all the big money with the new operation, he'll be left with scraps, and he'll manage to fuck up even that. The operation will be gone in six months.'

'Exactly, Ron. He'll have done the perfect job for us, breaking up the operation into a million little pieces. We move on to bigger and better things, no skeletons left in the closet. Crazy Ivan helps us to make our past disappear.'

'And when the smurf operation collapses?'

'We tell him we're not responsible for how he runs the business. He might not like it, but he won't have a choice.'

Now all Michael needed was for the Mallards deal to be concluded as quickly as possible. Apart from him, nobody seemed to be in a hurry. It was a family-run firm, old-fashioned working practices and selling the same stuff in the same way for two generations. The business was being decimated by new out-of-town furniture warehouses and trend-conscious chains like Brown Bear and Habitat. The family had decided to sell the company on while there was still a business to sell. Michael had asked around to find the best lawyer to conclude the deal, and now had the senior partner of Glasgow's top commercial firm grinding through the purchase process – and charging a fortune for the privilege.

The process was tortuous. At every stage, it took forever for his lawyer's opposite number to get instructions from the family, and during these interludes there would be a frustrating silence. They had due diligence, indemnities and warranties to sort out. Everything moved along at a sedate pace. And all the while Michael had Eddie breathing down his neck, asking what he was playing at, why it was taking so long as he pushed ahead, finding someone to run the organisation in each of the regions. He had Dick pointing out that Los Zetas were losing patience. For the first time in years, Michael was doing something legitimate, buying a real business, following all the proper procedure, and it was proving to be the single most stressful part of the enterprise.

Eventually, Michael signed the contract. Now he needed to visit the Mallards offices, finalise everything with Dick and Eddie, and approach Ivan to offer up the smurfs. Before that, however, he decided to celebrate.

Michael booked a VIP booth at Tiffany's and filled it with the latest hangers-on he had acquired. Some he liked, but most were there to ensure that he stayed connected to the social circles to which Charlotte had introduced him, and all of them were happy to freeload on his hospitality. When one of them left the group, the others would slag them off until they returned, when they would go back to their faux camaraderie. Not for the first time, Michael reflected on the close personal bonds he saw between many of the criminals he came in touch with, men who would do anything for each other, even to the point of sacrificing their liberty so not to betray their friends. The values and beliefs of the underclass, he reflected ruefully, could teach the rest of the world a thing or two. Charlotte had been different. He thought about her more than he cared to admit, but the few casual questions about what she was getting up to resulted in vague, disinterested replies. He hid his frustration that he couldn't find out more.

Michael pushed these thoughts from his mind and surveyed the dance floor. Flash and exuberance in all colours, fashion, sights and sounds. Disco seemed to revel in excess and euphoria – everything was bigger, brighter, funkier and a whole lot of fun. Van McCoy's 'The Hustle' was on the turntable and the guys were playing out their best moves, gold medallions swinging dangerously with every spin, the women batting their spider-leg eyelashes in appreciation. But grooving on the dance floor was not Michael's style. He preferred the VIP booth. It was expensive, but it always paid off. Invitations to join him were rarely turned down.

Then he spotted her. She looked very different from the rest. Fresh, natural, her dark brown eyes giving her an air of alluring innocence. Chestnut hair tumbled down to a figure-hugging yellow jumpsuit. And she was on her own. He was intrigued.

She had no shortage of attention, brushing off every guy who approached her with a friendly charm – but deliberately standing in a pool of light. Interesting. He saw her steal a glance at him, then another.

Michael sent someone down to invite her up. She glanced over and he raised his glass of tonic water in salute. She gave the slightest nod of acceptance and walked over to join him.

'Hello, pretty girl, I'm Michael,' he said. 'I haven't seen you here before. Your first time? I'm sure I would've remembered you.'

'Yes, first time. I'm Bobbie.'

'Bobbie. That's an unusual name for a girl.'

'Short for Roberta. I think my dad was disappointed I wasn't a boy.'

'Well, I'm not,' Michael said. 'Pleased to meet you, Roberta.'

'I prefer Bobbie.'

'But I prefer Roberta.'

She gave him a look of mild outrage.

'Is this your club?'

'Oh no.' He laughed. 'Far too exciting for me. I run an estate agency and a travel company. Boring stuff.'

'So, are you a leader of industry? Should I have heard of you?'

'I hope not,' Michael replied. The others laughed, aware of his reputation for keeping a low business profile. 'As I say, just a boring businessman. But sometimes I get lucky with a big deal, and that's why I'm here tonight. Celebrating a very successful business transaction.'

He liked her. Smart and sassy, but full of wide-eyed innocence. Coy and demure as she slid into the back of his car as they were driven home, but bold and assertive as they enjoyed each other on the drive back to the house.

The driver remained in the car when they arrived at Michael's house, lest Roberta catch his eye and feel embarrassed at what he had witnessed in the rear-view mirror. Michael showed her inside; the lights already low in anticipation of his return. They headed to the bedroom without preamble. Roberta didn't seem like the sort of woman who needed to pretend to be seduced.

Michael poured her some champagne from a small bedside fridge and watched as she gulped it down. He smiled. Despite her poised exterior, she was finding the atmosphere just as intense as he was. He poured her a second glass, sat back as she took in the trappings of the room. Black satin sheets draped over a circular waterbed, erotic art on the wall, a blazing fire, lit on his instructions by his housekeeper an hour earlier. The room was a paean to sensual delights.

Roberta closing her eyes, opening them as he reached for the fastening of her jumpsuit, smiling and willing him on. It fell to the floor and she stood there, proud, confident. She moved forward to unbutton Michael's shirt, but he stepped back so that he was lit by the flames of the fire, and slipped the shirt over his head himself.

It was a trick he had played before. As the light of the flames danced over the grooves and hollows of his naked torso, he saw Roberta gasp in astonishment.

Michael removed the rest of her clothes with practised efficiency. He stepped back to admire her nakedness, then lifted her with effortless ease and carried her to the waterbed. As he dropped Roberta on the bed, it swayed gently from her weight and she giggled like a naughty schoolgirl.

He wanted to extend this moment, to caress her, plant a myriad of tiny kisses all over her body, but his desire was becoming overwhelming. When he was inside her, her body began to twitch and shudder with a convulsive force. A pause, and then the same again, this time together with a high keening cry, like a demon released from her soul. The intensity was too much for Michael. He felt a sudden wave of ecstasy flow out of him; fast, full, deep. He arched himself towards her as he came, and as Roberta felt the blurry warmth of his climax, she moved up the bed a little and gave herself a small, secret smile of congratulation. She clasped herself around him, squeezing, refusing to let him go. Michael stared in wonder at her sweet, innocent face after the sexual voracity he had just experienced. She kissed him on his collarbone, licked the little hollow in his shoulder, then gave a soft, sweet, kittenish purr.

He could already feel himself stirring again.

chapter nineteen

The next morning, Michael watched as Roberta was driven away in his car. He turned and smiled to himself. Usually, a Tiffany's conquest did not get to spend the night, but there had been something alluring about the way she made love. Animalistic, cathartic, like it was an attempt to exorcise some torment in her soul. The contrast with her nice-girl demeanour had been enthralling. He sent her some roses to keep her on ice until he had time to see her again.

It wouldn't be for a while. As the Mallards new owner, Michael needed to get up to speed with the business he had bought so he would be fully prepared for the meeting with Dick and Eddie. Old Mr Mallard was taking early retirement, and his son would take over for the first six months or until Michael could move in to replace him. Michael wanted all the operations people to stay in place so the business could continue to be run to all appearances like any normal furniture chain. Jenkins would be parachuted in as finance director, with the job of setting up a double-accounting system so that only he would see the extra money going through the business from outside.

Michael headed down to the Mallards Surrey offices to get the ball rolling, Jenkins in tow. The business was a shambles. Despite knowing nothing about the furniture trade, Michael could see straight away where some things could be done better. When he met with the managers, there was undisguised euphoria that the business had been sold and that somebody, anybody, would try to rescue it from the doldrums. Michael found himself getting more and more drawn into thinking about how he could turn it around, make it a force to be reckoned with, then smiled at his foolishness. Even if it could become a going concern, the profits from selling the furniture would never be more than a tenth of what he'd really be using the business for. He was tempted, though.

Ron called to let Michael know that he'd got in touch with Ivan and had arranged for them to meet on Friday afternoon. As Michael travelled back on the first train to Glasgow on Friday morning, he went over in his head one last time how he was going to handle the conversation. That passed the time, but planning was mostly futile. Every encounter with Crazy Ivan was completely unpredictable.

He went straight from the train station to the hotel where they were to meet. After so many months of his intimidation, it seemed unreal to be meeting with Ivan face to face again. Michael cut to the chase as soon as he arrived. He wanted this over with as quickly as possible.

'I'm getting out of the business,' Michael said. 'Going straight, heading down to England to start a new life. Ron's taken up an offer to be part of someone else's firm, so he wants out as well. If you want to take over, the business is yours. You can have our manpower, I'll go over every detail of how it all works, and one of your boys can be running it before I pack it in. You win. I haven't the stomach for fighting off your thugs anymore.'

It galled Michael to have to put up this pretence, to give this brute the satisfaction of thinking he had got one over on him, but it would be worth it. With one fell swoop, he'd be rid of the smurfs and could put his past behind him. He steeled himself to keep up the charade.

'Mikey, Mikey, Mikey,' replied Ivan, as he tried to hide his gloating. 'A few wee bits o' high jinks, that was all, just to yank your chain. So you wouldn't forget me. I hope your no' sore wi' me. I'd hate that.'

'No, not at all,' Michael said with curt formality. 'I should be grateful. Now I can get out while I still can. I want to offer you a deal. Leave me alone, let me get the business sorted out after all your aggravation so I can make some money while I get ready for my future, and you take over a business that's stable and running smoothly. That also gives you some time to find someone to run it.'

'It's a great wee set-up you've got going there, Mikey boy. Everybody loves it. And they're going to have to love me now, if they want to keep using it. Aye, there's a few pricks out there that I'm going to enjoy seeing having to swallow their pride when they give me their business. I tend to rub people up the wrong way. Can't think why, I'm a pussycat really. Some cunts cannae take a joke.'

'Well, it's yours. We can settle this here and now. Promise you'll back off and leave me alone, and when I'm ready to move, the business is yours.'

'And how long do you expect me to sit about waiting?'

'Nine months. I'm talking about starting a new life. It takes time to get these things organised.'

'Nine months? You could make a bairn in that time. How do I know this is no' a con, just to make me piss off out your life? I wouldn't wait that long for an audience wi' the Pope.'

'These things take time, Ivan. Don't worry; I'll move as fast as I can.'

'Let's do this. I give you six months, and you start now, telling my man how things work. As long as you promise no' to scarper in the meantime. Cos I'd no' be a happy bunny. And you don't want to see me unhappy. I lose all of my roguish charm.'

'Very generous of you, Ivan. Okay, it's a deal. And let bygones be bygones. No hard feelings. When do you want to start?'

Michael told Ron the good news afterwards.

'It's all agreed. Ivan backs off from today, and I hand the smurfs over to him once we've got the Mallards operation up and running. Reckon that will be early next year, when I move to Surrey to take over as the managing director. We've got to move fast. All the clients we want to hang on to are going to have their money moved through the Mallards Glasgow store, and we increase the money going through the Avalon businesses as much as we think we can get away with. All the nutcases, loose cannons and head-bangers that we've picked up as clients get handed off to Ivan. You tell all the customers we want to keep that we're moving to a new operation and if they want to be part of it, secrecy is key.'

'Ivan is going to be furious when he sees how much business is disappearing from under his nose. We can hardly hide that from him. Expect trouble, Michael.'

'The story is going to be that people don't want to deal with him. That means losing all these customers is his fault, not ours. It might teach him a lesson.'

'You don't teach Crazy Ivan a lesson, Michael. That's all I'm saying.'

Michael had just finished his conversation with Ron when he got a call from the manager at Tiffany's. The girl he'd met the previous weekend had turned up at the disco and had been asking if he was going to be in the VIP booth that evening. She'd looked disappointed, the manager said, when he had told her no, but she hadn't left. Michael glanced at his watch. It had been a long, stressful day, but Roberta could be the ideal solution to that and his driver could get him there in half an hour. He shook his head. The most important meeting of his life was a week away; the last thing he needed was another distraction. Then he remembered their night together. Some distractions were worth it. He arrived as she was leaving, alone and sullen-faced.

'Roberta,' Michael said. 'How nice to see you. Where are you going?'

'Michael, you bastard, where have you been? Why didn't you call me?'

Michael stepped out of the car, trying to keep a straight face. 'What on earth do you mean?' he said. 'Didn't you get my note saying I was away and that I would meet you at Tiffany's tonight?'

'I got your flowers, but there wasn't any note.' Her voice was petulant, embarrassed.

He shook his head in exasperation. 'I'll have a quiet word with my florist. That's disgraceful he forgot to attach the note. But here you are anyway. Are you leaving? The night has just begun.'

Confusion was written all over her face. 'Maybe next time you want to meet me you should try calling, rather than relying on someone to give me a note.'

By now Michael was thoroughly enjoying the game he was playing.

'You're right, Roberta, I've behaved abominably. Things are a little ... complicated at the moment and I've not been as attentive to you as I should have been. Let me make it up to you. You look cold standing there. And you shouldn't be getting on the Underground dressed like that. Who knows what sort of undesirable attention you would attract, looking so beautiful on an empty train late at night. Come on, let me give you a lift at least.'

Michael gave himself the luxury of spending Sunday with her; then it was time to plan for the meeting with Dick and Eddie. He'd invited them to Scotland to finalise the deal, and Dick suggested the Turnberry Hotel on the Ayrshire coast so he could have a round of golf before heading back to Spain. The meeting would be mostly a formality, but Michael wanted to leave nothing to chance. By the end of the weekend, the bones of the new operation would be in place.

Ron tried to insist on attending the meeting.

'You don't know the street operation, Michael,' he said. 'I do. If we want to replicate what we do here in the rest of the country, then you need me along.'

'We're not getting into that sort of detail,' Michael said. 'Don't worry. There's going to be plenty of time for you to sit down with Eddie to get the specifics right. Once we've got the main points of the deal agreed, you'll be fully involved.' Michael needed to show Dick and Eddie he relied on no one. He'd go alone.

At least that's what he thought until Dick called mid-week.

'It's going to be a weekend of celebration,' he told Michael over a crackly phone line from Marbella. 'So, Eddie and I thought we should bring our girls along. You've already met Sharon, and Eddie has his bit of stuff to keep him out of mischief. That's not a problem, is it?'

Michael's patience with Dick was running thin. Playing golf, no doubt half-cut most of the weekend, now bringing along this Sharon bimbo. He was beginning to wonder if Dick was taking the whole proposition seriously. In the end, he relented. If Eddie had agreed, he must have thought there would be enough time for the serious discussions. And maybe, Michael thought, he was overly obsessive about the meeting. It was right, what he'd told Ron – everything had been worked out. He was trusting these two guys with his livelihood, his freedom, maybe even his life. It might be good to get to know them better.

'Then I'd better bring someone,' Michael told Dick. 'But she's a civilian, knows nothing of my operation, doesn't suspect a thing. As long as there's no talk of business when she's around. Do I have your word on that?'

'Unwritten rule of our business anyway, Michael. Tell the women-folk nothing. Sharon, bless her, is a lovely girl and knows how to keep an old man happy, but I wouldn't trust her with a secret if my life depended on it. And I don't think Eddie's one's for pillow talk either. Looking forward to meeting your lovely lady.'

Roberta was surprisingly difficult to convince to come along; it turned out she had a prior engagement which it took all of Michael's charm to convince her to cancel. But the promise of five-star luxury eventually made her relent. As he put the phone down after their conversation, Michael reflected that maybe he was being too uptight about the meeting, seeing how relaxed everyone seemed to be about completing the deal.

He decided he'd get the deal done and enjoy himself while doing it. It was shaping up to be a memorable weekend.

chapter twenty

Roberta and Michael looked an incongruous pair as they stepped out of the car and breathed in the sea air at Turnberry. Michael had dressed for a business meeting; he wanted Dick and Eddie to know they were dealing with a professional. He hadn't told Roberta to do the same and she had turned up in flared jeans and a red-checked cheesecloth shirt, three-inch platform shoes and woollen stripy socks. She looked horrified when she saw how straight Michael looked, relieved when he reminded her he had said he had business to attend to. She had given him her undivided attention in the two-hour drive from Glasgow, and he was beginning to regret his decision not to be there on his own. He needed a clear head for this weekend and Roberta would be a distraction, albeit a pleasant one.

Dick and Eddie had already arrived and checked in, so Michael dropped off their bags, left Roberta to settle in and headed down to the room he'd booked for the meeting. He set out the typed agenda next to the Mallards business plan document he'd prepared. He wasn't sure if this was how crime lords operated, but this was a business, and he wanted to run it that way.

Dick and Eddie arrived, strutting into the room like a pair of Roman emperors, displaying the unhurried calm of two men who had nothing to prove. They could not have looked more different. Dick, a bull of a man slowly going to seed, a half-empty glass of Campari in his hand at eleven in the morning, wore a paisley-pattern cravat and brass-buttoned blazer. Alan Wicker on steroids. Eddie, a few years younger, was trim and dapper, his manicured nails and slicked-back hair giving him all the appearance of a respectable businessman, spoilt a little by the slight trace of a scar under his left eye. Their two girls, Sharon and Cindy, were sent off to the hotel's beauty parlour and, after a few anodyne pleasantries, it was straight down to business.

Michael produced the memorandum of sale to show that the Mallards purchase had been completed and then ran through how the business was to be operated. 'We are going to ring-fence the retail operation,' he explained, 'so that everyone employed by the company feels they are part of a normal business. We run a set of parallel accounts which will be seen only by my accountant, where we move twenty times the revenue made in the stores through the accounts. For the day-to-day money laundering, the money will move through the business as if it was cash sales from people shopping at Mallards. When we have a client with a substantial cash sum he wants us to handle, that gets treated as a payment to our overseas Spanish wholesaler, paid first into a Spanish bank account and from there into our Swiss bank accounts so it can be sent anywhere in the world.'

'And you reckon you can do this without anyone else from Mallards catching on?' Eddie was focussing on every word. Dick's concentration was already starting to wander around the room.

'Definitely,' Michael replied. 'The managing director is the son of the owner. He's going to stay on for six months to show me the ropes. Then I take over, and we start putting our clients' money through the business. Every store manager only ever sees the management accounts of their store's actual sales and revenue. They get consolidated at head office by their finance manager and he hands them over to Jenkins, my accountant, to go into the group accounts. That's when we add in the extra costs and revenue to hide our clients' money. Nobody in Mallards ever sees the accounts after that. It's part of a privately traded group of companies, owned by me. The group accounts are confidential. For our eyes only.'

'You're putting a lot of faith in this accountant of yours. Is he up to it? And can you trust him?'

'You'll meet him once everything is set up. Yes, you can trust him. He likes the idea of earning a lot of money for doing very little work. He's got no ambition beyond that. And he was Kenny McGowan's accountant for years. He knows not to ask too many questions.' In this sort of company, Michael reckoned it was safe to mention McGowan's name.

Eddie looked thoughtful. 'Okay then. Dick, have you any questions?'

'Eh? Yeah, can I get another Campari? More ice this time.'

Michael wasn't buying the show of indifference, but he went out to the lobby, asked them to organise another drink. Eddie and Dick broke off their conversation when he returned.

Michael was beginning to feel uncomfortable, an outsider. 'I think it's time you both showed me your parts of the plan,' he said.

'Let's finish off with your side first,' Eddie replied. 'So, you've been going a year; it's your first venture, you've got Kenny McGowan backing you and every hoodlum in Glasgow loves you and wants you to squirrel away their cash. And you think, if this is so easy, let's do it in other places. And that's where Dick and I come in. Have I got it right?'

'Not quite. Kenny McGowan's got nothing to do with the operation. He just made our introductions as a favour from when I was a bank manager, helping out some old lag mates of his get bank accounts. I have someone on my staff who's connected enough to find our clients in Glasgow and I've got a … compliance officer, shall we say, to handle any problems that come our way. And that's been enough to clean up in the west of Scotland. But I think there's more opportunity out there. And for that, I need some help.'

Michael had explained all this at their first meeting. He was getting distinctly exasperated that he had progressed his plan this far, only to find he wasn't being taken seriously. But he saw Dick catch Eddie's eye, give him a barely imperceptible nod. Eddie swung his briefcase up onto the table and opened it.

'Good, Michael. Good. Wanted to check your story matched what we knew, that's all. No funny stuff, no embellishments. Okay, let me show you what I can do for you.'

Eddie produced a dossier on every proposed regional operator across ten English cities. A photo, a summary of their criminal record if they had one, a brief outline of how they operated. It was like looking through the personnel files of a large corporation. Michael was impressed by his thoroughness and professionalism. And, if he was honest, a little surprised.

Eddie must have picked up on it. 'You're not dealing with an amateur, Michael. I run a business. I've seen lots of tough, smart guys meet an unsavoury end from the streets or the cops, and that doesn't happen to me. I plan, I organise. If you deal with me, you're dealing with a professional.'

'Great minds,' Michael replied.

Eddie talked through his plan to base an operation around each of the Mallards stores, having someone in each city responsible for handling the business there, reporting back to him. Ten per cent of the fees went to the local guy, the rest they split three ways.

That left only Dick to go through his proposal. He stifled a belch as he fished out a brochure from his briefcase. The trade catalogue of Galicia Muebles was spread out on the boardroom table, covering the new range that Mallards would be selling.

'Take your pick from anything that takes your fancy,' Dick told Michael. 'Just be sure to choose the chests of drawers and the sideboards. That's where the big H is stashed when it's shipped across the border. Galicia Muebles' handling agent in the UK knows which items have got concealed compartments in the drawers. He takes them out and replaces them so they can be sold on to unsuspecting customers. Works a treat.'

'And it's okay for my purchasing guy to visit them in Spain?' Michael asked. 'They're a genuine furniture manufacturer?'

'As far as your guy is concerned, yes they are. You just need to explain to him he doesn't have a choice about using them as a supplier. Tell him they are owned by a sleeping partner who put up part of the cash to help you buy Mallards, or some such bullshit. They make their stuff look solid and respectable, but it's veneered woodchip and plywood. We don't want him getting stroppy with them about quality and buggering up Los Zetas' shipment schedule. They wouldn't like that.'

'And there's no way he could find out about Los Zetas from these furniture guys? You're sure about that?'

Dick gave him a withering stare. 'Los Zetas only ever deal with me. They're an old-school organised crime operation based in La Coruña, third generation crime lords, with a strict tradition of *silencio*. They imported drugs from South America in lumber shipments and used the furniture business to send the stuff around Europe. That's all you need to know. Galicia Muebles is the front, run by one of the family, and your guy will find they look completely legit. They'll raise invoices for fictitious furniture orders and send them directly to your accountant, as long as you use the real shipments for their drug operation. That's the deal.'

It was Michael's turn to be on the receiving end of the questions.

'So this Ron Smith, this partner of yours. The guy who handles your street operation.' Eddie gave a theatrical glance around the room. 'I don't see him here. What's the problem with him?'

'No problem,' Michael replied. 'He's a career criminal who I brought on board to have someone who would know who to talk to in Glasgow about our services. He's an employee, not a partner.'

'Would he agree with that? He gets a share of the operation and he's pretty key to you. Sounds like a partner to me. Why's he not at this meeting?'

'He's someone who does what I tell him. He knows we're meeting, and that what we're discussing doesn't concern him. He runs the Glasgow operation, and he still will after we've decided everything today. I don't get involved in that side of the operation and he doesn't get involved with what I do.'

'But it's not going to stay separate now, is it? I'm going to be in charge of operations and it'll be what I want to do in Glasgow that counts, not Mr Ron Smith. I need to look him over before he becomes part of the operation.'

'We discussed this at our last meeting.' Michael shifted in his seat, feeling he was being railroaded. 'I said we'd keep things the same in Glasgow. Leave you to focus on getting the operation set up in the rest of the country, at least in the meantime.'

'You don't have two operations in this business. It causes friction, even a bit of rivalry. Before you know where you are you start poaching customers, trampling on each other's patch.' He shook his head. 'I know what we agreed at our last meeting, but Ron's days at the top table are over. He'll be working for me from now on.'

Michael thought for a moment. He didn't feel comfortable handing over everything he'd built to Eddie, at least not straight away. Not before he knew he could trust him. He didn't like one bit that Eddie was going back on what they'd agreed. But the man was right – it did make more sense to have the one operation and it would speed up the day when Ron got retribution for what happened with Charlotte.

'Agreed. He works for you. I tell him when I get back to Glasgow.'

Dick had hardly uttered a word after explaining about Los Zetas. It was becoming apparent that what mattered most to Dick was Dick having an easy time. He'd made his stack of cash and now his days consisted of Ambre Solaire and getting roasted in the Spanish sun, squiring an endless succession of mercenary floozies half his age. Michael guessed that Los Zetas provided protection against anyone with an outstanding grievance from Dick's past, and his involvement in smuggling drugs into the UK was part of his efforts to keep them sweet. Now he was getting a split of the Mallards profits for doing no more than he was doing already. But Michael needed a Spanish partner to supply the false invoices, and Galicia Muebles and Los Zetas were perfect. Galling as it was, Dick had to get a cut of the action.

The rest of the weekend was spent in bed with Roberta while Dick and Eddie caught up on old times on the hotel's golf course. Dinner gave Michael a chance to get a handle on the sort of women these guys hung out with. Pneumatic blonde trophies who didn't ask too many questions. Roberta's face was a picture when she saw who she was being compared with, and Michael tried to imagine Sharon and Cindy turning up at one of his dinner parties. He found the thought farcical. Maybe he had become too much of a snob, but the girlfriend stereotype of this life was not for him.

Michael was full of anticipation about the future. This was the big league. His new business partners might not be the sort of people he'd introduce in polite society, but this was to be his world from now on.

chapter twenty-one

Immediately after Turnberry, Michael headed off to Switzerland to put the banking arrangements in place. He met up with Roberta on his return. He was starting to like her. She made a change from the usual Tiffany conquest – empty sex and vacuous small talk. And she showed at Turnberry that she wouldn't run a mile when she got a hint of who he really was.

That had turned out to be important. When Michael had given her a tour of the house, it was centrepiece of his collection that had impressed her the most. She had recognised the artist as soon as she saw it.

'Wow, a Magritte,' she had said, bouncing on tiptoes. 'But not a real one, surely?'

When Michael had told her it was, he could see she was impressed. She reached out and touched the painting. 'Your travel agency and estate agents must do awfully well for you to afford all this,' she said. 'Your place is seriously cool.'

'Oh, that was a very satisfactory outcome from someone's misfortune.' Michael replied. 'I'm in the process of setting up an art gallery, selling exclusive, upmarket stuff to the well-heeled Scottish gentry. One of my prospective clients fell on hard times and needed someone to take it off his hands in a hurry. A quick and very discreet sale.'

It was what she had said next that piqued Michael's interest.

'Art gallery? What a coincidence. I'm the assistant manager at the Third Eye Centre.'

Michael thought back to that conversation as they sat across from each other in a restaurant. She was the perfect person to front up the art gallery project. Knowing enough about art to be credible as the manager and nothing in her background to suggest she could be a front for a criminal operation.

She seemed to be becoming more infatuated every time they met. But it was one thing getting a glimpse of his world by meeting Dick and Eddie, and another seeing right in front of her what was going on. He had been lucky with Charlotte – she had suspected what he really did for a living, but the repercussions had been personal, not professional. He couldn't afford to take that chance again. If he played it slowly, he could draw Roberta into his world little by little. Then, and only then, would she discover what she was part of.

Dinner was the first test. Michael had brought along a diamond and ruby necklace – a jewel thief's payment in lieu. He was keen to see if she baulked at such over-the-top generosity. That would be the first indication of whether she was willing to look the other way when the price was right.

He produced the necklace at the end of the evening, saying he had a one-month anniversary present for her.

She gasped. 'You are joking, aren't you? I mean, get me a new Snoopy doll if you want to give me a present. I can't take something like this.'

'Relax. It's just something left over from a business deal. One of my business partners had a little liquidity problem and gave me this to settle some debts. It would have been too … problematic to dispose of it and I think it will look good on you. Please keep it.'

'It's not me, Michael,' she replied, biting on her lip. 'And whoever it belonged to before will have hated to have parted with it. It doesn't seem right to wear something with a sad history.'

'Look out the window, Roberta,' Michael replied. 'All of these dots of lights out there are people, in their houses, in their cars. Do they mean anything to you?' He pointed out the window. 'Would you give this necklace to that dot of light there if you knew it would help their problems? Or even give them the cost of this meal? Of course not. You have no connection with them. Our only real connection is with ourselves. Morals and scruples are all very well, but they never put food on the table. And we've got expensive tastes.'

He had prepared the speech carefully, using Orson Welles for inspiration. *The Third Man* was his favourite movie and Harry Lime his favourite character. He had been deliberately provocative – he wanted to be absolutely sure she would accept his criminal world, become complicit by accepting his gift, before he finally brought her into his operation. He lifted his glass of water in a kind of toast to her agreement to their Faustian pact, scrutinising her face for a reaction. The air crackled with expectancy.

Roberta fiddled with the necklace, staring at the ruby centrepiece. 'It's beautiful, Michael, thank you,' she said softly, slipping it around her neck. Michael got up and stood behind her, guiding her fingers to secure the clasp. He returned to his seat and gazed at her in admiration.

'No more beautiful than you,' he said.

Roberta had passed the first test.

★ ★ ★

Michael spent two weeks gently teasing out of Roberta more about her past. On the surface, she was as nice as apple pie, visiting her granny every week, caring for everyone she met. But hanging out in Tiffany's, looking for a pick-up, wasn't a one-off aberration. Nights like Tiffany's, she told Michael, had been her way of dealing with remorse over a tragic love affair that had gone badly wrong. She had promised herself she'd never have to be responsible for a failed love affair again, and one-night stands had been her way of dealing with her guilt.

Michael saw she was someone who avoided problems rather than confront them. That was good. The longer she avoided facing up to the world that Michael was drawing her into, the deeper she would become embroiled, the more difficult it would be for her to summon the will to leave.

But her dream to be an actress was the final piece of proof Michael needed. Her passion for acting consumed her, and she confessed that she had just failed an audition for a movie part when the director, Frank Fontaine, made it clear to her what favours would be required in return. Persuading the director to change his mind was easy.

One visit from Big Jockie and it was all portrayed as a big misunderstanding. Roberta got the part.

Michael was cooking supper, enjoying bustling around in the kitchen and whipping up an omelette Arnold Bennett, when Roberta told him the director had offered her the role.

'You got the part in the movie, Roberta? Congratulations. Well deserved.'

'It might be well deserved, Michael, but you and I both know I didn't get it off my own bat. They'd already cast someone else for the part and it was suspicious Fontaine changed his mind after I told you about him. I need to know, Michael: What did you say to him?'

Michael took the omelette out from under the grill and left it to settle. 'I can make inconvenient things happen to people who bother me, Roberta. Fontaine was out of order in his behaviour, and he needed someone to point that out to him.'

Roberta looked him in the eye, but the stare was a different one from the time he had given her the necklace. That one had been full of worry, uncertainty, unease. This look was more self-assured, confident, and aware. She went to speak, but caught herself before she uttered a syllable. Instead, she gave a smile of gratitude, came over and kissed him on the neck.

'Thank you,' she said.

Michael knew then that he'd captured her, that all he had to do was dangle dreams of acting fame in front of her and she would be putty in his hands. She was the perfect front for another of his Avalon businesses, and he could coax her along to run the art gallery operation, at least until Mallards made it redundant. Now all he had to do was give her one final little push to get her on board.

It was easy. She'd told him that on the following Friday evening there was to be a private preview at the art gallery where she worked. The previous show wasn't coming down till the Thursday, so she had arranged for the entire team to be in early Friday morning to begin hanging the new work. She set her alarm for 6 a.m. A simple flick of the switch on the clock and Michael made sure it never went off. Roberta woke late and panicked. Michael pretended to do his best to help her make up time, but as he had anticipated, there was a major bust-up when she finally got to work. When Roberta met Michael again, two days later, she was still fretting that her boss had not accepted her repeated apologies.

'I think he's under a lot of pressure at the moment,' said Michael. 'The word on the street is that his gallery is struggling.'

'I've not heard that. In fact, we seem to be getting busier all the time. Are you sure?'

Michael decided the time was right to make his move. 'I can only say what I've heard. Actually, now is as good a time as any to tell you about my latest business venture. Have I mentioned my new art gallery, the Avalon?'

'You mentioned something about it when we first met. What is it?'

'A high-quality art gallery selling top-end nineteenth-century Scottish art. The Glasgow Boys, Henry Raeburn, that sort of thing. London has traditional galleries like this in Mayfair and Old Bond Street, but we've got nothing like it in Scotland. What do you think?'

Michael looked her straight in the eye.

'I'd like you to be the curator,' he said. 'What do you say?'

'Oh, Michael, I couldn't do that. I'm not qualified.'

He played his trump card.

'And you'll have all the time you need for your acting career; you can even close the gallery for the day for an audition or to go to rehearsals. And think of the contacts you can make at exhibition openings and the like.'

Roberta took a deep breath. 'Michael, don't take this the wrong way …'

He smiled, knowing what was coming next.

Roberta looked at the floor as she spoke. 'Is your business completely legit?'

'What a question.' Michael laughed. 'I don't know what you've been imagining, but you don't need to worry. I want you to run my art gallery, that's all. Organise the hangings, chat to whoever comes in to have a look. Be a real curator, make the artistic decisions. You'll be a legitimate employee, pay your taxes. The books will show the business being a bit more successful than it is in reality, that's the only thing, because it's tax efficient to divert part of my overall income stream through a start-up company. But that's normal practice. What do you say?'

'I'm not sure. The job sounds too good to be true. And I'm worried about this "income stream" thing you mentioned.'

'Well, you shouldn't be. Do you think the girls at the travel agency are criminals? Or the people at the estate agents? Of course not.'

The look in her eye showed that she was tempted.

'And when the acting becomes full time, you can help me find your replacement and, puff, off you go. To be a star. Just think about it.' Michael took a sip of his soda water and raised his glass, as if to acknowledge she'd said yes.

He needed to make sure Roberta didn't have any secrets that could turn out to be problems further down the line, so he'd checked into her background, had her watched. Nothing concerning, apart from the fact that she was seeing someone else, a guy her age. When Michael dug deeper, it turned out to be an old school friend she'd known for years.

He arranged to have some photographs taken of her meeting with him, found out his name – Duncan Jones – and before he met Roberta that evening, he prepared a test. She arrived wearing a new outfit and sashayed into the hallway, waiting for Michael to congratulate her on how glamorous she looked.

'Who's Duncan Jones?' Michael said instead.

He saw the look of complete shock on her face.

'Duncan? He's a friend. How do you know him?'

Michael placed the photos on the table of Duncan and Roberta having coffee the previous day. 'You seem to be very close. Quite an intense conversation you were having.'

'What is this, Michael? Are you spying on me?'

He deliberately spoke with a slight menace. 'Please be calm, Roberta. There's one thing which is very important to me, and which I put a lot of effort into getting right, and that's security. Glasgow can be a mean city. Robbery, kidnapping, that sort of thing. Now you're starting to work for me; I've had someone keep an eye on you for your protection.'

He could see he was having the desired effect.

'This is too heavy, Michael. You're scaring me.' Her voice trembled as she spoke.

'I'm sorry if these pictures startled you. One of my business associates is being a little … troublesome at the moment and I'm probably more thorough in my surveillance than normal. I hope you'll forgive me. You look beautiful in that dress, by the way.'

'Michael, who exactly are your customers?' She was sounding more frantic now. 'Are we talking about murderers and armed robbers here?'

'Of course not. You've met Eddie and Dick, the guys I'm talking to about expanding my businesses. They might look like a couple of rough diamonds, but that's just their way. They're not criminals by any stretch of the imagination. So, if you don't mind me asking, who is Duncan and what does he do?'

'I've known him since school. My best friend. And only my friend.'

Michael acted as if he was finding this out for the first time. 'Good. I'm pleased to hear that. I'm so glad we've sorted out this misunderstanding. I've got no problem with you seeing Duncan, or any of your friends. But I care about you, Roberta, and I want to make sure no one takes advantage of you.'

As he expected, the whole thing had freaked her out. 'Michael, I'm scared,' she said. She started sobbing. 'I don't want the job anymore.'

'Please don't overreact, Roberta. I think you know by now I like my world to be organised, maybe a little too organised perhaps. I'm the first to admit I probably overdo my security. Let's call it my foible.'

'So, can I leave?'

'If you want to.' This would be the telling moment. 'But your old boss has hired someone to take your place, hasn't he? Everything's ready for our opening tomorrow; you've got these wonderful clothes. I think I'd need to ask you to work your notice period at least. And those Scottish Arts people who are coming to the opening night party, do you want to tell them you're quitting on your first day? But it's up to you.'

He could see her hesitating. 'I'm not sure, really I'm not, Michael.'

'Look, are we going to let one stupid incident spoil everything we have together?' He kissed her gently on the lips. 'Roberta, if I thought there was the slightest problem with you taking the job, I wouldn't want you to do it. If I say once more I'm sorry about the Duncan incident, will you at least consider staying on?'

She wiped her eyes.

'God, would you look at me! Okay then. Yes – I'll give it a try.'

chapter twenty-two

Five weeks after Roberta started work, Michael had Jenkins go to the gallery to get her to countersign fake invoices to cover some clients' money going through the books. He'd deliberately kept the amount low but, as anticipated, she panicked and said no.

Michael went to the gallery an hour later.

'Roberta, Jenkins tells me you have a problem with the paperwork. Can we have a quiet word?'

'It's not a problem with paperwork, Michael. He wants me to lie on a tax return. Say I've sold paintings I've not even seen. I can't do that, Michael, that's not what I agreed to.'

'Yes, it is, Roberta. I was very clear when I explained the job to you, that we would be accounting for additional revenue. You do remember us having that conversation, don't you?'

'Yes, I do, but I didn't realise you needed me to get this involved. You never explained that to me, Michael. Can't someone else sign the invoices?'

'It has to be you, Roberta. You are the gallery manager; it would be expected you would be the person to sign. But don't worry, all the paperwork ties together, that's what Jenkins is good at. If it makes you feel any better, I can tell you they were sales done directly with the purchasers away from the gallery. That's why you didn't see them.'

'I don't want to, Michael.'

'Then the gallery closes until we find another manager. I'm sorry, Roberta, but that's the harsh reality. Is that what you want? To tell your parents you were fired after a month? Lose all the contacts you made with Scottish Arts? Disappoint me? It's no problem, Roberta, I wouldn't ask you to do anything risky. Could you possibly imagine I'd ask that of you, of all people?'

'Are you sure I won't get into trouble?'

'Trust me, Roberta. Jenkins has given me the invoices. Just sign here.'

She signed.

'There you are, Michael,' she said, handing them to him. 'But I'm really, really not happy about this.'

'I can tell. I'm sorry if it's upset you, Roberta. I should have made it clearer when I explained the job to you. But I'll make it up to you this weekend. Have you ever been deer-stalking?'

'What? No, of course not.'

'Then let's go away for the weekend. I want you to put this unpleasant moment behind us. Let's have a very nice weekend, another experience for you to enjoy. It's the least I can do to make it up to you.'

'I'm not sure I'll be good company at the moment. I'm still in shock about these invoices.'

'Next weekend then. Look, close the gallery for the day, let's do something more low key. Take the dogs for a walk, go for a meal afterwards. What do you say?'

Michael made sure he was especially attentive to her for the rest of the week and took her off to his favourite place in the world, Glensporret House. A traditional Victorian shooting lodge, it was the perfect combination of Highland remoteness and pampered luxury, a sea of tartan and tweed jackets, festooned with stags' heads.

'It's *Brigadoon* come to life,' Roberta said when she saw it.

He took her stalking the next day. They shot a stag together, and the intense thrill of the kill created a new type of intimacy between them. When they came back to their room, the atmosphere was ripe with expectancy.

Roberta took a sip of wine to steady her nerves. 'Michael,' she said, 'if we're to continue seeing each other, I need to know what you do for a living. Really *do*, I mean.'

'I was wondering why it took you so long.' Michael smiled to reassure her, but felt strangely nervous, like a penitent beginning confession. 'The first thing you need to know is I'm not a criminal,' he began. 'I don't rob anyone; I don't harm anyone. All I do is provide financial services to some people who, for whatever reason, have activities that operate outside of the normal banking systems.'

He could see she was willing herself to accept what he was telling her. 'I don't understand,' she said. 'What sort of services?'

'I take someone's money, money that perhaps they've made a little ... creatively, shall we say, and make it disappear for a while. And when it comes back, it is nice and respectable. Stocks and bonds, Treasury bills, certificates of deposit and the like, which my clients are free to spend as they like.'

She frowned, but didn't look shocked. 'But that's money laundering, isn't it? It's against the law.'

Michael shrugged. 'Technically it might be, I suppose. But whatever my clients do to make their money is no concern of mine. And it would carry on if I wasn't there. I provide a service. I don't get mixed up in any unpleasant business.'

'I'm sorry, Michael, that sounds too smooth. How does this make you any less of a criminal than the thugs who do the dirty work to get the money?'

He leant forward and looked her in the eye. This was the moment to convince her. 'I think you're missing the point. All I do is run a financial process that I sell to clients. Just like any other service business does. Is that so bad?'

She gulped down a glass of wine. He topped it up.

'But it's illegal,' she persisted. 'If you get caught, you go to jail. And so do the people around you. Me, for example.'

'Let me tell you a few of life's realities,' Michael replied. 'They passed a law in America a few years ago. The Bank Secrecy Act, making banks responsible for reporting large cash transactions, for keeping records to show the authorities. Do you know what law we have like that here? No? Because we have nothing like that.' He was in full flow now. If he kept talking, he might even convince himself it was all completely justified, morally and ethically. 'You can walk into a bank with a suitcase full of cash, and they'll be delighted to have your business, no questions asked. And you know why? It's the establishment protecting itself. Politicians and coppers getting kickbacks. Businessmen not paying their taxes.

Everyone's at it, Roberta, I'm just better at it than most people.'

She was quiet for a moment, picking at the room-service meal. 'But if it's that easy, that commonplace, why doesn't everyone else do it?' she eventually said. 'How can you afford all this, doing something that simple?'

'Because it's only simple when it's small. Take the suitcase of cash I mentioned. That only works when it's not very often, or not very much. So, yes, a petty criminal can pay his ill-gotten gains into a secret bank account and hope he'll get away with it. But when the police come looking, he'll stand out like a sore thumb.'

'How do you do it?'

He told her about the smurfs and how he was setting up other businesses to make the operation bigger and better in future. He didn't tell her about Mallards, not yet. Michael was trusting her with a lot of information; he'd take his time before revealing everything.

'And that's what the money was, the invoices I signed?'

'Yes, it was. But it's not something you ever need to worry about. As far as the outside world is concerned, you bring experience and glamour to Scotland's top independent art gallery. You'll never see or be involved in any other aspect of my business.'

'Will you let me get out of this, Michael, as you promised? When I make it as an actress, I can quit as your … money launderer? Or even if I don't, I can still get out?'

'Of course. As we discussed before, our objectives at this moment are happily coinciding. The day you want to stop, when you don't need any more help in becoming an actress, when you feel you want to go it alone in the world, then you can go.'

It was a strange experience, for the first time describing and having to justify what his life entailed. But Michael guessed that after the initial shock, Roberta would understand.

A fortnight later, Michael offered her a chance to move from her grotty Maryhill flat into the one with the surveillance room attached, which he'd had specially refurbished to make it into a high-class city pad. He knew he'd got her just where he wanted her. A gilded cage, somewhere she could go when he didn't want her around, somewhere he could keep an eye on her if needs be.

Roberta had solved one organisational problem – how to securely start up the Avalon Gallery – but there was another one coming to a head. Ron had not been happy with the Turnberry deal. And he was even less happy about being told that he wouldn't be Michael's right-hand man going forward.

'We've built this together, Michael. We're partners. Okay, you might be the brains of the operation, but you couldn't have done this without me. It should be me running the new operation, not Eddie.'

'He's got the contacts all over the country; you haven't. It's nothing personal, it's just the most efficient business model. In six months, I'll be moving to the Mallards head office in Surrey; I can't have you run one operation in Glasgow and Eddie run another in the rest of the country. It doesn't make good business sense.'

'What makes sense is working with who you know. I've proved I can run the smurfs in Glasgow. I could run them everywhere else as well.'

'The smurfs are the past, Ron. Soon all the money will be moving through the Avalon companies.'

Ron's stony expression showed he didn't agree.

★ ★ ★

Finally, Michael was ready to start putting clients' money through the Mallards Glasgow store. He had been waiting for this moment for so long, it didn't feel real when it began to happen. No hassles, no security problems – and no need to have any smurfs involved. Even Ron would see it was better.

It was time to bundle the smurfs up with a bow and hand them over to Ivan. Michael booked a hotel suite for the meeting. There was a lot to get through, and he wanted no chance that their conversation could be overheard. Ivan brought along Dougie Stevenson, who was going to take over from Ron. A dour, characterless individual with the imagination of a clockwork toy. Dim Dougie. Once things started to unravel, he wouldn't have a clue how to deal with the situation.

Michael handed Ivan the dossier with all the smurf contact details, a detailed document outlining how the transit process worked, and a list of dos and don'ts on setting up bank accounts. A complete manual on how to run a money-laundering operation, his life's work. And the client list – the ones he didn't care that Ivan knew about. Ron had already told the rest that he would be making changes to streamline the operation, and to be even more discreet than usual. All the problem customers, the ones who were more hassle than they were worth – those were the ones that Ivan would be getting.

For all Ivan's bluster, Michael could see he lacked the business sense of Dick and Eddie. The trappings of the handover, all the neatly typed and bound documents, the draft ledger accounts waiting to be filled in once he took over the operation – they all seriously impressed him. Detailed paperwork and codified process documents were not part of the typical armed robbery.

'Way to go, Mikey, my lad,' he said, flicking through the documents. 'Very fucking professional. We're dealing wi' top drawer lads here, Dougie. See? More money to be made doing this in a week than all the post office stick-ups we could do in a month. Cracking wee job, you've done, Mikey. I cannae wait to get started. Doug, you go meet all they smurfs and introduce yourself as their new boss.' He laughed. 'Smurfs … What sort of doss cunt name is that? I'm no' being a called a smurfmaster, that's the first thing I'll change. So, Mikey, what's new for you now? What could be better than making all this money for nothing?'

'I've tried your life, Ivan, and it's not for me. I'm going straight, getting into a retail operation. All completely legit and above board. But you'll understand if I don't want to give you more details.'

'I could take offence at that, but I'll let it pass. Shows what a good mood I'm in. One final wee detail. I've got a bean counter to run the numbers side of things. He's no' invited to this meeting, doesn't like the limelight. He'll need to meet with your guy to sort all that stuff out.'

'I'll answer all his questions. I set up the operation, so I know all the details. All part of the service, Ivan.'

Ivan started cracking his knuckles and then moved forward, his face an inch from Michael's.

'My guy meets your guy.'

Michael had wanted to keep Jenkins away from the handover in case he panicked and told Ivan's accountant all about the Mallards operation. He laughed, trying to sound unconcerned. 'Believe me, Ivan, having to spend a few tedious hours with your accountant is not something I'm looking forward to. But I need my guy to do the books for my new business venture. He's easily swayed, and I wouldn't want you to turn on the charm offensive to get him to jump ship. Do me this one favour, will you please? Once your accountant says he's comfortable with the detail, let me and my team go off and do our own thing.'

Ivan's nostrils were flaring now, his face reddening as he tried to keep his temper under control. It took a good twenty seconds before he was able to speak again. 'You don't need to worry, Mikey,' he said, baring his teeth. 'I promised I'd leave you alone and I'm a man of my word. And I'm happy to let you sail off into the sunset wi' your new life. Just want to make sure my boys know all the clever stuff you've been doing. If my guy tells me you've given him all the answers, I'll let you off wi' your cheek.'

Michael left the meeting and breathed a sigh of relief. He reckoned it would be a couple of months at most before the operation self-destructed; then, he might have an Ivan to deal with who really had lost his temper.

In the meantime, he had Roberta. It was the first time since Charlotte that he was seeing a woman on a regular basis, and he was enjoying himself. He was keeping a close eye on her, making sure she wasn't having second thoughts about the world she'd become part of. But he needn't have worried. Apart from her friend Duncan, there was no one else she spent any time with.

Occasionally, he would slip into the surveillance room to check what she was up to when he wasn't around, listening on the headphones to her phone conversations or just watching as she moved about her flat, blissfully unaware of his presence. He couldn't work out why he enjoyed the voyeuristic thrill so much until it dawned on him. He had his cage of finches at home. He could admire them for hours, relishing their beauty, taking care of them. Now he had his own human finch. The ultimate little plaything.

Ron seemed to be finally accepting his new role in the organisation, and the hassles and stresses of the smurfs became a distant memory as Michael and Eddie set up the national operation. After Christmas, Michael promised himself, he'd move to Surrey and the full potential of the business would become a reality.

It was going to be a great new year.

1976

chapter twenty-three

Michael threw down the newspaper in disgust. Detective Sergeant Grant had been suspended from the force after being arrested for drink-driving. He could not believe Grant's stupidity, throwing away his career by an act of such recklessness. And it could not have come at a worse time. With the smurf operation unravelling, Ivan was out for blood. Michael's growing involvement with two of Britain's top criminals left him feeling exposed. He needed someone on the inside.

It was Eddie who suggested Detective Chief Inspector McDonald, known in the criminal fraternity as 'The Gardener' due to his habit of planting evidence on suspects he was investigating. His infamy had spread south of the border.

'Why him?' Michael asked. 'If he hates criminals so much he plants evidence, why on earth would he agree to go on our payroll?'

'Because he's the biggest hypocrite in the whole Scottish police force, and lazy to boot. He plants evidence to make it easy to get convictions once he's decided who the guilty party is. And then he basks in the glory from the press. Any top-level criminal knows he'll take a bribe to get charges against them dropped on a technicality, but he doesn't get involved in any street operation. He portrays himself as a family man to the press, a pillar of society, but he likes a bit of crumpet sent along to a hotel room when he gets someone off the hook. Crooked as hell, but likes to pretend he takes the moral high ground. You two are a match made in heaven.'

Michael didn't rise to it. 'So, if this guy is as high-powered as you say he is, I need to be careful about approaching him. He sounds like a dangerous man to come to the attention of.'

'You could say that.'

Michael contacted his previous informer, now plain Mr Grant and looking at a bleak future as a security manager at a Govan shipyard. The chance of one final payout, Michael told him. Five grand to approach DCI McDonald to be an informant, another five if McDonald said yes. Michael's name to be kept secret – only once they were sure McDonald was on board would he reveal himself.

To the surprise of both, the approach was rebuffed. Michael was sure that Grant must have screwed up the approach, but Grant insisted otherwise. 'McDonald is as bent a copper as they come,' Grant told Michael when they met. 'Trust me, I know. We've both been on the receiving end of the same payoffs over the years, that's how I knew I could even have the conversation. I couldn't believe it when he said no. Maybe he's getting scared someone's breathing down his neck, I don't know. But he's adamant. No means no.'

'And you said nothing that could identify me? Think carefully. There's a nasty smell about this.'

'Definitely not. I described you as a white-collar criminal, looking for information, no heavy stuff. Just like you told me. There's no way he should have said no – you're just the sort of operation he'd feel comfortable with. Give me another name and I'll try again. I need that five grand.'

Michael went through some other names with Eddie. None had McDonald's level of connections.

'We need to get something on him,' Michael said. 'Something to make him change his mind. Leave it with me, I'll think of something.'

The obvious answer was to set McDonald up using the surveillance room, but that would have meant getting Roberta to move out for a few weeks while he organised the sting with a hooker. It would raise Roberta's suspicions, and in any case McDonald sounded like a savvier operator than Grant. There was a chance he would spot a honeytrap.

Michael toyed with the idea of getting Roberta to move out in any case. If it weren't for her usefulness in running the art gallery, Michael would have finished with the relationship by now. He had begun an affair with a woman who had started to come to openings at the gallery, an up-and-coming painter named Judy Allen. She was everything that Roberta was not: strong-willed, uncompromising, obdurate. Michael hinted at hanging one of her paintings in the gallery to get her to go to bed with him, an offer she emphatically rejected. Then two weeks later she took the initiative to have sex, but only because she said she found him interesting. She was her own woman, a worthy equal. He liked that. Roberta was now a business asset, nothing more.

Michael had taken Judy to see *Emmanuelle* – the prelude to a night of passion. As he watched, he began to conceive the perfect sting for McDonald. In the film, Emmanuelle's prospective lover decides to enjoy watching her having sex with other men, and arranges a boxing contest between two candidates to determine who would bed her. It gave Michael an idea. If he could get Roberta to seduce McDonald in the flat, there would be no need for her to move out, no need to pay a hooker and no chance that McDonald would suspect he was being played by a professional.

That just left getting Roberta to agree. He called her up and arranged to take her to see *Emmanuelle*, and afterwards he casually mentioned the scene in the movie.

'Remember where Mario talked the Thai boxers into fighting each other for the right to have sex with Emmanuelle while he watched? I'd like you to let me do that.'

Roberta laughed. 'Michael, stop it.' Then she looked at him sideways. 'Do what, exactly?'

'Watch you screwing another guy.'

Roberta clearly found it amusing. 'Oh yeah? Let me think … There are a couple of cute guys on your staff who I wouldn't say no to. Just as long as I don't get crushed under Big Jockie.'

'I'm being serious. No one we know. Definitely no one who works for me. They'd see it as a weakness, not an adventure. It would have to be a stranger.'

'So, you're pimping me out now, Michael?' She was teasing him.

Michael decided to show he was perfectly serious. 'No, I want a performance. And it wouldn't just be

264

for me. You're an actress. This would be the ultimate challenge. I would choose someone who's a complete nobody, someone who would never be in your league, and watch you seduce him.' He paused for a second, as if a thought had just struck him. 'No, even better. I won't watch. I'll keep away, but you have to tell me every little detail afterwards. Then you and I go to bed, so that I can wipe his memory from your mind.'

'Wha—' Roberta was wide-eyed. 'No. Michael, no. You've taken me to some dark places recently, but I only go there with you. I'm not a whore. I'm not going to screw anyone you want.'

Time to back off.

'You're quite right, Roberta,' Michael said. 'There are some things you shouldn't do if they make you feel uncomfortable. Let's keep it as our fantasy, okay?'

'Your fantasy.'

Michael kept a low profile for a week. Then Roberta called him to see if he was okay. A few days later, a second call; she was worried, hurt that he was ignoring her. Then she called a third time, pleading with him to get in touch.

Finally, without explanation, he called Roberta and asked her to come round. They had sex when she arrived: cold, mechanical, Michael making it obvious he was going through the motions. When they finished, Roberta turned away from him, her head buried in the pillow. Michael heard her muffled sobs.

'Glad you could make it at such short notice,' he said to her, standing up to get dressed. 'I have gallery business to discuss with you and thought it best to do so face to

265

face. I hear congratulations are in order; that you've finally sold a painting.'

Roberta rubbed her eyes and looked at him, shocked at the coolness in his voice.

'I'm sorry, boss, it won't happen again,' she said, making a weary attempt at humour.

Michael remained impassive.

'That's a joke, Michael,' she said. She was struggling to hold back the tears. 'And it was no easy feat to sell a major painting like that. I hope you're proud of me.'

'Of course I am. The more we sell the better.' Michael gave her a patronising smile.

He walked towards the bedroom door. 'The painting we're going to replace it with is in the bird room. Come on, put your clothes on and we'll have a look.'

Roberta leapt up. 'But, Michael, you said I could choose any new paintings. Or at least have a say. There's a Sotheby's auction in Edinburgh next week. I was hoping to go.'

'Hush, hush, I'm sure you'll like what I've chosen.'

Michael showed her the Judy Allen painting leaning against the wall; a series of gestural brushstrokes in bold colours at right-angles to each other.

'Are you sure, Michael?' Roberta peered at the signature. 'Who's Judy Allen? I've never heard of her.'

'A future star in the Scottish art firmament. Still in her twenties but very talented. And she's so grateful for a chance to be shown in your gallery.'

'You know her? You've never mentioned her before.'

Michael turned to the birdcage, his sudden move provoking a medley of song. 'Will you listen to that,

Roberta? My little Society finches with their beautiful song. My favourite finch at the moment. Lovely, isn't it?'

Roberta seemed to consciously straighten up. 'If it's your choice, Michael, of course I'm happy to show it. Is that enough business for tonight?'

'Yes. Thanks for indulging me. I'll call John to take you home.'

Roberta looked shocked; she always spent the night.

'I'm sorry, Roberta.' He had already turned his back. 'I've got a lot on my plate at the moment, I need to catch up on my sleep. You don't mind heading home, do you?'

When he closed the door after her, Michael felt disgusted with himself. His behaviour had been brutal, degrading, and he had hated having to go through with it. He told himself she was just as manipulative as he was, having no qualms about using him to further her acting career. But he knew that wasn't true. He had hurt her, so that she would agree to anything to get their relationship back on track. And that 'anything' was going to be to play her part in his DCI McDonald *Emmanuelle* fantasy.

When he raised the idea with her again a few days later, his behaviour could not have been more different. An evening spent cooking for her, just like old times. Attentive, caring, like nothing had happened. And then the proposition whispered to her again as they lay in the afterglow of their lovemaking.

This time she said yes.

Michael told Ron his plan and was suitably gratified to see the look of astonishment on his face.

'And I'll be taking the pictures, in case you're wondering,' Michael said, smiling grimly.

That left arranging the meeting. It turned out to be easy. McDonald always drank at the same bar when off duty, so Roberta just had to be there, primed and ready to pounce. Ron got the job of driving her to the bar, keeping up the pretence they were heading somewhere random to pick up an unsuspecting stranger. Michael set up the spying room looking into the bedroom to get the incriminating evidence – tape recorder primed, camera on a tripod, pointing at the two-way mirror. The detritus from the previous session with DS Grant and the hooker was still lying around the room, but Michael left it untouched. He liked that it gave the room a sordid air.

Roberta arrived with McDonald and wasted little time in getting him into bed. When she was in full flow, he felt not a pang of jealousy or resentment while taking the photos, recording the sounds – even allowing himself the occasional smile of recognition at some of Roberta's moves. Within ten minutes he had all that he needed and left. It would be a long time before he would feel like sleeping with Roberta again.

Ron was given the job of confronting McDonald with the tape and photos. Michael waited at home for news of how it went.

'Perfect,' said Ron when he arrived. 'The guy was poleaxed by the photos.' He grinned. 'Pity I never got to see the action.' Michael ignored the comment. 'I gave him twenty-four hours to think about it, but I think we've got him in the bag. Mr Pillar of Society is never going to risk this coming out.'

Now all Michael had left to deal with was Ivan. He'd agreed to a face-to-face meeting to deal with Ivan's suspicions he'd been conned. It wouldn't be an easy encounter, but Michael had to at least try to get him to accept the situation. With the new operation invisible, Ivan would have no way to retaliate, but it wouldn't do any harm if he came to that conclusion sooner rather than later.

He came to Michael's house and they sat down in his study. Ivan had a glint in his eye, and it wasn't a playful one.

'I want the real money-laundering business, Michael,' he said. 'The set-up you punted over to me is a crock of shit, and you know it. There's fuck-all money coming from your clients. I want your new operation, whatever it is. And a wee sweetener on top for trying to make me look ridiculous.'

Michael sighed. 'Ivan, if that's all you've come to talk about, we're wasting your time and mine. The business was in great shape when you took it over. If you've driven it into the ground, that's your problem, not mine. Tell me that's not all you've come to say.'

'Maybe these will change your mind.' Ivan threw the pictures of Roberta and DCI McDonald onto his desk.

Michael couldn't hide his shock. 'How did you get these?' he asked. But the answer was already obvious.

'From McDonald. Came to see me straight after your pathetic attempt at blackmail. He knew I'd look after him, like I've been doing for years. I scratch his back, he scratches mine. How do you think I've managed to stay out of trouble all these years? But his faith in me was touching, if a wee bit misplaced. I had a flash of inspiration that even you'd be proud of. He's lying on his back in his car down some county lane at the moment, a bullet through his brain. And if you don't pay up, these photographs will be on their way to the cops to incriminate you. Photos of McDonald and that whore of yours, fucking away in a flat you own. All pointing to your involvement. So if you don't want to attract any undue attention for McDonald's death, you'll tell me everything. I start running your operation, and I start now.'

The colour drained from Michael's face. He could never have foreseen this. It was lunacy for Ivan to make such a move, to ruthlessly eliminate a key asset of his and take such a huge risk just to bring him down. But Ivan *was* a lunatic. Michael had underestimated him and he would have to deal with that mistake.

He kept his composure as his mind swirled with what action he could take, how he could respond. He used all of his self-control to make sure Ivan could not see how much he was rattled.

'Big play, Ivan, I've got to hand it to you. How long do I have to think about it?'

'Oh, I'm a reasonable man. The banks open at nine thirty tomorrow morning. I want fifty grand paid into my account as your way of saying sorry, and we meet the same day for me to get the gen on the new way you're doing business. You follow?'

Michael said nothing. He got up and gestured to the door. He needed to think. He needed to act.

Ivan couldn't help but crow about his victory. 'And a cracking place you have here, I might add. All these paintings and that war memorabilia. You're not short of a bob or two, Michael, so I don't want any bullshit in the morning about how difficult it is to get the cash.'

As they walked down the stairs to the hallway, Michael saw Lucifer and Satan watching from the door into the living room.

'Bark!' he yelled, and the two dogs did as they'd been trained to do: they leapt forward and set themselves between Ivan and the door, snarling and growling. Ivan turned towards them and started to pull a gun out from under his jacket.

It only took Michael a few seconds to act. Beside the swords and antique muskets hanging on the wall next to him was a Colt Derringer, and that one was different. Michael kept it loaded and primed.

He pulled it off the wall and in one motion turned to face Ivan. Ivan had been pointing his gun at the dogs, and as he turned around Michael fired. The bullet ripped into Ivan's shoulder, causing him to drop the gun. Michael's move had been instinctive, a desperate attempt at survival; he'd had no time to think about what he was doing. As he saw the blood seep through Ivan's jacket, he stared in horror at what he'd just done.

The dogs disappeared up the stairs, startled by the gunshot. Ivan fell to his knees, then reached out to pick up his gun, but his actions were slowed by shock and pain. Michael snapped himself out of his daze and fired again, more carefully this time, into Ivan's body. Ivan slumped back, summoning all of his remaining strength to pick his gun off the floor. The effort proved too much for him; his body bowed, flecks of blood appearing in a froth around his mouth. He let out a half-groan, half-roar as he looked at Michael, his eyes channelling a hatred, a frustration that he could do no more. Michael fired again, more coolly this time, aiming for the heart. Blood flowed freely from his chest and onto the marble tiles, and as Michael stood over him. Ivan's face turned grey and his eyes became a death stare.

Michael ran into the bathroom and grabbed some towels to slow the flow of blood across the hallway floor. His stomach heaved when he looked at Ivan's gaping mouth and glassy eyes. He piled more towels and sheets around the body, then called Ron and Big Jockie, telling them to get round straight away.

As he waited, he had a chance to contemplate what he had just done. Murder. Ivan was evil and would have probably killed Michael once he'd bled him dry financially, but that didn't make it right. He'd become what he promised himself he would never be. Not a smart businessman, playing by his own set of rules. A cold-blooded killer.

He sat on the bottom tread of the staircase, staring at Ivan's lifeless body. He kept telling himself he should be pleased, that he'd finally rid himself of a dangerous psychopath who would one day have brought about his demise. But he couldn't feel any elation. He went over and laid the corpse out, giving it some dignity as it lay on the floor. Then he went back and sat on the stair again, never taking his eyes off the body. He pressed his fingers into his temples and waited.

Disposing of a body was uncharted territory for Michael and for once he let others take control. Ron found the keys to Ivan's car and they bundled the body into the boot. Ron's advice was for Michael to stay at the house and keep the door bolted. Ivan had come alone to the meeting – he obviously wanted no one, not even his own men, to know that he had killed a cop. Michael's image of being the brains, not the brawn, of the operation, had lulled him into a false sense of security. His best chance of remaining undetected was to act as if the meeting with Ivan had never taken place.

Ron drove off in Ivan's car to dispose of the body, Big Jockie following. Michael got rid of all traces of blood from the floor, bundled the blood-soaked towels and sheets into bin bags and took the bags down to the basement. He'd dispose of them in the morning. The photos, he threw on the fire.

As he lay in bed that night, he pondered the magnitude of what he had done. Getting into this world had been easy, and he'd always fought Ivan with brains, not brawn. He had rid himself of the need to resort to brutality to control the smurfs, and now he had an operation that had run without any recourse to violence. Until that afternoon. Now he was a murderer, and there was a dead cop that would need to be explained away at some point.

For the first time ever, he regretted his decision to become a criminal. But it was too late now; he needed to stay focused on getting out of this mess. Michael tossed and turned fitfully all night. His world had changed forever.

chapter twenty-four

Ivan was buried in lonely moorland, his car turned into a cube of metal by a cooperative scrap-metal dealer, the murder weapon thrown in the Clyde. His disappearance sparked off a rumour that he had fled Glasgow after being involved in a cop killing, as the story of DCI McDonald's shooting dominated the news. A careful word from Ron here and there, and soon every criminal with an opinion was putting the word about that McDonald had been in Ivan's pay, they'd had a bust-up, Ivan had killed him in a typically hot-headed rage, and he'd had to leave Glasgow as a result. Nobody mourned his departure.

The heat from the police investigation into McDonald's killing meant that crime proceeds dried up to almost nothing; nobody was risking a job with this white-hot intensity of police activity going on. But it was a small price to pay. With Ivan gone, the few remaining smurfs disappeared into the shadows. Nobody suspected Michael had anything to do with Ivan's disappearance. Things had played out beautifully.

Except for Roberta. As Michael anticipated, she saw the photos of McDonald in the papers and was on the phone straight away.

'Michael, it's me,' she said, her voice quavering. 'Have you seen the newspapers today?'

'Of course,' Michael replied. 'The first Concorde flight to New York. Wonderful, isn't it?'

'That's not what I mean. DCI McDonald, the detective they found dead. That's what I'm calling about.'

There would be a limit as to how much she would believe that he wasn't involved. Michael decided to see what he could get away with, so he'd know the level of danger that Roberta's suspicions would represent.

'What a strange thing to call me about, Roberta,' he said. 'Yes, I saw that as well. A few of my clients won't shed any tears, I'm afraid. He'd been rather successful over the years at putting more than a few undesirables behind bars. I hope they find out what's happened. He might not have been good for business, but it's always a sad moment when someone dies before their time. But why are you calling me about it?'

'Because he's the guy Ron chose for me to sleep with as part of your sex game. And now he's dead. What's going on, Michael?'

Michael concentrated all his efforts on trying to sound surprised. 'Good Lord! Are you sure? I told Ron to take you off the beaten track. How did you manage to end up with him?'

'Because Ron chose him for me. Please, Michael. No games. What's going on?'

'I can assure you this is a complete shock. You're not suggesting I had anything to do with his death, are you Roberta? You know I hate any sort of violence. I could never do anything as dreadful as that.'

'Michael, please. This is too much of a coincidence. Tell me what's going on.'

'Look, Roberta. I don't know McDonald. I've heard of him, but that's because of his reputation for bringing down Glasgow hard men. That's what he did. Went after razor-wielding thugs, murderers. It's a dangerous line of work. But that's not my business, and you know that.'

She didn't sound convinced. 'But I met him three days ago and now he's dead,' she insisted. 'That's too much of a coincidence.'

'Look, we shouldn't talk about this over the phone. I'll talk to Ron and see if he has any clue as to who the guy was he picked for you, see if that sheds any light on this. But don't do anything rash, Roberta. If you think you can help the police, then by all means talk to them.' He paused for a second, waiting for a response. 'But think about the shame for your family, the scandal affecting your acting career. Being under suspicion for a crime you didn't commit, all because of a dreadful coincidence. Let me look into it and get back to you.'

The call had gone as well as he could have hoped for. There was a chance, just a chance, that she would not go to the police. The longer she waited, the less likely it would be that she would break her silence, the less a threat she would represent.

Ron did not agree.

'You've got blood on your hands,' he said. 'She's the one person who can link you and me to DCI McDonald. She's got to go.'

Michael shook his head. 'I've never seen anyone easier to control. Jangle jewels and the high life in front of her, indulge her in her fantasy that one day she's going to be a Hollywood actress, and she's putty. Believe me, Ron, I can control her. When she found out about McDonald she called *me*, not the police, just as I knew she would. She'll stay in line.'

'You should have discussed it with me first,' Ron replied. 'I'm in this up to my neck. You're playing with my freedom as well. You might think you've got her twisted around your little finger, but I'm not going to take the chance. Let's call in Big Jockie.'

'That's even more of a risk, Ron. People have seen us together. If anything happened to her, I would be questioned and I don't want our business put under the microscope. She's rattled alright, but I can control her.'

Michael had someone glance in the door at Avalon Gallery the next morning. Roberta was there, he was told, looking tense but otherwise okay. She's seen sense, he thought.

He called her that evening and was frustrated there was no reply. He tried again later and made a final call at eleven. Wherever she'd been, she should be home by now. Michael headed over to the flat, taking his own key just in case. He knocked at her door. Knocked again, then again. Then he let himself in.

The flat was empty. All her possessions gone, just a few odds and sods left behind that she probably didn't have the time or space to pack. Michael glanced at the mirror in the bedroom; it had a crack running across it. He went over to investigate. The crack spread out from one of the screws securing it to the wall. The mirror had been removed and then the screw over-tightened when it was put back. Roberta had found the spy room, panicked and fled.

Michael called Ron from a phone box and headed back home. When they met, Michael was on the defensive. Ron proposed a wave of terror against everyone who knew her.

'Someone must know where she is,' he said, 'and when we find her, no kid gloves this time.'

'I'm not so sure,' Michael said. 'I don't know whether to be worried or pleased by this. If she's disappeared by herself, she's done our work for us, as long as she stays invisible. If we start beating people up to find her it makes it doubly likely that we could tip her over into going to the cops. Oh, I'd like to find her, don't get me wrong. But let's see how good a job she's done of disappearing. We'll track her down carefully, not all guns blazing. Okay?'

Ron was having none of it. 'I think all the time you've spent in the sack with her has addled your brain,' he replied. 'You killed somebody, that somebody killed a cop, and the only person who can link us to that has disappeared and you want to be all softly softly about catching up with her? You're losing your mind, Michael.'

Michael told him to leave, but Ron refused.

'This has gone too far for you to think you can talk her out of betraying us,' he told Michael. 'I'm going to track her down, with or without your help. Starting with that bloke she's always hanging out with.'

'If you do that, you're finished,' Michael replied. His voice was raised. He realised he was in danger of losing control and tried to calm himself down. 'Okay, Ron, let me promise you this. I'll track down everyone who could know where she's gone, play the part of the worried boyfriend concerned for her whereabouts. If that doesn't work, we'll try things your way. Give me a few days.'

'One day. We talk tomorrow, and if your sob story hasn't turned up anything, then I go in hard. And be grateful I'm even giving you that.'

Michael decided not to argue. Every hour Roberta was on her own, she could end up convincing herself to go to the police. He knew Ron was right; she'd made things worse by running away. And it wasn't just Roberta he had to worry about. Every minute he kept Dick and Eddie in the dark would make it worse for him when they found out. They'd have even fewer scruples than Ron.

He hired a private investigator to track her down as a matter of urgency. The detective made a breakthrough straight away.

'Looks like she's moving to Edinburgh,' he told Michael the next day. 'I called three property solicitors this morning, and a Bobbie Sinclair has asked them to send her particulars of one-bedroom flats to rent in the city. Couldn't get the address she wanted them sent to, but I'm working on it. She might be at her parents; I'll try there. But if she's not, the minute she surfaces and starts looking at properties, I'll have her tracked down. Should have results soon.'

Then there was another development. The detective had told Michael to keep the gallery open, just in case it acted as a magnet for a lead, and that paid off too. Michael had asked his secretary, Mildred, to wait there, and she called early afternoon. 'Mr Mitchell, there's a young man called Duncan here, asking for you. Says he wants to track down someone he calls Bobbie. He must mean Roberta. What do you want me to do?'

'I'll come straight over. Tell him not to leave.'

Duncan. Roberta's friend, Michael thought. The detective was trying to track him down, and instead he'd turned up asking to see him. Something was not right.

Michael arrived at the gallery and Mildred nodded to a denim-clad hippy sitting on a chair in the waiting room, casually flicking through a music magazine. Michael walked over to him.

'You must be Duncan,' he said, flashing a cheery smile. 'Roberta's told me all about you. Pleased to meet you. I'm Michael Mitchell.'

Duncan stuffed his copy of *Sounds* into a denim knapsack and shook Michael's hand. 'And I've heard all about you. But you call Bobbie Roberta? She didn't tell me that.'

Michael smiled again. If this Duncan was in on Roberta's escape, he was hiding it well. 'She's a lady of many parts,' he said. 'Anyway, Duncan, what can I do for you?'

'Well, it's all very odd. She phoned last night to say she was heading off to London and would be gone for a while.' He looked sheepish. 'I was a bit stoned, and she didn't get much out of me. I think she said it would be a while before she was back in touch. When I woke this morning, I wasn't sure if I'd remembered correctly. When I phoned her, there was no reply. I went around to her flat, and when I looked through the letter box, it looked like she'd moved out. I'm worried about her, it all seems very sudden. Then I thought of you. Do you know where she might be?'

Michael scrutinised his face. Duncan's concern seemed genuine enough.

'No, I'd no idea she was gone. I only spoke to her yesterday and she didn't say anything about leaving, certainly not for England. Are you sure she said London, not Edinburgh? She's often said she thought that would be a good place to live as an actress, what with the Fringe and the Festival and everything.'

Duncan shrugged. 'No, I'm sure she said London. Something about an audition.'

'She's got her movie coming up. She wouldn't just suddenly move to London on the off-chance of getting a part in a play.'

He was getting suspicious now. Duncan telling him this all seemed too convenient, a smokescreen to cover her tracks.

'I'm worried about her, Duncan,' he confided. 'She can be impetuous sometimes, as I'm sure you know. If you find out anything, get in touch. I'll have someone go down to London to see if he can find her and check she's all right. And let's keep this between ourselves. If she needs help, it would be better if one of us turns up to see her without her knowing about it. If she's run away once, she could do it again.'

Duncan took Michael's business card and gave him his phone number to get in touch. When he left, Michael stared after him. No way would she leave without telling her best friend what was going on. Duncan knew.

The detective called again in the early evening. He had been busy, had managed to find an excuse to visit Roberta's parents to enquire about her whereabouts. He was told the London story also. Off to star in a West-End play, her excited parents told him.

'She's gone to London,' Michael told Ron that evening. 'Laid a smokescreen for me that she was looking at flats in Edinburgh, but she's invented some cock-and-bull story for her parents that she's landed a West-End acting role at short notice. They seem to believe her. This guy Duncan, her best friend, has been in touch and he told me about London before I found out from the parents. I'm guessing he doesn't yet know exactly where she is, or what the reason is, otherwise there would be no way he'd volunteer to get in touch. So, if she's gone to London, she means to stay disappeared. The longer she stays disappeared, the deeper she's in this with us, and the less a threat she becomes.'

'I don't like it. If you can't track her down in London, we need to try a little rough stuff with this Duncan guy. Nothing too severe if he's as much of a pussy as you say he is. Trust me: if I say boo to him, he'll freak out and tell us everything he knows.'

'I don't want any more violence, Ron. If I can track her down without that, I've got a chance to persuade her that she's not in any danger from us. And if I can't track her down, she's made the problem go away.' He didn't tell Ron his suspicions that Duncan's story could be one big double-bluff. If he had to put pressure on Duncan eventually, he wanted it to be on his terms.

He could see that Ron was not convinced, and that worried him. Michael would be moving to Surrey to become Mallards new managing director in a few weeks, and he wouldn't be able to keep an eye on Ron from four hundred miles away. He decided to tell Eddie that they'd had a security breach, but that he had everything under control, and he needed Eddie to make sure that Ron didn't step out of line and risk everything by using violence to track Roberta down. Eddie agreed that there was no point in using force if it wasn't necessary, and that Ron needed to be kept an eye on. Michael was relieved. If a hardened criminal like Eddie thought it best not to resort to violence just yet, it told Michael his decision wasn't just sentimental weakness.

He doubled the fee he'd agreed with the private investigator and sent him to London to track Roberta down, told him to find someone else to keep an eye open in Edinburgh, just in case. If these early successes were anything to go by, this would be the way to find her, smart and discreet. Michael was leaving Glasgow to put his past behind him, and the last thing he wanted was more violence and recriminations.

There were a few loose ends, but to get rid of them would create more problems than they would solve. Eddie was not hot-headed. He'd help Ron reach the same conclusion.

chapter twenty-five

It looked like Roberta had disappeared for good. There had been a brief sighting at a jeweller as she tried to sell the necklace Michael had given her, proving she was in London; but other than that, nothing. The trail had gone cold, and there was no sign of her appearing anywhere on the London stage. Michael promised himself he would make one final attempt to find her, and if that didn't work, he'd forget about her.

That's why he was furious when he found out Ron had been back to see Duncan and had told Big Jockie that Michael had agreed to Duncan being roughed up to force him to disclose whatever he knew about her whereabouts. Big Jockie did not do subtle, and the reports were that Duncan was in hospital, nursing a broken jaw and two cracked ribs. That meant that the police could be involved and it increased the risk that if Duncan did know something, he would run scared and tell them. This time, Ron had not just been insubordinate – he had deliberately gone against Michael's wishes, and had lied to Big Jockie about his approval.

'You took an unnecessary risk with this attack,' Michael told Ron. 'It's not your job to make judgements like that.'

'I think you lack the bottle for the hard stuff and that's been clouding your judgement. You should stick to the brains stuff, Michael. Leave the heavy stuff to the professionals.'

He had gone too far. Amongst criminals, cleverness won respect. But only strength and ruthlessness garnered obedience. For that, Michael needed Eddie's help.

Eddie told Michael he was right to be concerned. He said he'd learnt over the years that when a subordinate started to act on their own initiative, it was usually a sign of worse to come. Disobedience led to disloyalty, disloyalty to treachery. Michael had to decide.

'If it were up to me I'd get rid of him,' Eddie told him. 'I've got someone who can step in and run his operation and Ron's on a much bigger pay packet than the other regional bosses. He thinks he's special because the two of you set this up together. It's time to tell him he's not.'

It didn't take Michael long to agree. Eddie gave him the low-down on the guy who would be taking over, someone from Liverpool who had good connections with the Glasgow criminal fraternity. He could start straight away. It would be best to do the handover swiftly and efficiently, they agreed. Tell Ron he was fired face to face, sweeten the message with a goodbye payment if he cooperated. Michael arranged to meet Ron in a couple of days. Soon another part of his past would be behind him.

Michael realised he should let Dick know of the change, so he called him in Spain. As usual, Dick behaved as if he couldn't care less. But when he called Michael back the next day, Michael hardly recognised his voice. Gone was the boozy drawl, the oafish demeanour. His voice was crisp and clear, his words razor sharp. It was like an actor had come backstage and removed his robes. For the first time Michael heard the real Dick talking, not the façade he displayed to hide his keen criminal mind.

'When do you catch the train to meet Ron?'

Straight and to the point.

'I'm taking the sleeper tonight. Seeing Ron in the evening. What's going on?'

'When you meet Ron, you're to be whacked. The driver who's picking you up is going to take a detour. Out to the Barrhead woods again. You'll be keeping Ivan company.'

Michael couldn't believe what he was hearing. 'How do you know this?'

'I learnt over the years to always have an insurance policy. I've never trusted Eddie, and so I've had someone on the inside of his operation from day one, keeping an eye out for anything he might be trying to pull. And the word is that he and Ron have become pretty pally since they started working together. Ron started bad-mouthing you a couple of months ago, saying you were spineless and love-struck over some floozy. I decided I could tolerate a little hot-headed disloyalty to you and let it go. But then the slagging off stopped and the silence was ominous. I had my guy dig deeper. Eddie's convinced Ron that you're surplus to requirements. Now that you've set up an operation that's fully automated and runs like clockwork, he thinks the business doesn't need you anymore. All you do is play at being a businessman in Surrey, the people doing the real work are the people like him. You're an unnecessary overhead, a relic from the past. Eddie's convinced Ron that if he bumps you off and makes it look like retaliation for Ivan, he'll put Ron in charge of the whole UK operation as a reward. Eddie would take over your role in the organisation and I'd go along with all of this for a quiet life.'

'But he's taking a risk that you'd agree to that. You're not going to work with someone who bumps off his partners when he thinks he doesn't need them anymore. Why would he think you'd agree?'

'Because there's a second part to the plan. The minute Ron disposes of you, Eddie has him done next. The story would be that Ron took you out because of all the bad blood between the two of you in recent months and Eddie moved swiftly to deal with him for his treachery. Then him and me have to pick up the pieces of the organisation and find a way of keeping it going, no doubt with Eddie in charge and taking the lion's share of the profits. Eddie's a businessman, Michael. He always tries to eliminate unnecessary overheads. And that includes you.'

Michael could hardly speak. 'And you're sure about this?'

'Definitely. Got to say I'm impressed with Eddie's chutzpah; it's the sort of play I've not seen since the Soho gangland wars in the sixties. But I'm old school. It doesn't matter to me that you might have brought this on your own head. It doesn't even matter that I might stand to do well out of the changes. You never betray your partners. If Eddie does for you and I let him, I can't complain if one day he does the same to me. I'm saving your skin, Michael. Not because you deserve it, but because it's the way I do things.'

Michael was shaken. But it made sense. Ron had been too easily cowed by the punishment over the Duncan beating. This was his revenge.

'Is there any chance at all your man could have got it wrong?'

'None. I like working with people like you – rational, smart, everything thought through. My partners feel the same way. You have to deal with some crazies in this business, that's why I opted for a quiet life in Spain. I'm surprised by Eddie but as I say, I never trust anyone.'

'I have to admit, it's a smart move.' Now it was Michael's turn to coolly and calculatingly appraise the situation. 'I was always a businessman to him; I could tell he felt I didn't have the street savvy that you and Ron have got. Okay, so I shouldn't go to Glasgow. Now what?'

'Oh no, tell Ron you're on that train. We need to act now, before they get suspicious. Los Zetas have a service they can offer to deal with issues like this. Say the word, I can have one of their button men in Glasgow by the time you're due to meet Ron, and one of them in Eddie's manor as well. We do the hit against the two of them simultaneously. There will be a fee, of course. Last time I checked, fifty grand was the going rate for two hits. You say you'll pay it, problem solved.'

Michael needed to be sure. For all he knew, this could be a play by Dick; *he* could be the traitor. He called his driver in Glasgow, the man who chauffeured Ron around when Michael was in Surrey. Michael asked him if he could pass a message on to Ron as he wasn't answering his phone, telling him to call. Michael felt his chest tighten when the driver told him that Ron wasn't in Glasgow, he was down south with Eddie, and wouldn't be back until the middle of next week.

Michael called Dick. 'You wouldn't have had much joy trying to track Ron down in Glasgow,' he said. 'He's holed up with Eddie, waiting for the call I've been taken out, no doubt putting four hundred miles between himself and my murder. That clinches it. Call Los Zetas.'

Dick said to leave everything to him, and that was that. Michael put the phone down and stared into the distance. He thought back to that first meeting with Ron in the bank, when his initial hostility turned into a partnership that had made their fortunes. Then the last dinner with Eddie, talking about the future. Soon they'd be breathing their last. One word to Dick, that's all it had taken. He shivered at the thought.

Killing Ivan in cold blood, abusing Roberta's feelings for him and making her flee for her life, now signing two death warrants. Michael tried to tell himself he hadn't become a monster. He repeated Nietzsche's morality of consequences philosophy like a mantra, but to no avail. His world was toxic, evil. And now he was too.

He received a quick call from Dick the next day.

'Our friends have gone on an extended holiday together,' Dick told him. 'We need to discuss their replacements. I've got a couple of names we could consider. Can we talk?'

'Dick, put in whoever the hell you want. The operation is yours.'

He'd had enough of this life. He wanted out, and as quickly as possible.

1977

chapter twenty-six

Under the new set-up, Michael stepped back from the day-to-day running of the money-laundering operation and concentrated on the legitimate side of the Mallards business. He identified the key numbers that defined how well a store was operating, had every store manager mail him these figures once a month and collated these into a ledger so that he had a quantitative snapshot of every Mallards branch and how they compared to each other. He visited a different store every week, finding out why one store was overperforming against one parameter, or underperforming against another. He walked around the shop floor, chatting to customers, finding out what they wanted from the store and where Mallards was letting them down. He would talk to anyone in the operation who had a good idea as to how to cut costs or make things more efficient, the best suggestions earning the originator a bonus, no matter what level in the organisation the initiative came from.

He was turning a failing company into a going concern, and he found it curiously compelling. Month after month there was a slow, steady improvement and when, after fifteen months, Jenkins produced a set of accounts that showed they had made a small but real profit in the previous quarter, Michael was delighted. The first time Mallards had made a profit in five years. Just under ten thousand pounds, but it meant more to him than the eight million he'd laundered in the same time.

It was time to get out. If he could make a company like Mallards profitable, Michael reasoned, he could do the same again. Make a clean break from all that he had been involved with in the past, find a new business to run that was entirely legitimate from day one. He just had to convince Dick.

Dick said no.

'Michael, this is the life we have chosen for ourselves,' he told him. 'It has its advantages, but it also comes with restrictions. And the biggest one is that you can never say goodbye. Someone always comes knocking at your door, asking for one last job. The only way you can escape from the past is to do time, usually a lot of time, and keep a low profile when you get out. That's not an option I want to contemplate. And I don't think you do either.'

'How would it be if I was to be around on an advisory basis, leave running the business to someone else? If I were to get someone to take over from me, someone you could trust, wouldn't that be pretty much the same as we've got at the moment? And I'd always be just one phone call away if you wanted the processes updated. That could be our deal, couldn't it?'

'Get me somebody I can trust and who can run the business? Tall order, Michael. I'd take a lot of convincing. We trusted Ron and Eddie, remember?'

Michael knew better than push Dick too far until he had a concrete proposal. When he did, he flew out to

Spain to persuade Dick of his plan: Eric Jenkins to be the new managing director. Dick was unimpressed.

'He's a bean counter, Michael. An empty suit. We need to grow the Mallards business, so the revenue from the furniture sales keeps up with the rest of the operation. Jenkins doesn't have your drive, your ambition. Take it as a compliment that I say no.'

Michael had anticipated Dick's reaction. 'All you need is someone who knows how our processes operate and can keep on top of the money flowing through the business. We ship in the same furniture every month, sell it at the same prices in the same stores. The business is so straightforward, you don't need a real managing director, you need someone who's good at hiding money. And Jenkins has been doing that for years. He's got it down to a fine art. He might not be the most dynamic businessman in the world, but he knows what's going on, he does what he's told, and he's good at what's important. That's all that matters.'

'But he's not you, Michael. We need more than that.'

'Here's what I suggest. The Mallards business needs to be doing five million a year in revenue to hide as much money as you could ever want to launder. I'll take a year to get it to that level, and at the same time I'll put a marketing team in place who can supply all the creativity and imagination that's missing with Jenkins. I give you my word I'll always be a phone call away if there's ever a problem you need sorting out. If I can do that, let me go. Buy out my part of the business for a million. It's worth a lot more than that. All you have to do, going forward, is pay Jenkins a decent salary rather than me keeping my piece of the action. You'll get the same as if I'm still here, but without any additional overhead. That was what Eddie was trying to achieve, but this way everybody's happy. Everybody wins. It's worth considering.'

'Kenny McGowan said you were a persuasive bugger,' Dick responded. 'But the answer is still no.' Michael grimaced. 'Okay, to put a lid on this once and for all. You're right. Five million a year of Mallards revenue would be enough to cover all the money we'd ever want to launder. Make it ten million and I'll let you go, and you can take a million quid with you. But if we need you to sort out a problem, or think up some new schemes, you need to be there for me. And if Jenkins screws up, you come back and sort out the mess. That, I could sell to Los Zetas.'

Michael got fired up to make it happen. He brought in a top design agency to give the stores a more modern image and a marketing team who knew what they were doing. He worked with a passion and ferocity that he hadn't felt since the early days at Royal Clydeside. This time there was no prejudiced hierarchy to stop him. He had proved he could succeed using one kind of morality. Now he was going to succeed with a more conventional kind. Ten million pounds a year was the price of his freedom. The business plan said he'd get there in five years. He was going to get there in one.

Advertising would be crucial to making that happen. Mallards were from the pile-it-high-and-sell-it-cheap school of retailing; their ads were cluttered and tacky, cramming as many photos of their product range into one ad as possible, announcing a new sale every other week and shouting about the best-ever discount if you bought your furniture now. Except that next month another sale would come along and say the whole thing all over again. Michael might be new to marketing, but he realised if Mallards were to ever to get to the sales he needed, they had to make a break from the past, find a way to appeal to the fashion-conscious young professionals who were buying up new starter homes in droves. That meant finding the best advertising campaign money could buy and spending whatever it took to drive the new message home.

He chose three ad agencies to pitch for his business: two of the biggest, who promised that their professionalism and experience would deliver the campaign he needed, and one of the newest and fastest-growing, who promised fresh ideas and radical thinking to solve his problems. They were called Campbell, Peters and Dixon, CPD, and Michael warmed to the managing director, Ben Campbell. Self-made entrepreneur, his agency had come along and shaken the big boys out of their complacency. They were the ones Michael thought would deliver.

His intuition turned out to be well founded. He went to the big ad agencies' presentations first: slick, well thought out, but lacking the spark of creativity that he was looking for. CPD was presenting the next morning; all his hopes were pinned on them coming up with the goods.

The meeting was in London; Soho, nine thirty. Michael turned up a few minutes late, he'd had to finish off a phone call to Dick to sort out some supply issues, and the rest of his marketing team and the agency were already assembled when he arrived. Ben Campbell met him in reception and extolled the virtues of the work that was about to be presented as he escorted Michael to the meeting room. It would be headed up by one of the agency's rising stars, Ben said, and he promised Michael he'd be amazed by what he was about to see.

They walked into the room, and Michael was, indeed, astounded. The hot-shot account director presenting the ads was Roberta. Dressed all very businesslike, and still as beautiful as ever. Michael saw the colour drain from her cheeks as she stared at him in horror. So this was the new life she'd found for herself in London. Not working on the stage, but reinventing herself so she wouldn't be discovered; a new career in advertising. And now fate had brought them together again.

Ben did an opening welcome and handed over to Roberta. She was a disaster, fumbled every page of the presentation, dropped her pile of overhead projector skins, stuttered and stumbled over her words as she tried to focus.

At the end, Ben stood up and took over. It was apparent he was trying to salvage something from the disaster. 'I'll just go over the final points, if that's okay,' he said to the room, pointedly ignoring Roberta.

He finished. After an awkward silence, Michael spoke. 'Thank you. I think we've seen enough.' He picked up Roberta's business card lying on the meeting-room table and left the presentation brochure behind. He stormed out, his bemused marketing team in his wake.

Michael called Ben that afternoon and said his decision not to appoint them was down to the disastrous presentation. No way was he going to give his business to an agency who chose the office junior to run the account,

Michael told him. He'd find another agency that took their business more seriously. Ben stammered out an apology that did little to disguise how furious he was with Roberta's performance.

When he got back to Surrey, Michael tried to push the day's events out of his head while he went through the other agency presentations from the day before, trying to decide which one to appoint. Nothing was that great, and he cursed that there would be another delay while he briefed some more agencies. Then there was a knock, and his brand manager stuck his head round the door.

'Michael, before you make any final decisions, I think you should look through the CPD pitch again. It might have been the worst presentation, but what they were recommending was good. See what you think.'

Looked at dispassionately, it was indeed impressive. 'Good taste never goes out of fashion' was the slogan, the ads linking Mallards furniture to timeless icons of good taste. Every single part of the campaign – the ads, the magazines and programmes they would be advertising in – all tying back to and reinforcing the same core idea. Simple and powerful. Michael had a grudging admiration for the new skills Roberta had displayed. She understood his business and was clear about what was required to grow it.

A thought struck him, ridiculous at first, but then seeming to make more and more sense. He needed a marketing director who had drive and creativity. He needed someone he could control. The people on the business side of Mallards were shielded from the real operation it was hiding, but there was always a theoretical risk that one of them could figure out what was going on. Roberta already knew, or at least could work it out, and she would never betray her part in what was going on and what had happened in the past. And now she had shown she could do the job; it would be her plan they would be implementing. She would be perfect.

Michael went back to CPD's offices the next day, asked the receptionist to tell Roberta he was there and wanted to talk to her.

'I can't tell him that, he's seen me talking to you,' Michael heard the receptionist say on the phone. Despite the tenseness of the situation, he smiled to himself. After fifteen minutes, Roberta appeared. First a nervous glance from the stairwell, then she strode towards him, a defiant look on her face.

This had to be handled carefully. 'I need to apologise for telling your boss you were the reason CPD didn't get our advertising, Roberta,' he said. 'That was a bit harsh. I hope it didn't cause any problems for you.'

'What do you want, Michael?'

She'd got tougher since he last saw her. That meant he could be tougher in response.

'Quite direct, aren't you? Well, in that case, let me tell you. We've got … an indiscretion in our past; I'm sure you remember what I'm talking about. All the other indiscretions that I used to commit when you knew me in Glasgow – they've been swept away. The smurfs are gone, and my services are now channelled through genuine businesses. Mallards is a legitimate company, and I'm its very respectable managing director.'

'I'm sure you are, Michael. Very respectable.'

'Look I know what you're thinking,' he replied. 'You think I had something to do with the tragic death of the detective we used in the little game we played. But it was a bizarre coincidence.' He looked over, saw her shaking her head in denial. 'Oh, I admit it was convenient. I was looking to get out of smurfing, and the detective's death did help. Some of the smurfs came to the same fanciful conclusion you did, and kept quiet during the investigation. No doubt due to a misguided belief that, if I could kill a cop, I could do the same to them.'

He could tell she didn't believe a word of it. He toyed for a moment with telling her about Ivan, that McDonald was a crooked cop who had met his end at the hands of his gangster paymaster, but decided not to. He could win her round with only what she already knew.

'Coincidences do happen, Roberta,' he went on. 'I mean, look at our meeting like this. I must admit I was upset you ran out on me. I trusted you with my secrets, just as you trusted me with yours. I thought that bonded us together. So I had some of my people ask around to see if they could find you. Even hired a private detective to look for you in London.'

'I know you did, Michael. I've spent the last fifteen months being chased by him, in case you've forgotten.'

'Don't be angry, Roberta. Yes, I had him look for you when you first moved down here. A last attempt at a reconciliation. But when I realised you didn't want to be found, I said to myself, no more. Even when I had new leads about where you might be in London, I stopped following them up. I'd given up on ever seeing you again, until our fortuitous encounter yesterday.'

'Michael, this is the biggest load of baloney I've ever heard in my life. You want me to believe DCI McDonald's death was a coincidence? Give me a break.'

She was getting more and more worked up now. Michael let her get all of her anger out of her system.

'And what about Duncan?' she cried. 'You had him beaten up so badly he ended up in hospital. And the disgusting room where you had someone photograph me having sex? Do you expect me to believe you knew nothing about any of that?'

'I didn't authorise any violence. Big Jockie got carried away, and let me assure you I was as shocked as you when I found out. But yes, I knew about the room and the two-way mirror. I was worried a previous girlfriend was being unfaithful, and the layout of the flat was convenient for setting up a surveillance operation. You know how I like to keep an eye on people, for their own good. But when she moved out, I had it locked up and had forgotten about it. I was mortified when I was told about the broken mirror and realised you'd found it. I can see how you could've jumped to the wrong conclusion.'

Michael knew this was the weakest point of his argument, so he quickly pressed on. 'Our deceased friend is ancient history now. Something no one wants to bring up again. I admit it looks unfortunate, our little game coinciding with such a tragic event. But think of how deeply involved you were with me back then, how long you've had these suspicions and haven't said anything. You talk to anyone about this and the police will think you were part of it as well.'

He paused to see her reaction.

'I would never do that, Michael.'

He detected the slightest faltering in her resolve. It was time for the mildest of threats.

'It's not me you have to worry about, Roberta. I just run a slightly unconventional financial services company. As I've always told you, I'm not into the blood business. It's my clients who should scare you. My operations would expose them to the authorities, and they would take a dim view of anyone who had the potential to make that happen. A very dim view. That's why I wanted to keep you close to me, why I made so much effort to track you down.'

He leant over and took her hand. She didn't pull it away.

'I want to keep you close to me, to protect you from yourself. I don't want you to wake up one morning full of irrational guilt and do something silly, something you'd come to regret. The best thing is for us to be together, Roberta. I need to make sure nobody develops bothersome conspiracy theories based on your speculation that I was connected to McDonald's death. As I'm sure you can appreciate, that troubles me.'

He told her his idea about her coming to work at Mallards, running the marketing side of the business. He could see the horror on her face and that it filled her with dread, but he persisted, said that she should at least come down to Surrey the next day and have a look at what was on offer. She mumbled her agreement.

He left it at that. He might be able to convince her, he might not. But at the very least he had shown her he was trying to be reasonable, that she had nothing to fear if she continued to keep silent about her past involvement. Now it was a question of waiting to see how she would react.

She didn't turn up. And when Michael checked, he found she'd disappeared again, walked out of the agency and no one had a clue where she had gone. For the second time, she was risking everything, throwing away all that she had worked for, so that she could escape from him. He cursed his foolhardiness at trying a rapprochement between them. She was running scared, no doubt going over in her mind whether she would ever be free of him, maybe even considering breaking her silence. He had to find her.

He told his London detective to check the ad agencies, and the one in Glasgow was instructed to keep an eye on her friend Duncan. After the lack of success last time, Michael didn't hold out much hope. She'd been smart when she came to London, avoiding the obvious option of finding work in the theatre. She'd think the same way again, start a new life doing something new. Meeting up with old friends or finding another job in advertising would make it easy for him to track her down.

So Michael was surprised when his Glasgow detective told him she'd moved back to Scotland, and was staying at Duncan's Glasgow flat. That made his concerns about her keeping her silence ever more acute. Duncan no doubt knew about McDonald, and the two of them together, desperate to find a way to put the threat of Michael behind them once and for all, could easily convince themselves that they should finally go to the police with what they knew.

Michael sat alone in his flat that evening, pondering what to do. Disposing of Ron and Eddie had been so easy, so clinical. One phone call from Dick to Los Zetas, one payment of fifty thousand pounds, and they were gone. He started doodling on a notepad, a few random words to try to organise his thinking, and he thought back to that evening, a lifetime ago, when he had sat down and worked out the pros and cons of a life of crime. Four people dead because of him, one of them killed by his own hand, and now two more murders just a phone call away. That had never been part of the equation.

He gave a rueful smile as he thought about his promise to himself to put his life of crime behind him and use his fortune to start a new business, a legitimate one. Now, only a few weeks later, he was contemplating killing again. He had to stop kidding himself. There would always be something else, one more horror he would have to be part of, every time telling himself it was the last. This decision was a test, a crossroads. If he ordered the execution of Roberta and Duncan, he knew it would never stop.

He made up his mind. He would have their every movement watched, do nothing unless he saw evidence that they were going to turn him in. He got back in touch with the advertising agency, told them he'd read through the presentation and wanted to give them a second chance. Then he waited to find out what his detective would uncover.

Roberta stayed silent. Michael learned that she moved out of Duncan's flat a few weeks later, got a place outside of Glasgow where she probably felt she would be less visible. The detective told Michael she'd gone back to college to get a psychology diploma, no doubt part of her plan to start her life all over again. It was time to let her go. Roberta was an irritation, a voice from the past that had spoken for the last time.

He was proud of his decision. He'd never have blood on his hands again.

1978

chapter twenty-seven

Michael stared at the full-page ad in *Country Life*. 'Stunning Highland estate. Ten thousand acres, early-Victorian house, three cottages, full stalking and fishing rights. £1,500,000.' Glensporret Estate was for sale.

His annual shooting trips there were one of the highlights of Michael's year. The intensity of stalking one of the world's most magnificent wild creatures – a Royal or an Imperial, very occasionally a 16-pointer, the sublime Monarch; the adrenaline of the kill; the atmosphere of privilege in the smoking room afterwards, rubbing shoulders with the higher echelons of society. And now, he could own all this.

He was close to reaching the ten-million turnover target Dick had said was the price of leaving the Mallards operation amicably. Running the Glensporret Estate would be the perfect legitimate business for him to take over. He could move into the lodge, wind down the rest of his business operations from there, and spend his days living off the estate's revenues. The life of a landed gentleman, mingling with the guests when it suited him, deciding which members of the establishment to make the acquaintance of. He wanted that life so badly he could taste it.

The lawyers handling the sale sent him the brochure and said he could view the accounts when he visited the estate. As he stood on a heather-covered knoll, overlooking the magnificent glen, the mighty River Sporret coursing through it, he felt he had found his home. Bidding closed in three months. He had to move quickly.

He had about a million pounds he could get his hands on – all the wealth he had accrued in the last few years. Half a million more would secure the estate, the same again to do the refurbishments and the PR for the launch.

He booked an appointment with Royal Clydeside for the following week. He had asked Jenkins to prepare the financial side of the business plan. He was seeking a half-million-pound loan to allow him to buy the estate, the property to act as security. Selling his share of the Mallards business to Dick would pay off the loan and cover the refurbishment, the launch and operating costs for the first year. That was going to happen in the next six months. The financial projections showed the estate would make a profit, even without assuming any growth. He'd proven he could run a business; the Mallards turnaround had been remarkable. It was a cast-iron business plan, with minimal risk.

Ian Mason, now the bank's regional director, had welcomed Michael back like a long-lost friend, and listened in astonishment as he outlined his success at turning the fortunes of Mallards around, and his ideas for turning Glensporret into Scotland's most exclusive shooting retreat. Michael left the meeting on a high, certain that the loan application would be bound to succeed.

The bank turned him down.

'I'm sorry, Michael,' Mason said when he called. 'But sometimes it's our responsibility to save our customers from their flights of fancy. You don't have the experience or the connections to make this sort of thing work. It's only been a few years since you were an assistant manager here. I have to say everyone at the bank is very impressed by how you've succeeded at the businesses you've been running; I take my hat off to you. But there's a big difference between selling furniture and running a Highland estate. And Glensporret has been in the same family for generations. I think a few of the patrons might think it's beyond the pale to have it run by a business whizz-kid from a council estate. No offence.'

'None taken,' Michael said, a red mist descending on his eyes. 'What do I have to do to make it work? What if I said I could find some extra cash to reduce the size of the loan? Maybe agree to a higher rate of interest?'

'No, the figures aren't the problem. On the face of it, your plan seems eminently feasible. It's just, well, it doesn't smell right. Your business partner at Mallards is not willing to come forward and indemnify us in case the sale of your share doesn't go through, and there's your reluctance to share the detailed accounts with us. It's a huge gamble to assume that you can learn the ropes about running an estate while at the same time reassuring the current guests that someone who is not one of them will not make regrettable changes to one of the jewels of the Scottish Highlands. So, I'm sorry, Michael, the answer is no. Why don't you try running a hotel up there as a first step, come back to us in a couple of years when you have a proven track record and you know for sure what the outcome of the Mallards sale is? I'm sure we'll be much more receptive.'

Dick couldn't be budged on letting Michael get out of the Mallards operation before reaching his revenue target. Michael thought about going to another bank, but if Royal Clydeside had rejected him, it was unlikely that a bank who didn't know him at all would make a different decision. For the first time in years, he'd looked to the establishment for help, and yet again they'd closed ranks against him. He seethed at the unfairness of it all.

Before Michael left Scotland for Surrey, he met with Big Jockie. He had been in two minds as to whether it was a good idea – he was part of the violent past Michael was trying to leave behind. But with Ron and Eddie gone, Big Jockie was the one person in the operation who knew the incriminating events of his past. They had parted on good terms when Michael had moved to Surrey. Michael had made a generous final payout to ensure Big Jockie didn't harbour a grudge at no longer being required once the smurfs had gone. It would be good to check what he was up to. And, God forbid, there was always a chance he might need him again.

What Big Jockie had to tell Michael sent a chill through his heart. He'd taken over Ron's loan-sharking business once it became clear that Ron had disappeared forever. To some extent Michael had to fill in the blanks, but clearly terrorising the unfortunates who got into arrears had given Big Jockie a thirst for violence which had become insatiable, and brutality had become more and more his opening gambit, rather than a measured last resort. His latest scheme was a perfect example. Some guy on the streets had come into the largest stash of heroin ever found in Scotland, with a street value of just over four million pounds. But heroin had only just started to arrive in Scotland in any quantity, and the guy had no idea how he was going to distribute it.

Big Jockie had apparently found out, and arranged a meeting to take it off his hands. But not the way the guy was expecting. Big Jockie 'persuaded' him until he revealed its whereabouts and once he had his hands on the drugs, the unfortunate dealer was no more. Big Jockie was now sitting on a mountain of heroin and didn't know what to do with it. Selling it on the streets of Glasgow would take a lifetime and the minute its arrival made the news, the authorities would move heaven and earth to find out who was pushing it.

Michael told him that it wasn't the sort of business he was interested in, but promised he'd ask around to see if he could find a buyer. He hadn't really been serious, but as he travelled back down to England, his mind started to wander. If he could sell it to a middle man for two million, fifty per cent of two million was enough to purchase Glensporret and implement the business plan. The heroin was a one-off, it wasn't Big Jockie's usual line of work, so there would be no repercussions if he never went anywhere near another drug deal in future. And he knew of a potential customer in the shape of Los Zetas.

He pushed the idea from his mind. His decision not to ruthlessly silence Roberta and her friend had been a turning point for him. He had stood on the brink of conscienceless and mercenary brutality, of being so desensitised to violence that he could unleash pain and death on anyone who stood in his way, without any doubts or misgivings. Every day since that decision he had pulled himself further and further away from his life of crime. He couldn't let himself get sucked back in.

And yet. He was only having to contemplate this action because, once again, he was being held back because of who he once was. Because of a prejudice that someone of his background had no right to be running a historical Highland estate. Once again, he was being forced to play by a different set of rules because of the iniquity around him.

He called Big Jockie, asked him to give him a week to see if he could come up with one single buyer at a price he liked. If he did, they'd split the proceeds fifty-fifty. Big Jockie said he'd give him a day.

Los Zetas said they were interested. Dick had put the proposition to them in return for Michael agreeing to forgo his cash payout when he transferred the Mallards business to him. It was a high price for a few phone calls, but Michael didn't object. The Mallards money would have been needed to buy Glensporret; this deal would do the same job.

'You've got a nice earner, there,' Dick told Michael when he called back with the news. 'They say they'll send a guy over to check it out, but for that amount of dope, they'll pay the two mill you're asking for.'

Michael told Big Jockie the news, and they congratulated each other on their good fortune. But Michael needed to be careful. The deal would make Big Jockie rich beyond his wildest dreams, but Michael still felt vulnerable. Big Jockie had shown how ruthless he was prepared to be to get the stuff in the first place. Michael needed to keep him away from Los Zetas. If Big Jockie knew who the buyer was, he could easily cut Michael out of the deal. Possibly in a very unpleasant way.

Big Jockie was unhappy that he would have to hand the heroin over to Michael to give to the mysterious buyers, but he finally relented. Michael told him that the buyers were paranoid about their confidentiality, wanted no one other than him to have any hint of who was involved. And he also persuaded Big Jockie that it would, in any case, be the smart thing for him to agree to. Michael was taking all the risk of handling the actual heroin, and Big Jockie was getting the same share without any of the danger of being caught red-handed making the consignment.

The implications of what he had agreed to only began to dawn on Michael when he drove round to the lock-up where Big Jockie had stored the heroin. Michael gasped when he saw how much there was to handle. When he drove off with it, it felt like there was a ticking bomb behind him. He drove home more carefully than he had ever driven a car in his life. He wanted this stuff out of his hands as quickly as possible.

He arranged to meet Diego, the Los Zetas contact, at his house. Los Zetas could probably find out where he lived anyway, and he wanted to move the drugs about as little as possible. Diego affected a weary indifference as he prepared to examine the drugs. He brought along a compatriot called Manuel, weasel-like and subservient, his eyes like hollows of madness, his hair like mouldy hay.

'I make test, here, yes?' Diego said, as he unlocked his briefcase.

Michael nodded. Diego chose one of one of the packets of heroin, slit it open with a scalpel and spooned a small quantity into three test tubes. He selected another parcel from a different part of the pile and repeated the operation.

'*Agua?*'

Michael fetched a jug of water and watched as Diego added three chemicals from his briefcase to each of the three test tubes, then a few drops of water, before holding them up to the light. Two turned an eggshell blue, the third a deep crimson red. '*Bueno, bueno,*' he muttered, repeating the test on the second batch and getting the same result.

'Scottish Red Chicken very good,' he said to Michael. 'We do one final test. Ready, Manuel?' He turned to Manuel, who had been watching with a strange, constrained yearning. Manuel nodded, an admiring imbecility escaping from his nose and lips.

'Manuel, he is a connoisseur of Red Chicken,' Diego told Michael. 'We let him try a little.'

Michael couldn't believe what he was seeing. Diego took another small spoonful of heroin, added a little water and produced a syringe. He sucked up the liquid into the barrel, gave it a tap to get rid of air bubbles, looking for all the world like a doctor ministering to a sick patient. He handed the syringe to Manuel, who clenched a fist, raised his arm and pushed the needle into a vein. Michael saw a plume of blood enter the syringe, spiralling around like some distant nebula, then

316

Manuel pushed the plunger fully in. His lips loosened in a furtively exultant smile.

'Ah. *Si*,' he groaned.

'*Perfecto*,' said Diego. He turned to Michael. 'You help me lie him on your sofa, while we finish this business.'

Michael looked at Manuel, whose eyes were glazed in a beatific dreaminess. 'How long is he going to be like this?' A room with enough heroin to send him to jail until the end of the century, a stoned junkie, and a professional drug dealer was not a place he wanted to stay in for too long.

'A little while. But I take care of him, no worries. Now we have to do big count of all your nice powder.'

Diego produced a set of scales and started methodically weighing each parcel in turn, noting down the results in a leather-bound notepad. Michael sank back into his chair. After ten minutes Diego had hardly made a dent in the mountain of heroin in front of him. Michael began to rue his decision to be so personally involved.

It took Diego just over an hour to complete the inventory.

'Now I tell you the price,' he said, getting out a slide rule and totalling up the figures. Michael heard a clock in the hallway strike the hour. Soon this would be over.

'*Excelente*,' said Diego eventually. 'Two hundred and twenty million pesetas.' He looked over at Michael. 'You want to know pounds?'

'I want to know pounds.'

'One million, seven hundred and forty thousand,' he said. 'I tell you what; I make it one-eight because I like your Glasgow Celtic, eh? Jock Stein, he very good manager.'

Michael didn't see the point of negotiating; it wasn't like he had any other options. He'd be two hundred thousand short, but if the worst came to worst, he'd find something to sell.

'Okay, it's a deal. You can pick up the heroin as soon as the money comes through.'

'Ah, no. Delivery is included in the price. I pay when you bring it to our warehouse in Oviedo.'

Michael was horrified. 'It would be easier for you to collect it here,' he said.

'No possible. Too many risks. I don't know you, who you tell. Maybe they tell someone. Any problems in Scotland, they your problems. I see you in Oviedo.'

Diego couldn't be persuaded. That meant going back to Big Jockie and finding someone they could trust to take it to Oviedo. Michael had risked everything to be this closely involved in a drug deal; no way was he going to put himself in further jeopardy by taking the drugs to Spain. All it would take was one random check at the border and there would be no way of avoiding a long, long jail sentence. Michael didn't do random. It would be pure chance to get to Spain undetected.

After Diego left, half-carrying the semi-comatose Manuel, he considered his options. Big Jockie couldn't do it; if anyone was likely to attract the attention of customs, it was someone looking like him. Finding someone else to make the trip would mean trusting whoever that was not to screw up, not to betray them, and even if they were successful, never to talk to anyone about what they had been part of.

He had been stupid to get this closely involved. Maybe he should tell Big Jockie and Los Zetas that the deal was off, that he wanted no further part of it, and if they wanted to sort something out between the two of them, to do so but not to involve him. The outlook was bleak. Two irate parties furious with him for letting them down. If they went ahead themselves, none of the money coming to him. Glensporret, a pipe-dream that had forever slipped through his grasp.

He'd taken risks before. He could take one more, one final risk, as long as it could be managed; as long as the odds of detection were acceptably low. Flying was the easiest way. Book a package holiday to northern Spain and he'd be able to get to Oviedo the same day. But far too risky. If he were asked to open his luggage at the airport, he'd be done for. That left driving, taking a ferry – either a short Channel crossing and a drive through France, or a longer trip across the Bay of Biscay. He decided the Calais crossing would be best. There would be another customs check at the France–Spain border, but that would be relatively busy, less chance of a thorough check.

Michael got one of his regional operatives to fit out his car with hidden compartments, a common enough practice among the brotherhood of thieves. It meant a long drive to Liverpool and back, but Michael wanted no one in Glasgow to have any inkling of what he was doing. It would be a long shot that he'd even be stopped at customs, and there would never be a thorough enough search to find the drugs unless the authorities had been tipped off, or he started acting in some way suspiciously. He could trust himself not to do that. He loaded up the bags the night before his drive to Dover. He'd break his journey south of Manchester and be on an afternoon crossing the next day. Two days of driving to reach Oviedo on Spain's north coast. Then he could complete the deal and relax on a ferry straight back to the south coast of England.

As he pulled into Dover, Michael could see the SeaLink ferry waiting in the dock, a long queue of cars snaking back from the ramp waiting to board. He joined the longest queue. He wanted to reach passport control with as little time as possible to spare before the ship sailed, hoping that would reduce the chances of a lengthy examination.

The queue started moving forward, car by car, to the customs booth looming ahead. Then it was one car before him. He held his passport and ticket in one hand, the other cradling the gear stick. He took a few deep breaths to keep calm, puffing out his cheeks when he exhaled. He realised that looked conspicuous and stopped. His nose had an insatiable itch.

The car in front had been at the customs booth for three, maybe five minutes; there seemed to be a problem. Michael saw the customs officer pick up the phone, the driver folding his hands behind his head as he waited. The cars behind pulled out into the now empty adjacent lanes, disappearing into the bowels of the ship. Just as Michael was beginning to think it was going to look odd if he was not doing the same, the guard put down the phone and handed some documents to the driver. He headed off, and Michael drove up to the booth, smiled forgiveness to the guard that he'd been kept waiting. He got a harassed wave to continue, and Michael tried not to grin too much as his front wheels bumped up onto the ramp.

Once in France, all the cars sped off without any more checks and Michael drove down through the country avoiding further incident. For the last few hours before reaching the Spanish border, he debated whether to turn off the motorway and cross the border on a rural road where he imagined there wouldn't be any checkpoints. But if there were, a British car might arouse suspicion. He weighed the pros and cons, but there was no clear answer. In the end, the decision was made for him. It was getting late as he neared the border and he didn't want to risk getting lost on some anonymous backway. He drove through the crossing just after the Basque town of Biarritz without any problems, and was checked into his hotel in San Sebastian as night was falling.

He set off before six the next morning as he wanted to complete the drive along Spain's northern coast and hand over his cargo by the end of the day. For the first time on the journey, Michael felt able to relax. Keep below the speed limit, he told himself, and there was nothing more to worry about until he reached his destination.

He came over the brow of a hill just outside Laredo and was met by a line of stationary traffic. Blue flashing lights in the distance told him it must be an accident of some sort, but at least the queue was moving slowly forward in sporadic bursts, and the delay didn't look too long. He did a quick mental calculation, worked out it would likely be one hour at most. Frustrating, but no need to change his plans.

After inching forward for half an hour, he stepped out of the car to stretch his legs. A few other drivers were doing the same, and Michael noticed that one of the cars behind him had a British number plate. 'Looks like there's been an accident,' he shouted over to the driver, a florid expat in blazer and cravat.

'No accident, old boy. Heard the news on the radio. ETA set off a bomb in the town this morning, absolute bloody carnage. This will be the roadblock the Civil Guard set up to search for the perpetrators. Waste of time if you ask me. The scoundrels will have scarpered long ago. Still, it makes it look like they're doing something. Bloody pain in the arse.'

Michael looked up and down the road. No way of turning off before the roadblock. No way to do a U-turn onto the other carriageway. He had no choice but to continue. He got back in the car as the queue started to move forward again. When it stopped, he was about four hundred yards short of the checkpoint. He fished out a pair of binoculars from the glove compartment and sized up what was going on.

They were searching every fifth car. Rigorously. Alsatian dogs were sniffing around, two guards, one on either side, were inspecting everything. He watched three cars being examined; sure enough, it was exactly one in five. Even if the dogs didn't detect the heroin, the search surely would. He got back in the car. They moved forward another hundred yards or so. He leapt out, started counting back to his car from the one being searched. A sickening realisation. His was the thirty-fifth car.

He slumped back into the driver's seat. There was no way to avoid the search. Abandoning the car was an even worse idea; once the heroin was found it would be traced back to him. His only option was to sit tight, and hope against hope that he'd get through undetected. But as he got closer to the checkpoint, he saw that was a forlorn possibility. It was taking a long time because the search was so thorough. Terrorists wouldn't leave anything incriminating in open view, and the police were making sure they missed nothing.

The whole situation was surreal. He could walk around his car, unfettered and ignored, but slowly, inexorably he was heading to his doom. He felt a sickening spasm of irony. Ever since day one, he had planned meticulously, left nothing to chance. Now it was all going to end on a dusty Spanish highway because of random bad luck.

The next wave of cars moving forward put Michael less than a hundred yards from the checkpoint. One more surge, two at the most, and it would be his turn. Then he saw two new guards approaching, sauntering insouciantly towards the checkpoint like they didn't have a care in the world. The two new guards approached the two conducting the searches, chatting with them before taking charge of the Alsatians and continuing the checks.

But they stopped the third car in line, not the fifth. Sure enough, once they got going, every fifth car was searched. But now that didn't include him. He got back in his car and slipped into a Zen-like trance of numbness. He wouldn't believe he was out of this until he was through the barricade. Things had changed once; they could change again.

Nothing. He was through. Once he was on his way, free to drive along to Oviedo, he let out a cathartic, primal scream. He started sobbing with relief, his body wracked by tears of gratitude. He would never go as close to the edge as that again.

chapter twenty-eight

The opening-night ball at Glensporret House had been a stunning success. Invitation only, it had attracted the great and the good of Scottish society and was even graced with the presence of a minor royal. The morning after saw the arrival of a fleet of Range Rovers to spirit away the revellers, with one rock star putting on a display of ostentatious one-upmanship by leaving the front lawn by helicopter.

Michael looked over the scene from the balcony window of his private apartment. It had been the greatest day of his life, the point when he had reached his destiny. He allowed himself a small smile of satisfaction as he slid back into bed to allow time for the last guests to depart. There was a slight stirring beside him, and an arm extracted itself from under a pillow and draped itself across his chest.

'Morning Charlotte,' he whispered.

'Morning darling. Has everybody gone?'

'Everybody but you, my love. I'm never going to let that happen again.'

Charlotte chuckled softly, and he started to coax her fully awake.

★ ★ ★

He went into the great hall, flicking through the thank-you notes left by satisfied quests. Most were written on lodge notepaper, but beside them lay a crisp white heavyweight envelope with his name typed on the front, marked *Private and Confidential*.

He sat down and opened it. It was from the chairman of one of Britain's big five banks, Sir Harold Carrington. Michael remembered exchanging a few pleasantries, recalling him as the archetypical silver-haired banker, oozing gravitas from every pore. The letter was an offer to discuss an important role at his bank, one it said he would find it easy to fit in around his obligations running the Glensporret Estate. If he was interested, could he call Sir Harold's private office and make an appointment? It was six months since Royal Clydeside had turned down his request for a bridging loan. Michael smiled at the irony.

He visited the bank's offices when he travelled to London a few weeks later. The liveried doorman pointed him towards a private elevator that whisked him up to the executive floor. From the reception area there was a panoramic outlook over the Thames, and the décor was an understated avowal of luxury and good taste. The room had about it a moneyed hush, as of a gateway leading to a world of wealth and power beyond.

The middle-aged receptionist spoke as he walked up to her desk.

'Mr Mitchell, isn't it? Welcome. Please take a seat. Sir Harold's secretary will be here in a moment.'

He sat down on a pale grey sofa, felt its aniline softness. He tried not to look too interested in the Old Master on the wall, ignored the Rodin sculpture in the corner. He did nothing, in fact, to show how impressed he was by the surroundings.

Sir Harold's secretary was in the same mould as the receptionist, elegant and charming but with a steely core of brisk efficiency. She showed Michael into Sir Harold's office, a combination of business modernity and traditional oak panelling. Sir Harold got up from his desk and came over to greet him. He ushered Michael over to two matching red-striped silk sofas facing each other. They sat down and Sir Harold began to talk.

'Thank you again for a wonderful weekend at Glensporret,' he said by way of introduction. 'Marvellous what you've done with the place in such a short period of time. I'm hosting the next chairmen's conference in the autumn. Thinking of your place for the venue. We can combine business with a few days' shooting.'

'I'd be delighted to have you,' Michael replied. 'Have one of your people contact me direct; I'll personally oversee the arrangements.'

Sir Harold nodded his appreciation. 'I know you're a busy man, Michael, so I'll get to the nub of what I've invited you here for. There's a vacancy on the board for a non-executive director, part-time, one or two days a month at most, quite an important corporate governance role. It requires someone with complete discretion, which is why I didn't go into too many details in my letter. Can I tell you more about it?'

'Please do.'

'There has been pressure put on the banks from the highest level to do something about money laundering. You might remember what that's all about from your time

327

at Royal Clydeside. The Scottish banks have shown up us English, I'm sure you'll be amused to hear, by working together to combat this blight on the banking system. They put in place inter-bank cooperation and processes years ago. Now we're catching up. Each of the major English banks has agreed to appoint a non-executive director, someone who's not a part of the day-to-day operation, to implement a common strategy. Someone who is an outsider to the banking world but who understands how it works so that we can root out corruption and malpractice. As you can imagine, a tricky brief. That's why your name came up. Someone from the world of business, but someone who also has had a stint in the banking world. What do you think?'

'I'm flattered.' Michael decided to play hard to get. 'But Glensporret House takes up a lot of my time, especially at the moment. What would the post entail apart from two boards a month?'

'Oh, nothing too onerous. You'd receive a monthly briefing on our latest anti-laundering strategies, with which you'd be required to familiarise yourself, and once a quarter you'd need to meet with your counterparts from the other banks, so that we're all singing off the same hymn sheet. No point in us all doing our own thing. The rascals who we're out to catch would be able to play us all off against each other. You'd report back to the main board after your meeting, with any changes or new initiatives the group recommend, and we'd take it from there. So, one to two days a month of your time, for which you'd be paid £10,000 a year. Plus the knowledge that you're helping to get rid of this reprehensible practice. What do you say?'

'Well, the money's very attractive, but I think it's more my civic duty that makes me want to say yes. The banking industry has been very good to me, it gave me a start in life. I think it's fair to say that without the experience I had with Royal Clydeside, I wouldn't be where I am today. It would be nice to give something back. I'd be delighted, Sir Harold. When do I start?'

'Splendid. I like a chap who doesn't take long to make up his mind. Someone will be in touch to sort out the details.' He paused. Michael could see him trying to choose his next words carefully. 'There's one other thing, I'm afraid. You'll be seeing some highly sensitive and confidential documents. It's critical they don't fall into the wrong hands. Everything needs to be delivered to you in Scotland by personal courier, and you'll have to do the same sending anything back to us. You'll need to have a safe installed at Glensporret, at our expense of course, to store all your files. Only you to know the combination. And it goes without saying that you can't share this information with anyone, and no copies of any documents can be made. Sorry to have to mention this, but I'm sure you understand why.'

'Of course. You don't have to worry. I don't want to see more criminals getting into laundering any more than you do. It will be fascinating work, Sir Harold. And very satisfying. Delighted to be able to help.'

Michael flew out to Spain the next day. Dick thought it hilarious.

'This is like all our dreams come true,' he said as Michael outlined his role at the bank. 'Know every safeguard, every red flag, and at the same time make it tougher for anyone else to muscle in with a rival operation? Michael, if you weren't so ugly, I'd kiss you.'

'If we play this smart, it sets us up for life,' Michael replied. 'That's why I think we need to make some changes in how we operate. You told me I could never fully shake free of my past and I accepted that. But I think we should do things differently from now on.'

'How different?'

'I cut all my ties with your operation. Every single piece of paper involving me is destroyed. I don't have to come back to solve any problems; I never get involved operationally in the business ever again. As far as the rest of the organisation is concerned, I don't exist, never have. You are the only person who knows of my existence, and in return, I keep you one step ahead of the banks at all times. You never react in a way that would create suspicions you have someone on the inside. That means sometimes taking a hit rather than have any risk the banks change the people who are privy to what is going on. We never take any chance I could be detected.'

'Nobody gets a ticket out of an operation like ours, Michael, I've told you that. But, yes, this is a special situation. I don't want to take any gambles with this either. As long as you keep the information coming, you'll get your wish. And there will be a little something from time to time to show our gratitude. Don't want you to think of you forgetting about us, with your new fancy friends.'

'Very generous, Dick. And my money stays offshore, in the most secure haven we've got.' He stood up and shook Dick's hand. 'It's been good working with you. And the best is still to come.'

★ ★ ★

That was the last time Dick and Michael met face to face. At bank board meetings, Michael always provided some perceptive insight on laundering, usually based on one of the techniques that Dick's operation had stopped using. The banks were praised for leading the fight against corruption and laundering, and Michael was building his reputation as the person behind it all. There was even talk of an honour in recognition of his contribution to financial regulation. And with a steady accumulation of funds in a secret offshore account from an ever-grateful Dick, he could fund his every extravagance at Glensporret House. As the estate became more opulent and magnificent, it became more and more sought after by the world's elite. To stay in the main building, you had to be invited by Michael himself, and you had to pay for the privilege.

What Kenny McGowan had said all those years ago had proved to be right. It was the consequences of your actions that defined whether they were moral or not – not the actions themselves. By that measure, Michael had succeeded in what he set out to achieve. He'd battled against the world and won by playing according to a different moral code.

But what he didn't know, didn't even suspect, was that all of this would soon come crashing down.

Thank you!

This is not the end of Michael's story. *Silent Money* is the prequel to *Love's Long Road*. That book is also set in the 1970s and tells the story of Roberta or 'Bobbie', Michael's one-time lover. Read it and find out why she was alone on that fateful night she met Michael at Tiffany's; what happened to her in London; and how she still has a part to play in the next chapter of Michael's life.

The third part of this trilogy is *A Friend in Deed*, set over forty years later in a near-future Britain, again told from the viewpoint of a character from the first two books, this time Duncan, Roberta's best friend.

I hope you enjoyed reading *Silent Money*. If so, I would very much appreciate it if you posted a review.

You can follow the latest news on my website, www.gdharper.com and you can follow me on Twitter, where my handle is @harper_author. My Facebook page is @gdharperauthor.

If you would like to contact me directly with any comments on the books, please email me at gdharper@gdharper.com.

If you are a member of a book club, feel free to request an author chat by Skype when you are discussing any of my books. Just email to ask for an information pack.

Many thanks.

GD Harper

Acknowledgements

Thanks to Liz Allen, Sue Dawson, Jill Fricker, Trevor Hadley and Elena Kravchenko. Also to Debi Alper, Helen Baggot, Sheena Billett and Michael Faulkner, and to Matador and Spiffing Covers. And finally, my thanks to Agnes for all her love and support.